LEIF'S LEGACY

CALUMET EDITIONS

Minneapolis

First Edition September 2023

Leif's Legacy. Copyright © 2023 by R. Newell Searle.
All rights reserved.

This is a work of fiction. All of the characters, names, incidents, organizations, and dialogue are either the products of the author's imagination or are used fictitiously.

10 9 8 7 6 5 4 3 2 1

ISBN: 978-1-960250-96-4

Cover and book design by Gary Lindberg

LEIF'S LEGACY

Book 2 – The Alton County Murders

NEWELL SEARLE

CALUMET EDITIONS
Minneapolis

"Property is an aphrodisiac... It releases the other deadly sins—lust, pride, envy, greed and wrath. Just how deep and universal is the lust for land in Alton County—deep enough to kill for its title?"

—Boston Meade

To Edward S. Iversen, forester, mentor and friend of many campfires.

Also by Newell Searle

Saving Quetico-Superior: A Land Set Apart
Copy Desk Murders

CHAPTER 1

The woman hiked up the hill from the mailbox through the dawn's iron cold with the January ninth edition of the *Alton County Statesman* tucked under her arm. Snow squealed under her insulated boots, and her freckled cheeks tingled. Nestled inside the down coat, Ginger O'Meara exhaled and watched her breath drift away like small, white clouds. She already knew the paper's lead story because she was the *Statesman*'s managing editor. Her lover, Boston Meade, owned the paper and wrote it. Even so, she wanted to read it to him.

She hung the parka in the foyer of the hilltop house, entered the breakfast nook and gave Boston a good-morning kiss. He offered her a cup of fresh coffee in return. Though unmarried, they lived together in what she merrily called "a state of sin." Brushing some locks of chestnut hair away from her oval face, she unfolded the paper and her amber eyes sparkled with an impish glint. "Listen to this," she gushed and then read the story in the exaggerated tone of a TV news anchor:

> FUTURE OF TARN LAKE IN COURT.
> Featherstone – Dr. Harald Nielsen of Wa-
> terford has asked the court to set aside the
> will filed by his brother, the late Leif Niel-
> sen. He is challenging the will on behalf of
> himself and Mr. Nielsen's daughter, Karla
> Ronning of Minneapolis. He says develop-
> ment of Mr. Nielsen's property at Tarn Lake
> will provide an inheritance for Ms. Ronning
> and her son.

According to Dr. Nielsen, his brother was gravely ill and asked him to prepare a will for his signature. The draft named Dr. Nielsen as his personal representative with the power of attorney. However, after Mr. Nielsen recovered, he changed his personal representative without telling Dr. Nielsen and filed the will through his own attorney. Dr. Nielsen was unaware of the change until Mr. Nielsen's death last year, October 12, 1985. He claims his brother wasn't mentally competent when he changed his will.

"*Oooh,* now for the juicy part," she cooed:

Mr. Nielsen owned the only private property on Tarn Lake, a spring-fed body bordered by nature preserves. The lakeshore property is valued at several million dollars if developed for recreation and second homes. Mr. Nielsen's friends say he wanted the farm to remain undeveloped. The future of Tarn Lake itself may hinge on the court's determination of Mr. Nielsen's state of mind when he filed his will. District Judge Ray Knatvold will hear the case.

"Now," *that's* a story," she said with a grin.

"And that's not all of it," he replied as his expression turned serious and his gray eyes appeared even more opaque. "According to Jack, the probate challenge is only round one. He thinks several more shoes may drop before this is over."

"Whose shoes?"

"He's not saying. Only that the deputies are taking a closer look at a car accident and certain medications prescribed for Leif. But keep that in your purse for now."

2

"You'll stay on top of this, won't you?" she asked, knitting her brow. "The Nielsens have a high profile. You've already interviewed the major players."

"Oh, so now you're inviting me back as your unpaid investigative reporter!"

"Yes, with all the usual benefits," she added and puckered her cherry lips.

"I might as well," he conceded, removing the tortoise-shell glasses and polishing them on his bathrobe. "Sooner or later, Jack will drag me into it." Jack, his adopted brother, was in his third term as the Alton County Sheriff. He was born in Featherstone to a mixed-race couple who had moved there from Louisiana. Though baptized Jacques Baptiste DuBois, he called himself Jack. He and Boston bonded in grade school when they bloodied some noses to end the schoolyard taunts of "Sambo" and "Jungle Bunny." Jack was eight when his parents died in a wreck, and the Meades adopted him as their second son. The boys were the same age and inseparable.

"Jack wants me to cover his back," he said, settling the glasses on his Roman nose. "You know how he works."

"What about your profile of Leif?" she asked while rinsing her oatmeal bowl in the sink. "I hope you'll finish it. You've already interviewed everyone."

"That's the problem. I'm compromised as a reporter. If Jack draws me into this case, my gut says that what I already know could become evidence. What I know, even if I withhold it, will make me one of the players in the story. It's not what I wanted."

"In the paper or in the court, isn't it enough that your words serve the greater good?" She looked into his eyes and saw the inner struggle between personal desire and professional ethics. He was honorable that way, but she saw he paid a price for it.

"Yeah, I suppose you're right. The judge will rule on Leif's state of mind. There's no way I can be neutral now. If I share my interview notes, they'll strengthen Leif's case. If I don't, his brother may win. The judge's decision will either save or ruin Tarn Lake."

"Oh, for Pete's sake," she scolded, rolling her eyes. "Come down from Mount Rushmore! Do what's right. Write a book about him later—if that'll ease your conscience."

"I've thought of it," he said, rising from the table. "I wanted to write about him as a paradox. One of a kind. Tragic in a way. A scientific forester who became the consummate woodsman just as they were no longer needed."

"Good, start with that," she said, nudging him with her elbow. Then she bundled into her puffy coat and kissed him. "See ya later," she called on her way out the door.

Standing at the turret window in the living room's corner, he watched the Subaru wagon vanish down the hill and drive toward town. He hated to see her go each morning because she and Jester, her border collie, brought an energy that made the big house cozier. Jester whimpered, and Boston scratched his head. "She'll be back, boy," he said, as much to himself as to the dog.

He and Jack grew up in the three-story Queen Anne house his grandfather built for a family of eight with live-in servants. Besides the spacious rooms, it had a massive stone fireplace, a turret, a wrap-around veranda and dormers. It crowned a low ridge overlooking Featherstone that his grandfather dubbed San Juan Hill, a reminder of his service in Cuba under Teddy Roosevelt. He founded the *Statesman* as a bi-weekly in 1903, and Boston's father, London, later turned it into a daily that became famous for its reporting and learned editorials.

Boston fled Featherstone to Chicago after college and made his mark climbing the ranks at a national magazine, thinking he had escaped the expectation he would succeed his father. He returned home last summer to settle his father's estate and hire an editor for the *Statesman*. Ginger's last-minute application offered strong business experience, and he hired her despite their mutual distrust from a bitter parting in college twenty years before. Then, he suspended his Chicago career to track down the man who killed the paper's intern. In the process, nailing the killer redefined him in local eyes as it led him and Ginger to a mature reconciliation. Now they shared the house, her

4

dog and a bed, but not the *Statesman*. He had promised her a free hand, and she made certain he kept his promise.

Turning from the frosty window, he scanned the walnut bookcases flanking the fireplace. Yesterday he had just seen the book he wanted. It wasn't there today. Nor was it on the end tables by the wing chairs facing the hearth. Then he found Aldo Leopold's *A Sand County Almanac* in the den beneath the stairs. Leopold was a forester twenty years older than Leif, but both shared a land ethic that he wanted to work into the profile.

Ginger suggested the profile last summer as they sat on the veranda, barely clothed in the August heat. He remembered his frustration over the subject of his next syndicated column in *American Outlook*. Annoyed at his grumbling, she put down her cross-stitching and told him Emery Daniels was donating a chunk of bluff land as a nature preserve. Then, speaking as if he were a cub reporter, she suggested he talk to Daniels. After that, she resumed cross-stitching the affirmation she intended as a gift to a woman in her Alcoholics Anonymous group. And that was it.

He had interviewed Nielsen and those who knew him last autumn. Now he passed the morning at the desk reading his notes while Jester lay across his feet. After reading the notes from two interviews with Leif, he closed his eyes and imagined the story arc for the profile. Every story he had ever written began with several possible narratives from multiple points of view.

The truest stories are asymmetric, he thought. It's a rare tale that falls into an evenly balanced pro and con. Lazy reporters treat them as equal to avoid criticism instead of digging for the truth. That kind of objectivity is a lie. Even the presence of a reporter on the scene—especially a television reporter—may alter an event. He recalled a quantum physicist who claimed that even the observation of an experiment affected its outcome. There was so much more about the old ranger he wanted to know, but the interviews of Leif's friends had revealed different sides of him in specific contexts from distinct perspectives. Was it possible to profile the whole man from this handful of sources?

As he flipped through his notes, he saw the scribbled words were enough to trigger a complete recollection of the conversations. The first interview was with Emery Daniels in late August. It was hot that day when he entered the brick Commerce Bank that mimicked a simplified Greek temple. "Boston, so good to see you," the old man rumbled from his dimly lit office filled with heavy furniture from an age long past. "Tell me what I may do for you." His rheumy eyes behind the large glasses wedged beneath a hedge of bushy brows created the visage of an owl. He wore a wool suit, regardless of the heat. Despite the old banker's informality, Boston still couldn't call him Emery. He began by asking Daniels if he was going to donate land for a nature preserve.

Daniels asked, "And where did you hear that?"

Boston caught the note of displeasure and said, "Ginger told me... but didn't name her source. She asked me to check it out before it's public knowledge."

Daniels said, "*Hmm,* that's true." Then he cleared his throat. "I own the oxbow chasm on Hennessey Creek and all the land on either side. Few know about it. That's the way I want it." After completing an ecological survey, he would announce it and the county board enacted its management plan as an ordinance.

Seeing that Daniels wasn't upset with him, Boston asked who was writing the plan. "Leif Nielsen," Daniels said. "Do you know him?"

When Boston shook his head, the banker said, "Leif is a man after my own heart. His life is a story in its own right. I can arrange an interview if you like."

In the months since then, Boston had filled a stack of small notebooks from interviewing Leif and his circle of family and friends. Each person had a distinct perspective. Since then, what started as a short piece about the Oxbow kept taking unforeseen turns until it evolved into one about Leif and his farm and then Leif and his career. Now, instead of profiling a man and the Oxbow, it had become a story of fraternal struggle over title to a run-down farm on a spring-fed lake.

What am I going to do with the story, Boston wondered. Dad harped on the principle that an honest reporter researched his subject thoroughly. It's something I honed over twenty years at *American Outlook*. Leif seemed sharp enough when I interviewed him. Share my notes, and they support the will. Withhold them, and the doctor has an easier path to claim Leif suffered a mental decline. No matter what I do, it will affect the judge's decision. I've always tried to tell the story straight as a custodian of the public good, but what is the public good, and how can I serve it?

Boston stood and stretched his arms to rid himself of stress. Maybe Ginger's right about my overwrought impartiality, he thought. The story lost its purity last October when I decided Leif's life story and his farm were more important than the Oxbow. Now he's dead, and his will has touched off a struggle over the farm. The story is mine to tell. There aren't many facts in the backstory, so I'll have to imagine some of it based on the interviews. It now seems this story, like so much of history, is a conflict to take or defend hunting grounds, fields, duchies or nations. Property works like an aphrodisiac that releases other deadly sins—lust, pride, envy, greed and wrath. Just how deep is the lust for land in Alton County—deep enough to kill for its title?

CHAPTER 2

Memory. What a powerful gift, Boston thought as he reviewed last August's interview with Leif. The sparse notes captured specific details from which he reconstructed the whole interview. It was a feat any journalist would covet. Daniels had arranged the meeting and told him that Leif had a look-you-in-the-eye honesty and hated double-talk and waffling. Though often contrary and opinionated, he was an honest and honorable man whose word was his bond. Well, if Daniels set store by him, he has to be quite a man.

The drive to Tarn Lake took Boston across the Tatanka River and over the gravel hills in the county's northwest corner. On the way, he passed woodlots and pastures where he and Jack had hunted pheasants in high school. Then he turned south at Stavanger—three houses, a gas station and the Plowboy Bar—and, after two miles of gravel road, crossed a hayfield to the farmhouse atop a low knoll overlooking the lake.

He glanced at his notes of first impressions: "House needs white paint. Salt-box barn, hen house and lean-to sheds need paint... any color. Aero-motor windmill, minus vanes, grapevines, anchors TV antenna." When Leif stepped out the back door, Boston scribbled: "Handsome... nearly eighty. Well-proportioned face, silver hair, salt and pepper mustache. Canvas pants, plaid shirt, Red Wing boots. Clothing... a 1940's style." He wondered if Leif was unaware of changing modes or was his dress for dramatic effect.

Boston noted Leif's direct welcome. "Daniels says you're all right. If he vouches for you, that's good enough for me. I know you cracked that money-skimming case last year. Shows you don't break under pressure. Got coffee on the stove. Let's make medicine on the porch and look at the lake."

He followed the forester through the backdoor into the kitchen and wrote down details: "Canvas jacket, felt hat hang from pegs. Heavy China mug... camp coffee, full-bodied. Front room... large windows, low bookcase... forestry manuals, field guides, binoculars. Rump-sprung couch, threadbare armchair... organic growths... been there forever. Small room to one side... bed and a dresser. Another room... work table, chair. Bathroom between them."

Closing his eyes, Boston recalled his emotions at the first view of Tarn Lake: "Teardrop cupped among stony hills.... Sunlight glints off chop... breeze shivers water... Wooded hills on west shore dwindle... knobs at outlet down the lake."

He recalled feeling ill-equipped to start the conversation. "Mister Daniels told me you and only you were to do the survey and the management plan. Knowing Emery as I do, that's a huge compliment."

Leif said, "I guess him and me are birds of a feather. We're fly-fishermen old enough to appreciate life's unknowns." He slurped some coffee and wiped the tips of his mustache. "Know what you're looking at?" he asked before the next question.

Boston recalled shaking his head and saying, "It's beautiful. Hard to believe this is southern Minnesota."

"It's more than beautiful," Leif said, drawing on the pipe. "It's perfect." And then he related how he was born there, as were his two sisters and a brother. "*Far* an' *Mor*... *oh*, that's Norski for father and mother. Well, anyway, they bought this place because it was cheap." He waved an arm. "Those hills reminded them of Norway. I spoke Norski in the home and with the neighbors before I learned English in school."

"I think your brother treated my gunshot wounds last year," Boston said.

He snorted. "Yeah, probably him. He's rich but not content with making people well. Still wants to make his mark with the Mayo Clinic crowd."

Boston remembered writing as fast as Leif talked, and for whatever reason, the ranger skirted his questions about the Oxbow. He said he didn't want to say much until after the survey. Instead, he told intriguing but seemingly irrelevant tales of his boyhood on the farm. Then he pulled on his pipe and pointed with the stem. "When I was a kid, there were five or six families across the lake—dairy and chicken farms. The neighbors come here with my folks in 1901. We got most of what we needed from the lake, the woods and the gardens." Then he pointed toward a field of timothy and clover where he and his father cleared stones from the soil and built a low wall now covered with raspberry canes. "Goddamn, but those were good days," he whispered as he blew a plume of smoke.

The neighbors couldn't make it on low prices in the 1920s, so the state took their farms for taxes and later turned them into a wildlife refuge. His father rented out his fields and went to work on the country road gangs. After the elder Nielsens died, he and Harald divided the property. His brother wanted the eighty acres of good land as collateral to build a clinic, and Leif took the rocky homestead because he loved it.

The forester interrupted this reminiscing, drew on his pipe and pointed at the sooty terns and tree swallows that darted after insects just above the water's surface. "See them? Notice how plants and animals support each other. A place for everyone. All equal. That's how I come to forestry," he said. "Studying natural science will reveal more about God and his intentions than what's in the Bible or Luther's catechism. If you're looking for revelation, it's all around you… in the creation."

After another moment of observation, he led Boston down the gentle knoll to a large boulder of pink granite. "The glaciers carried this down from the far north," Leif said as he sat on it. Then he leaned forward and rested his elbows on his knees. "I like to start the day here looking at the lake. It gets my mind in the right place. Now, you try it," he said, standing and lighting his pipe. "See those smaller stones… that's where my folks and one sister are buried. When my time comes, I'll lie there with 'em."

They walked onto a short dock. "This lake has walleyes, pickerel, bass and suckers," Leif said. "Fresh or smoked, they're good eating.

It's the pure water that gives 'em a sweet flavor." Then he said he plumbed the lake through the ice and found its deepest point was over a hundred feet.

Afterward, as they walked along the shore, Boston listened as the ranger seemed to be talking to himself as if his mind were in another place or time. He wondered if the old man felt his end approaching. Then he stopped and faced Boston. "You know, it's paradoxical that we humans lived out-of-doors for countless ages. Then we moved inside and became miserable. Makes you wonder, doesn't it?"

After that, Boston followed him through prairie grass as the ranger called out the names of flowers as if they were the neighbors along his road. Then he swept his arm around the farm and said this was what much of southern Minnesota used to look like. Boston glanced at his notes: "The farm… nothing but a stone-studded patch of prairie full of charms."

"People ask me why I don't sell it for de-*velopment*," Leif said, spitting out the last syllables of the word. "We've got enough of that already. Two guys from Rochester offered a hundred grand for ten acres. *Ten acres*! Just for cottages. I said no. Cottages, septic systems and motorboats would kill the last pristine lake in southern Minnesota. I won't let money destroy something so goddamn perfect. This place should belong to people who respect the web of life. They're few and getting fewer. I intend to see it's kept as it is."

"I understand," Boston said. "How are you going to do that?"

"Well, I haven't quite figured it out yet. My daughter lives in the Twin Cities but can't afford it. And Harald, hell, he'd sell it to some developer. No, I need to leave it to someone who respects it the way I do. Someone I trust."

Boston read the last entry from that interview. Though the property was hardly a farm, Leif had spoken of it in the voice of one talking about a child or possibly a lover. He had evaded questions about the Oxbow, and that's when it seemed the Oxbow story would be incomplete without a profile of Leif. Boston scratched his head. Most of what I know about him comes from those who knew him. How much can I believe?

CHAPTER 3

Leif Nielsen lowered his butt onto a limestone outcrop. "*Jeez*-zus, it's dry," he muttered, thumbing back the sweat-stained hat and taking a tally book from his shirt pocket. He dated the page "8/27/1985" and recorded the township, range and section, and quarter section. Then he noted the details of trees, rocks and wildlife in the tract he had just surveyed. He dribbled canteen water onto a bandana and wiped his face. Southeast Minnesota was baking in the summer's heat, and the drooping oak leaves seemed ready to fall without a killing frost. The spring brook in the coulee a hundred feet below him flowed with less water than usual. "*Key*-ryst, this is as bad as the summer of thirty-six." A bad fire year. Back then, he didn't even break a sweat hustling up ridges like this one. But not now. Seventy-seven years might slow me, but I'm not going to stop. Not and take it easy like brother Harald. No sir. Struggle brings out the flavor of life. Keep moving or die.

He sipped from the canteen, swished the water around in his mouth and spit. After another swig, he wiped droplets from the graying mustache, packed the bowl of his pipe and struck a match. There's good medicine in a smoke, he thought. It opens the mind.

He thought about yesterday's interview with Boston Meade. Didn't mind his company at all because the fella asked smart questions and knew when to leave. Not much to tell him anyway. Daniels wants to keep a lid on it until the survey is done. After that, he can have the whole story. No harm in telling Boston about growing up outdoors, working beside *Far* and getting through the lean years on pioneer skills. More and more these days, he thought of his career patrolling forest districts on foot, horseback and canoe. "*Jeez*-zus, that was a good life," he said under his breath. "Great until the goddamn desk rangers took over."

He had left the Forest Service after twenty-odd years because the leaders practiced politics instead of science. He had set up as a consulting forester in Featherstone, but it didn't pay off the way he figured. Even so, he had no regrets except one. He lost Lilja, and, without her, he lost a part of himself. It was a sadness that didn't go away.

Resting his elbows on his knees, he drew on the pipe and wished Sandy Brewster had come with him. We've worked in the woods ever since he was a sapling. Took him under my wing just in time, too. His dad was dead, Abby had her hands full and the pup was already in trouble. Calling him Saginaw after the lumber town seemed just right. He liked that. And he liked working for me on the farm. Work is what turned him around. Now he's a history professor. I know he'd be here now if he wasn't bucking for tenure. Well, we can take to the woods another time.

His memories always become stories, even the surprise phone call from Emery Daniels. It's been a long time since I've had real work. Some say Daniels is a business sage, and others say he's a tightwad. He could be both, of course, but he had a proposition. So, I went to meet him looking like a professional—whipcord trousers, a Pendleton shirt and oiled Red Wing boots. Sage or tightwad, he looked like good hickory timber—straight, sound and tough. And he probably looked at me like a credit risk.

That banker is no bullshitter, though. Real direct. He began by saying, "I'm told you're the best woods cruiser around." Then he came to the point. "I own two thousand acres that include the Oxbow chasm on Hennessey Creek. Know it?"

I told him, "I know the place. Been to both ends but never through it. I hear the chasm holds twilight all day, the creek runs fast and the pools have big trout." I like Daniels because he fell in love with the place years ago and bought the land around it to protect it. I'd of done the same if I had his money. He's shrewd, too. A biological inventory and a management plan will make certain the county follows his wishes. His donation hinges on my survey and management plan. I didn't expect that.

He recalled saying, "Thank you. I'm flattered, but the county parks staff could do this at no cost. Or maybe a prof from Seabury College. Why me?"

Daniels's bushy eyebrows jerked up and down, and then he cleared his throat. "That's because you know the area and bought land for the state forest. There is no other place like it in Minnesota. Few people know I own it. Keep that confidential. They say you keep confidences. I need someone who doesn't have a vested interest. You don't. Last of all, the protection plan has to consider the connections between organisms. I'm told you've got the experience, and your word is good. Are you interested?"

A stunning offer. I said, "Why yes. Of course."

"Good. I've prepared a contract for—"

"—I don't need a contract. A handshake will do."

"I agree. However, even though you work for me, the county will oversee your payment, and they require a contract." So, I filled in my daily fee and signed the contract in his office. Either one of us could cancel, but only in writing with two weeks' notice. I told him the survey would take a month, and the fee would be $20,000. A lot of money next to a few hundred dollars here and there from advising city crews how to manage their trees.

This is good work, he thought. It might be my last big job. The last good job, anyway. Honest work. Restorative work. This is what I was born to do. Though he couldn't name the feeling, it was a sensation of wholeness in flesh and spirit. Whatever it was, it restored some of the swagger he felt as a district ranger.

Daniels has an eye for land, he mused as he smoked. He's got three square miles of hillside prairies, oak woods and valley forests, limestone ridges and springs, sink holes and caves smack in the center of the state forest. Best of all, the Oxbow Chasm is some kind of Ice Age anomaly. The glaciers never covered this area, but when they melted, their waters found a way into an underground river that undermined the limestone. The gorge runs northeasterly, turns southerly and then northeasterly again and exits into a broad valley. It was nearly two hundred feet deep and a hundred feet across in places. Leif drew on the pipe, feeling privileged to survey it.

Mapping the Oxbow gave him a sense of kinship with the old-time surveyors who had divided the nation into townships and sections using only a transit, compass, rods and chains. Each township had thirty-six sections—each section a square mile of 640 acres. Twenty-one tracts surveyed, twenty-nine to go, he thought as he cleaned his pipe.

He pulled a small, hinged case from his rucksack. Its light frame with a stiff cowhide cover was a field desk he had made fifty years ago in therapy while recovering from burns in a forest fire. He opened it and removed a sheet of paper and colored pencils. Then he consulted a pocket notebook filled with enigmatic letters and numbers for the location of trees, shrubs, plants and animals in the parcel he had just surveyed. Field mapping, even small parcels, was more of an art than a science. For accuracy, he subdivided the Oxbow lands into fifty parcels of forty acres and made a map of each parcel. A large square on a sheet of paper represented forty acres that he subdivided into four parcels of ten acres. At that scale, he could accurately sketch in the land's contours in brown lines with hash marks for the escarpments. Curly green lines limned the timbered areas with notes on species. Blue spots and lines located springs, seeps and brooks. Red stars meant a special feature like a cave or colonies of rare plants. Each map had a companion page of detailed notes.

Leif rose from the ledge and blazed two sides of a tree with his small axe to mark the corner of a parcel. From there, he took 264 paces along a compass course and cut a blaze. Walking with a woodsman's high-stepping pace, he went another 264 paces and cut a double blaze. Then he turned ninety degrees and paced his way along another side until he went around the parcel. Afterward, he crisscrossed the center of the parcel from one middle blaze to another and recorded everything he saw. It took over an hour to inventory a tract. He took pride in his accuracy, using this old but effective method.

Getting into the field and living close to the earth renewed him like a colt let onto spring grass. After four long days of climbing and descending ridges, he stumbled into his camp at day's end, gasping like a beached carp. The wheeze that began in the morning now seemed worse. He leaned against the '72 Chevy van and coughed to clear his lungs. "Goddamn, a summer cold," he muttered and pulled off his boots, skinned out of his sweaty clothes and sponged himself from a pail of sun-warmed water.

The easiest part of the Oxbow is done, he thought, putting on fresh clothes. Eight hundred acres along the chasm's east side. The west side will be rougher. That'll take five days. Then three more for the chasm. He hacked up a gob of phlegm. "God-damnit! Couldn't have asked for better weather." He opened the van's rear doors, set a portable typewriter on a box and cranked in a sheet of paper. Pecking at the keys, he transcribed the notes from today's surveys. Then he clipped the sheets—one per forty acres—to their corresponding maps and added them to a three-ring binder.

He poured whiskey into a steel cup and cut it with spring water. Tonight's stew of tomatoes, potatoes, onions and Polish sausage bubbled on the Coleman stove. As he ate, his mind turned to his farm on Tarn Lake. He owned 180 acres of level, rocky soil that had defied plowing. Most of it was still wild grassland on 4,000 feet of lakeshore. His farm, the state wildlife refuge and a Nature Conservancy preserve protected the lake. This contract was a lot of money but not enough to keep the farm undeveloped forever.

If only I could leave it to someone who can afford to keep it the way it is, he brooded. The way it's always been. Better figure it out. *Damn.* If only I knew someone with that kind of money.

.

CHAPTER 4

The intercom in the Waterford Medical Clinic paged Dr. Nielsen for an emergency phone call. He looked up from examining a patient and picked up the phone. "Yes… I understand… I'll take responsibility for him, of course. Make him comfortable. I'll be there shortly." He hung up, finished his examination and told his assistant to cancel the day's other appointments. Then he raced twenty miles to the county hospital in Featherstone.

The station nurse stopped him just outside Leif's room. "A neighbor stopped by and found him," she said. "He could barely stand when we admitted him." Harald entered, read the intake report, checked his vitals and listened to the rattle in his lungs. He shivered at the sight of his brother's hollow cheeks and sallow complexion. He might not last the night. The next twenty-four hours would be critical.

"Pneumonia," Harald told him, taking the stethoscope from his ears. "You'll be here a while."

Leif barely opened his eyes. "Hullo, Harald."

Harald assured him he would call Karla that evening. Giving grave news about a loved one requires skill. Although he was good at it, he disliked doing it because he didn't always feel authentic compassion when he did it. A patient's death was unacceptable, and he took it personally, like a failure on his part.

He gave Karla the news, and from her voice, he knew it alarmed her. She said she would be down right away.

"Wait until tomorrow," he told her. "I think the old bull will rally once the antibiotics kick in. Then we'll know if he has the strength for visitors."

"All right, you know best," she said. "I don't want to lose him without saying goodbye, whether he can hear me or not."

Leif was asleep when Harald stopped in the morning. He noticed his brother's breathing sounded clearer, so he went about his rounds. When he returned, the old ranger was sitting up in bed and fully alert. It seemed like a miracle.

Harald stood at the foot of the bed and looked him in the eye. "You're better already," he said in surprise and checked the charts. "That's an incredible rebound. You can go home in a few days."

"Good," he grunted. "I don't like it here."

"You better take it easy from now on. You're not a young buck anymore. No more camping."

"We'll see about that," he snorted and then started coughing.

"Be serious," Harald pleaded. "Think about how to live your last years. Think about what happens to the farm after you're gone."

"Why?" he asked testily. "I'm not dying any time soon."

"It could happen. You're at a point where it isn't safe to live alone."

"The hell I can't," he bristled. "I'll live there 'til I die—and that ain't soon. Hell, even sick, I'm stronger than you." He sat straighter to make his point. "A life without struggle isn't worth much. When the day comes that I can't… that's when I pack it in. I'm not—"

"—Think about this. If you sold the farm, you could get enough to buy a place in town. You could have someone to cook and clean for you," Harald said, giving Leif's leg a gentle pat. "Think it over. Be sensible. You're pushing eighty and—"

"—And I'm old enough to know my mind," he snapped. "Goddamnit, I'm not going to let you shove me into a compost bin you call a nursing home. *Jeez*-zus *Key*-ryst! You ought to know me better than that. I entered the world at the lake, and by God, that's where I'll leave it."

"Easy. Don't get all worked up. I'm sorry. I just don't understand your attachment to that place. It's an old house on a lonely lake."

Leif fixed him with his good eye. The monitor beeped in the silence as the brothers engaged in a stare-down. The doctor shifted from one foot to the other, then stuck his soft hands into the pockets of his lab coat.

"No, Harald," he said in a hoarse voice. "You don't understand. If you did, you wouldn't ask me to sell out. The farm is more than land."

"Maybe you can explain that sometime," he said, pulling the stethoscope from the coat pocket and hooking it around his neck. "I've got to make the rounds now."

"I'll explain it when you drive me home," he called after him. Then he lay back against the pillows. The argument used up his energy, and he felt weak again. He dozed until an orderly wheeled in his lunch. He looked at the tray of soft foods with disgust. Picking through it, he pondered how he and his brother could be strangers when the same mother gave them life. We're men of different generations, he thought. Too bad our lives don't overlap enough for a sense of real kinship. We're like those twins in the Bible. He is the younger, clever one. I'm the wild man of the field. But who are you really, Harald? What makes you tick?

Leif's outburst chafed Harald for the rest of the day and on the half-hour drive home to Waterford. We aren't close in age or interests, he thought, but we always got along. Sure, he still acts like an older brother. He can't help it. But it's not likely we'll ever be of one mind about the farm, the lake or—or maybe life itself. Wish it weren't so, but too much has happened in between.

If Leif sold a couple of lakeside lots, he would have enough money to live comfortably, Harald thought. But selling a lot here and there gets him small change. The big money comes from selling it all to a developer. There's a couple million's worth in lakeshore alone, even more with high-end houses on a private lake. There's enough shoreline for a small village. An ideal getaway. Why, I know Mayo doctors and IBM execs who'd pay through the nose for a place on that lake. There's even space for a private golf course. And why not? After all these years, that place could make real money and give pleasure to those who can afford it.

Harald shook his head. Leif's sitting on a gold mine and doesn't know it. The farm is too valuable to let it go. If he doesn't make provisions for it, then it's up to me to see it stays in the family. By rights, it should come to me when he goes. I was born there. The folks are buried there. He has it because he didn't want to sell it. Karla doesn't want it and can't afford it if she did. No, I've got as much moral right to the farm as he does. But he'll never go for a partnership.

Harald parked the cobalt blue Lincoln beside the black Mercedes in the triple garage. Entering the chateau-style house, he went directly to the paneled salon where Regina waited with the evening's pitcher of martinis. She arched her neck and poured a drink for Harald. She had weaned off rum and Coke in favor of cocktails. As the daughter of a wealthy lawyer, she considered his preferences *declassee*, and during their courtship, she introduced him to cocktails, tailored suits and the social skills necessary to fit into her social circle. Though she no longer practiced law, she kept her license and used her legal contacts to build a power base within the Republican Party.

Harald plopped into his favorite chair and laid out the idea for getting Leif to sell the farm so they could develop it.

"And how did *that* go?" she asked, raising a neatly plucked eyebrow.

He wiped a hand across his high forehead. "He said, no... well, he didn't say no. He yelled, hell no. *Never.*"

She laughed without mirth. "I'm not surprised. He's shiftless. So what? The farm isn't worth much anyway." She got up and went to the kitchen to check on the maid and see about dinner. "Does he have a will?"

"I don't think so, but the farm is valuable."

"What, that rock pile?"

"Exactly. He owns the only land that can be developed on a spring-fed lake. Not another one like it at this end of the state. It's got huge value." He ate the martini olive. "He doesn't know what he's got."

22

"Really. What's the value?" She put the glass to her lips and gazed at him.

"Book value on lakefront runs one-hundred-twenty a foot. That's easily six hundred grand without buildings."

"And with buildings?"

"*Mmm*, you could easily sell twenty-five lots with two hundred feet of frontage for fifty grand apiece. That's over a million dollars with a hundred acres left over for putting greens and tennis courts. It could be wrapped into a package with a beach and a small marina for added revenue."

"And with houses?" she asked, shifting to the edge of her seat.

"Millions if the property is sold or developed as a package," he said, warming to the idea. "Twenty-five houses—fifty grand for the lots and say an average of four hundred grand for each house. That comes to…" he began counting his fingers.

"Easily ten million dollars, dear," she said, rising from the chair and refreshing her drink. "But if he dies without a will, the state will take a third and allocate the property between you and Karla as the next of kin." She pressed her lips into a hard line.

"Yeah, I know."

"So, without a will, we might get two hundred thousand in cash and lose the opportunity to develop the farm as a package."

"I'm afraid so, sweetheart." He sighed, and his shoulders slumped.

"Is that all you can say," she snapped, impaling him with an icy glare.

"Well, he wouldn't say what he planned to do with the place. He's stubborn. Doesn't know when he's well off. Never has. It's harder now that he's older."

"Yes," she said with a smile. "Yes. That's even better."

"What's better?"

"He's old. It's likely he's lost mental acuity. In fact, I'm sure of it," she added, nodding her head. "Don't you see, he's incompetent. A rational person would sell and live well. It's clear he's at the point where he needs your guidance to make business decisions." She smiled and then kissed his forehead.

He drained his martini and held up the glass. "He wants to be buried there. Said we could be, too, if we wanted." He let out a belly laugh.

"That's not funny. What are you going to do?"

"I'll ask him to make a will. It's all I can do."

"Wake up, Harald. Don't *ask*, dear. *Act*. Take the initiative. Honestly… sometimes you are so passive—like my mother when she was sober. Daddy taught me to act. Instead of waiting for things to happen, make them happen. Take charge."

"Well, what do you suggest?"

"*Ugh*. Ask Sam to draft a will. Something simple but airtight. Make sure Karla gets the family heirlooms and any cash. He probably doesn't have much, but she should have it. Don't specify anything for yourself. Just make certain you are his personal representative with authority to act in his best interest when that becomes necessary. I can't prepare the will because I didn't practice that kind of law. Sam is skilled at that. Besides, you know your brother wouldn't sign it if he thought I drafted it."

"*Hmm*. Yeah, but he's not incompetent. Just bull-headed."

"A court will decide that when the time comes," she said. "We need Karla to agree. Maybe she could petition the court to name you his guardian. We live closer to him than she does. She needs money and is entitled to some share of selling the undeveloped property. She could use a fifty-or sixty-thousand-dollar windfall."

"I don't think she'd go for a petition," he said. "She's protective of their relations. As a paralegal, she might resist or raise questions."

"Well, you know her better than I do."

He paced the floor still holding the empty martini glass. "Yeah, I think he'll sign a will if he knows that I'm his personal representative."

"Just think of it, dear, if we do this right, the farm will stay in the family, and we stand to gain millions."

He gazed at Regina for a moment, flushed with gratitude for the good fortune to marry such a bold thinker. That's what had drawn him to her. Besides that, she was also beautiful and cultured. Thanks to her wit, they could be ten million richer when nature took its course.

CHAPTER 5

Boston's house baked in the early September heat, and he sat on the covered veranda in nothing but boxers. He looked up from a magazine at the sound of Ginger's car coming up the hill. She would be tired after an hour with her mother at the Franciscan Villas. The nursing home visits usually drained her high spirits.

She got out of the car and whistled. "Wow, you're *hot!*"

"I'm roasting."

"I meant your looks, not the temperature. You've got the right idea. I'll join you," she said and quickly stripped to her bra and panties.

"Keep going!"

She flipped him the bird and ran inside to change clothes.

"How was Mama?" he asked when she returned wearing a slip.

"Well… silent, as usual," she said with a fatalistic sigh. "We may never have a conversation. I can't remember when she wasn't angry. I think her dementia is rooted in anger since childhood. She was disappointed in Daddy and furious when I didn't become a nun or marry you. It's permanent; it's fossilized in her psyche. You know the rest," she sniffled and wiped her eyes.

"I'm sorry for you both. If only she could see the woman you are," he said, reaching for her hand.

"Thanks, lover. Caring for her is my half of reconciliation."

"You know I admire you for it. And I know the feeling, too. Dad withdrew emotionally after Mom died. He just doubled down on his work." He squeezed her hand, and she squeezed back. "You and Jack got me through that."

"I heard Leif is in the hospital," she said, propping her bare feet on the railing and wiggling her painted toes. "Pneumonia, I heard."

"Oh? He seemed all right last week."

"I overheard it at the Streamliner, but no details."

"I better see him before anything happens to him," and he got up to call Harald.

The doctor turned down the request to visit him but offered to be interviewed instead. In fact, Boston thought he seemed eager to talk about him. Why not? Harald was well-regarded as a doctor and as the former mayor of Waterford. Now, he was a county commissioner. Besides his medical practice, he owned the Waterford Clinic and half-owned a Rexall pharmacy. Boston thought a brother's perspective might be a penetrating one. Maybe Harald could tell him more than the forester had. Besides that, he looked forward to meeting Regina. He heard she had practiced criminal law before marriage and was now politically influential. Some day, she might be a source for a political story.

Waterford had changed a lot since Boston's last visit a decade ago. During Harald's mayorship, the town transformed from a modest rural commercial center into an upscale bedroom community that capitalized on developing amenities along the placid Wacouta River. As doctors, professionals and executives from Rochester moved in, Victorian houses became bed-and-breakfast inns, and empty storefronts became new specialty shops and restaurants. He passed through the downtown and drove east on River Street to the curving driveway with "Nielsen" chiseled into an upright slab of dolomite. The cut-stone house sat on a terrace facing the riverside parkland. Its mansard roof, dormers and multiple chimneys reminded him of a chateaux he had seen in France.

"Welcome. Come in, come in now," Harald called and led him into the living room with tall windows that framed a view of the tree-lined river.

"What an incredible view," Boston said, gazing through an arched window at a couple strolling hand-in-hand along the river path. He noticed the room's thick Persian rugs, original impressionist art and colonial furniture. It didn't feel like a cozy family room as much as a showplace for entertaining, if not impressing others. "You have an extraordinarily beautiful home," he said.

"It's Regina's work," Harald said, beaming. "She's a visionary. You can tell her. She'll be along later." The young maid brought in a carafe of coffee and poured a cup for Boston and then one for Harald. They faced each other in matching spindle-back chairs. "As I understand it, you're profiling my brother," he began. "Of course, he'd be your best source."

"I talked with him a few weeks ago. He's a most interesting and remarkable man. He told me a lot about the farm but evaded questions about his personal life. You don't often meet a scientific forester who is also an old-school woodsman."

"Oh, he's all of that," he said with a chuckle. "Sometimes I don't know which brother I'm talking to—the scientist or the woodsman."

Boston asked him to talk about Leif in whatever way he felt comfortable without betraying confidences. As the doctor talked, Boston noted his appearance: "About Leif's height… pale blue eyes, thinning hair. Expensive suit… size too large. Rotund body lacks coordination… waddles like a penguin, splay-footed, stiff-armed. Pleasant face, genial nature, like Porky Pig." Where Leif laced his conversations with pungent terms and profanity, Harald spoke in banal phrases that wouldn't offend anyone. It seemed strange they could be brothers.

Harald said Leif was born in 1908, and he was born in 1923 but had no recollection of his older brother's childhood. He was four when Leif went to the university, and he saw even less of him after he joined the Forest Service. Harald recalled his life on the farm as constant hardship and poverty caused by drought, poor crops and low prices. He was eight when his father got steady work on the roads, and they moved to town. "Leif says the early years were the good ones," Harald said. "Maybe so. But I knew only hard times." After that, questions about Leif became segues for Harald to talk about his medical studies, building his practice, the clinic and all he did for Waterford as its mayor. Though this wasn't what Boston wanted from him, he made notes. Then he asked about Leif's health.

"Oh, he'll be fine once he settles down. He's pushing eighty but thinks he's twenty-one." Harald laughed. "Despite his age and years of drinking and smoking, he's still as sharp as a tack. I'm trying to convince him to sell that place and move into town. If he'd cooperate, why, we could develop the farm and make millions, you know. Wouldn't you like a second home on that lake?"

The question struck Boston like an off-key piano chord. It seemed to him Harald admired a version of his older brother but didn't really know him, and there was little he could tell him about Leif. Taking another tack, he asked Harald for the names of people outside the family who knew him, people he might talk to.

"Let's see... there's his daughter Karla in Minneapolis. She's all right, but I'm not sure they're particularly close. There's Abigail Brewster here in town. Her late husband was one of his closest friends. Her son Sandy is kind of like his woods protégé. He's a professor at Seabury College. Oh, and Morrie Isaacs. He's a lawyer in Featherstone that Leif taught to fish. And then there's Fred Bosch. He owns the Plowboy Bar. Beyond that... I really can't say."

"That's helpful. Thanks."

"Oh, that will be Regina," Harald said at the sound of the garage door rolling up. An inside door opened and closed a moment later. "We're in the salon," he called.

Everything about her entrance impressed Boston. Her golden complexion, mauve suit of raw silk and erect carriage were striking but in restrained good taste. Slender and exquisitely made-up, with her dark hair gathered in a bun at the nape of her neck, everything about her seemed regal. In her narrow, dark eyes, he sensed a commanding presence that made him feel he should immediately get to his feet to await her pleasure. He guessed she was over fifty, but it was hard to tell. Everything about her seemed groomed, plucked and tailored to silently express her wealth, power and command.

"Welcome to Nielsen Manor," she said with a smile and extended a jeweled hand. "I see you have coffee. We usually have cocktails now, so I hope you will join us," she said and sat on the loveseat.

"Thank you, but I have an evening engagement in Featherstone," he lied from an inexplicable on-set of emotional disquiet. She and Harald struck him as an odd couple, a toad and a princess. Their union, whether spiritual or carnal, is none of my business, he reminded himself. People probably wonder about Ginger and me.

"Boston is writing a profile about Leif—as a woodsman and scientific forester. I was telling him a little about him and the farm."

"Oh, I see," she said evenly, arching her brows. "It will be interesting, I'm sure."

"He seems like a remarkable man," he said but saw a flash of annoyance in her eyes like an electric spark and wondered if there was more to it. He chatted with them for a few more minutes and then stood to leave.

"I hope you come again," Harald said. "If there's anything more you want to know, just call."

"Yes, come again," she said. "And stay for cocktails next time."

Boston paused beside the Jeep to admire the manor set among some maples. So, this is how the other Nielsen's live, he thought. The backyard had a formal garden complete with a fountain and pool in the center of a flagstone patio surrounded by a lush lawn with flower beds and enclosed by a low hedge of yew. Farther back and partially visible through some oaks stood a solid-looking house wearing a coat of light gray paint with dark green trim. Harald said they had a guest house, and Boston guessed it was the original farmhouse that came with their twenty-acre lot.

On the drive home, Boston noted that Leif had avoided saying much about his personal life, but Harald talked about himself and little else. And then there was Regina. She had an aura he couldn't fathom, but noticed a tone of distaste after he mentioned Leif. There's a story there as well, he thought, but then dropped it. Probably nothing more than the usual dysfunctions among in-laws in every family. He saw no reason to return for another interview.

It was midafternoon when Boston returned home and began preparing supper. He took on all the cooking a year ago when Ginger moved in. Though she appreciated good food, her timid culinary skills rarely ventured much beyond salads, brown rice and roasted chicken breasts. For his part, he enjoyed preparing something elaborate to share with her. Besides, she spent her days managing his newspaper while he stayed home and wrote syndicated columns for *American Outlook*. He thought it a fair arrangement.

"Learn anything interesting?" she asked while setting the table.

"Not much. Harald talked a lot about what he's done for Waterford. He's filthy rich. You ought to see their house. It's a regular chateau with a live-in maid. The only things missing are liveried footmen and a vineyard. Our house is a chicken coop by comparison. And then there's his wife."

"Did you meet her—what's she like?" she asked, eyes bright with anticipation. "I hear she's a political wheel."

"She's... *uh*... unforgettable... unforgettable like the queen in Snow White."

"Explain that. I don't get the connection."

"She's cold, imperious and... I caught a bitter undertone in her voice."

"Oh. Why do you think he wouldn't or didn't talk about Leif?"

"They didn't grow up together. There's a fifteen-year difference in their ages. Everything he told me sounded too polished, too curated to be the whole story. In fact, they almost have conflicting childhood narratives. On top of that, I don't think Harald knows much about his brother because he was four when Leif left the farm."

"So, they're hiding something."

"I don't know," he said but later added her comment to his notes.

CHAPTER 6

News of Leif's condition rattled Karla's tightly organized life. She took a vacation day and drove to the Featherstone hospital. Behind the wheel, she fretted at the thought of losing him. Though she was too young to grasp the complexities of marriage at fourteen, she still regretted all the years she had avoided him. Even after he said the divorce was his fault, it was easier to blame him for it—and every other problem, too. She even asked Harald to walk her to the altar to spite him. Then she smiled. *Daddy didn't give up. He had my back when I divorced the bastard I married. That must be what they call karma. That's when I grew up. Divorce meant dropping out of law school and working to support Ted. I can't afford to send Ted to a private college, but Harald has no children. Maybe he will have some ideas about how to help Ted.*

She felt a rush of relief when Leif opened his eyes at the sound of her entrance. "Hey, gal. You look good," he wheezed and gave her a weary smile. "How's Ted?"

"Hi, Daddy," she answered and kissed his forehead. "He's great. I'll bring him next time. He wants to see you." She took his hand, the one with the band on the wrist. "This gave me a shock," she said. "Tell me what happened."

"Not as bad as Harald says. Doctors like to dramatize. Makes 'em look heroic."

"Be serious now, Daddy. This could kill you."

31

"That'll be the day," he snorted and touched her thick blond hair. They sat in silence for a moment before he asked about Ted's plans for college.

"He's been accepted at the university. We're exploring private colleges, but they're so expensive. He's got good grades but not enough for big scholarships." She talked fast to cover her unease at his appearance. He seemed smaller and thinner than she remembered. At this rate, he might last only a few months. A couple years at most. After that... But she kept the thought to herself and thought of preparations. "Daddy, do you have a will?"

He looked at her as if she had two heads and then shook his head.

"Daddy, if you don't have a will, the state will sell the farm and..."

"Did Harald put you to this?" He squinted at her, annoyed.

"He mentioned it."

"No rush, gal. I'll be out in a couple days. I'm not going to die any time soon."

"Face it, Daddy. It could happen any day," she said, now stern. "In my legal work, I see what happens when there isn't a will. Please put things in order. Spell out what you want. If you don't, it'll leave a mess for the rest of us. Will you do that, please? For Ted's sake," she begged, playing to his soft spot.

"Okay. I promise," he said and smiled. "I'll do it as soon as I get outta here."

Leif couldn't look at Karla without seeing her mother, Lilja Haakala. Damn, but if she isn't the spitting image of her. Got her mother's figure, golden hair and those high cheekbones. Just wish she'd smile more often. She's damn good-looking when she does.

He had never been able to forget Lilja for long. They met at a dance in northern Michigan when he was a ranger, and she was a public health nurse. Her smile could light up a dark room. They fell in love and married ten months later. He still recalled the details of her face, her voice and even her scent after making love. For almost twenty years, every day had felt like May—warm, bright and full of promise. He hadn't felt such joy since. God, but she was a classy woman.

The remembrance of Lilja took him back to the summer of 1936. It was the year of the big burn that took his right eye. He remembered how she nursed him through the skin grafts and restored his confidence. Then Karla came, and Lilja put up with my griping and pushing back against the wink-and-nod foresters and their politically expedient decisions. It cost me a couple of promotions. She didn't want me to quit the service. And just as she feared, I couldn't make a go of it as a consulting forester. I should've listened to her. Losing the house was a minor thing compared to losing each other. It was my single, angry slap that did it. She filed for divorce and took Karla with her. When was the last time I saw her, he wondered. Had to be at Karla's wedding. Twenty years ago. God, she was still good-looking at fifty-two.

Seeing Karla and thinking of her mother revived him, and he slept well for several nights as his lungs cleared. Waking on the fourth day, he felt ready to go home, sit on the porch and look at the lake. It was an innate urge, like the migratory impulse of wild geese. He sat up, threw his legs over the edge of the bed and stood. No dizziness. He huffed in a deep breath. No rattling, no wheezing and no coughing. After a few short steps, he judged his legs were as strong as before. He was looking out the window when the nurse entered behind him.

"Damn-it. Can't a man have a little privacy," he barked, whipping the gown across his naked backside.

"You should be in bed," she scolded with mirth in her voice. "The doctor won't like you up and around."

"Doctor," he scoffed. "He's just a kid brother. It'll be a cold day in hell when he tells me what to do and makes it stick."

She laughed again, told him to stay in his room and closed the door as she left. Putting on his old clothes restored his sense of himself. Then, he sat on a chair and read the *Statesman* until Harald arrived.

"You look much better," he said from the doorway and jammed his pink hands in the pockets of the white coat. "I'll take you home tomorrow. Oh, Karla told me you don't have a will. That right?"

He nodded. "I'll get it done this week."

"Here's something to get you started," Harald said, drawing some folded papers from the lab coat pocket. "My attorney drafted an outline for you," he explained. "It's pretty much the same boilerplate language that's in my will. All you need to do is fill in some particulars. Those are the blank spaces. Put down who gets your personal items and so forth. When you're done, we'll go to my lawyer's office to sign and file it."

"Thanks," he said, taking the papers and putting them on the bed. "I'll read it when I finish with this," he said, holding up the newspaper.

Leif put on his glasses and read every word of the draft. Well, it's got the usual convoluted legal bullshit, he thought. It's airtight and covers just about everything important. He read it again, folded it carefully and put it with his other personal effects.

CHAPTER 7

Harald parked the Lincoln behind the farmhouse, and the Nielsen brothers got out. Leif lit his pipe, and Harald scolded him for smoking, but he saw robust color in his brother's face and joy in his voice. They went inside, and Leif brewed a pot of camp coffee, filled two ceramic mugs and led his brother to the porch.

"That's a fine-looking garden," Harald said, waving toward the overgrown patch of potatoes, squash, pole beans, cabbages and onions. "The squash looks ripe. You sure take after *Mor* in that respect."

Leif slurped deeply from his mug. "This place is the best medicine," he said. "I need this more than pills—no disrespect, kid. I'm grateful for what you've done. Just send me the bill."

"No, that's okay. Keep your money. Never know when you'll need it."

Leif waved his pipestem at the lake. "*Far* and *Mor* got something more than land with this."

"What—it's nothing but rocky ground."

Leif swept an arm at the lake. "Look at that. *Dette er himmelen på jorden*—this is heaven on earth. Still looks as new as the day God made it. Unspoiled. Good medicine."

"So tell me why it's so special to you," Harald said. "Tell me—in English."

Leif hacked and spit. "You don't remember speaking Norski, do you? Well, growing up here was a happy time. The lake and wooded hills reminded *Far* and *Mor* of their old home near Trondheim. They

35

were happy because they had friends on farms across the lake. There were parties and dances. There was a country school and a Lutheran chapel up the road where the Plowboy is now."

"I don't recall them, sorry."

"That was before you were born. *Key*-ryst, but those were good years," he said, rubbing a hand over his mouth. "*Bare gyllent*—just golden."

"I have different memories," Harald said with an edge in his voice. "We didn't have money for shoes. *Mor* cried a lot, and *Far* was angry all the time. Things got real bad right after you went into the Forest Service."

He drew on his pipe and ran fingers through his silver hair. "Yeah, I know. Our world was perfect up 'til twenty-seven or so. Just goddamn perfect," he said and then coughed until he gasped like a beached fish.

"You all right?"

"Yeah," Leif wheezed. "You know why it was perfect?" He fixed Harald with his hard, blue eye. "Because we had a community. *Mor* cooked and canned the ducks and geese and pheasants we shot. We caught and smoked fish. Our garden gave us all the vegetables we could eat. The cows gave us milk and butter and cheese. Our chickens gave us eggs and fryers. The soil, the lake, the woods and the neighbors gave us everything we needed. It was perfect. All we had to do was make it useful. Life had a clear purpose. That's perfection."

Harald nodded. "Oh, I see. Hunting and fishing and—"

"—*Key*-ryst, it wasn't the hunting and fishing," he said, annoyed. "I don't have the exact words for it. It was like we were living a special life. Like a life ordained by God or something. It had order and purpose and purity. Like we lived under a dome where nothing could touch us."

"Well, the dome broke after you left," he retorted.

"Yeah, things changed about then. But not all at once. The bottom fell out of milk and corn prices right after *Far* bought those good fields. The ones you got. That was after he already bought a tractor on time. Then he couldn't pay the interest on it."

"I remember the crops didn't do well, and he couldn't pay taxes."

36

"That was the drought," Leif explained. "*Far* was a damn good farmer but a piss-poor businessman. He always believed tomorrow would be better. It's a good quality, generally, but it didn't help him. I sent him money every month after I went to the Forest Service. It wasn't a lot, but it got you by."

"I didn't know that." He patted his older brother's leg. "Thanks."

"Him and me made a plan. When he got the county job, he sold the cows and the machinery, rented out the land and moved you to town. That's what saved the farm."

"I remember the move," Harald said. "A happy day. I was lonely out here—especially after you left."

"I've never been lonely here. Not with a lake full of geese, a pelican now and then, some deer and a few turkeys. Come on now, this is beautiful."

"Yeah, it has possibilities. Some development could really make it shine."

"*Development!*" Leif spat out the word. "You can't improve this. It's already perfect." Silence followed his outburst. Then he drew a breath. "*Far* hated to leave this place because he put sweat into it. That's what land does. You work it until it owns you."

"I recall *Far* and *Mor* were happier after the move."

"She was happier on account of you," he agreed. "But she missed the lake, her garden and the wildflowers. That's why they're buried here next to Cora."

"And that's why you want to stay."

Leif coughed. "I damn well plan to stay here to my end."

"But you aren't well enough to live alone. You—"

"—I want to die when I can't take care of myself. And when I'm dead, I want to lie here next to *Mor* and *Far*." He paused to catch his breath. "And when your time comes, you and yours are welcome to lie next to me," he added with a sly smile.

"Thanks. I'll give it some thought."

Leif knew Harald wouldn't be buried there. Not if Regina had anything to say about it—and he knew she would.

CHAPTER 8

Twenty-four hours at Tarn Lake and Leif felt like a man in his fifties. Yesterday's chat with Harald replayed in his mind while he hoed the garden. He's hot to develop this place—except he doesn't own it. So, what's he up to? When he finished hoeing, he made coffee and drank it on the porch. He read the will twice, called his attorney in Featherstone and made an appointment.

Morris Isaacs had a private law practice on the second floor of the Heath Block, a yellow brick building with tall, arched windows and brick filigree at the cornices. The lawyer was a trim man in his early sixties who wore brownish suits the color of his thinning hair and mellow eyes. These last fifteen years of private practice were much quieter than the previous fifteen as the state's deputy attorney general. And yet, he missed the excitement. He heard the street door open and then shut, followed by a slow tread up the stairs. Leif, he thought when he heard the client catch his breath at the landing.

Their unlikely friendship began shortly after Isaacs moved to Featherstone. He asked the ranger to teach him the art of fly fishing. Leif had just bought the Chevy van and told him he had "jewed down the price and got a great deal." Isaacs had heard that slur all his life. An insult on so many levels.

He had looked Leif in the eye and said, "I take that comment personally. In case you don't know it, I'm Jewish." Leif opened and shut his mouth. With some heat, Isaacs said his immigrant grandfather went from town to town peddling dry goods from a

39

wagon until he opened a store in Rochester. His father ran the store, bought a house and sent Isaacs to college. He remembered how Leif hung his head and said he was sorry. It was something he heard at home. To drive the point home, Isaacs said he didn't tolerate prejudice but offered his hand. After that, the friendship ripened while fishing together.

"I want to make my will," Leif said as he accepted the proffered cup of instant Nescafe. "Harald's convinced I'm going to croak any minute now," he laughed as if the idea were ridiculous, but mirth produced coughing. "I promised Karla I'd do it. Now Harald had his lawyer draft this one without consulting me." He shoved the papers toward Isaacs. "Take a look."

"I see," Isaacs said after he read it. "This one's complete. All you have to do is fill in a couple of blanks and sign it. Is this what you want?"

"No. First off, he didn't consult me. Some of the language is all right, I guess. Second of all, I want to make a few changes." He picked up Isaacs' fountain pen, crossed out several words and wrote others in the space above them. Then he pushed the pages across the desk.

"This is fine, but I think we should discuss the implications."

"Nope. This is what I want to do if it looks legal to you."

"Yes, this is fine. I'll have a revised version typed up. Come back after lunch. I'll have witnesses and a notary for your signature."

That's what I like about Morrie, he thought, going down the stairs. No double-talk, no pussyfooting. Just straight to the point. He walked the length of the Green to The Streamliner Restaurant, pleased his joints and muscles felt in working order. The restaurant, a 1930s dining car fused into the sides of a brick building, was the downtown hub for breakfast and lunch. He was ahead of the noon rush and bantered with the sassy younger woman who owned it. Then he returned to the law office, read the revised will and signed it. Isaacs said he would take care of the rest. Leif drove home, pleased he had kept his promise to Karla. Now to complete the survey.

Daniels called Boston with the news that Leif was out of the hospital and offered to arrange another visit. Boston finished the call bemused and grateful to the codger, who sometimes acted like a fierce guardian angel. He reviewed the notes from the previous interview and prepared the questions he wanted to ask him. The most puzzling thing about the ranger was his sense of time. His clothes and his stories harked back to the 1930s, yet he talked about them as if they had happened yesterday. It made Boston think the old ranger was living in the past and not as sharp as he and the others thought.

Leif looked up from loading camping gear into the van as Boston arrived. "How are you doing, young fella?" he asked in a hearty voice. "As you see, I'm good as new in spite of anything my brother says. I'm going to the Oxbow tomorrow. You can come along if you like. That is, if you can sleep on the ground and eat simple grub." He laughed until he started coughing.

"Thanks. Wish I could spare a week. Maybe I can meet up with you for a day."

"Well, I dunno. It's a question of where I'll be and when. Let me think about that while we talk." Leif glanced at the sky. "Say, it's late enough for some whiskey now. Let's have a snort."

They sat on the porch drinking whiskey from ceramic coffee mugs and watched as a small vee of geese wheeled in for the evening. Neither man said anything. Leif watched the geese the way a father watched his firstborn. Boston interpreted the silence between them as a gentle bond of comradeship, something mutually understood that needed no words. He had felt something like it as a reporter traveling with the Marines in Vietnam. They let their actions say what they felt. He honored the moment by holding his questions in check until they had finished the drinks.

"Last time we met, you told me a lot about this farm but not much about the Oxbow or yourself," Boston said. "I'm interested in all three—your career, your farm, the Oxbow and how they all fit together. Are you all right with that? I won't publish a word without letting you see any statements I attribute to you."

"I'll go you one better. I won't tell you anything I'm afraid to have repeated."

"All right. I talked with your brother while you were in hospital. He didn't tell me much about you that I didn't already know. I did learn an awful lot about him. He suggested talking to your daughter, Sanford Brewster and his mother. Oh, and Morris Isaacs."

"They're all fine people. I trust 'em. Saginaw—that's what I call Sandy—he's kind of like a son to me. His dad and I were close. When he died, I kind of stepped in when the pup headed the wrong way, if you know what I mean. Morrie is my lawyer, so he might be reluctant to say too much, you know, that attorney-client thing."

"I'd like to talk to your daughter."

"Go ahead. I'll give you the numberk but don't be put off if she won't talk. Things are good between us, but it wasn't always that way. We both had a lot to learn. She has a son. A good kid."

"When we talked last, you weren't sure what to do with this farm. If I may ask, any further thoughts on that?"

"Yeah. Thanks, I've found a solution to keeping the farm as it is," he said, but his tone of voice didn't invite further questions.

"All right. Can you tell me about the Oxbow and how you came by the survey?"

"Sure. See, most of our state forests are up north on pine lands that were never sold or were cut clear and abandoned for taxes. This one is a hardwood forest. I bought a lot of private land from willing sellers. See, when I was buying forest land, I found out Daniels was buying up property around the Oxbow. I guess that's how he heard of me. Have you seen the Oxbow?"

"Yeah, my brother and I have fished trout a few times at the lower end. It's hard to get into the upper end."

"Yeah, and it's too good to let it get spoiled by summer homes and that sort of trash. That kinda reminds me of what happened to a place in Michigan…" and he went off on a tale of his ranger days before returning to talk about the Oxbow's depth and the plants and birds he had seen there. Boston realized Leif's conversations were elliptical discourses of one thing reminding him of another.

Sensing the ranger was eager to finish packing, Boston left after an hour of several tales and a little more information about the Oxbow. On the drive home, he realized the old ranger preferred to talk about himself by telling his stories. Each tale was like a parable or a metaphor that revealed his values and beliefs. The secret to understanding Leif was hidden in his stories—if they were true.

CHAPTER 9

Bunches of blue-winged teal dabbled among the rushes as they gathered for the fall migration. The autumn equinox had come and gone, daylight lasted less than twelve hours and the September rains could begin any day. Leif read the signs with a sense of urgency. *I told Daniels it would take a month. Well, it's been a month, and it's only halfway done. Can't say I'm completely over the pneumonia, but never mind that. If I don't get moving, I won't finish it this year.*

He started for the Oxbow in the morning, and the fair weather continued with cooler temperatures. A week of scrambling up and down the ridges set his heart pounding beneath his ribs. Now and then, a sharp pain in his chest made him stop to catch his breath. After five days of this, he was coughing again and scarcely had the energy to cook an evening meal. "You're an old fool," he said out loud. *A fool, but, by God, the job's nearly finished. Just the chasm is left. That's all. Two days of dry weather is all I need.* He had studied the chasm from the rim and understood the challenge. Traversing the length of the gorge would be strenuous. The idea excited him as he crawled under the blankets. Tomorrow, he would move camp to the chasm's upper end.

Dawn came and went, but Leif stayed under the blankets. He rose at midmorning, still exhausted. His lungs rattled, and he coughed until his diaphragm ached. His head swam, and he gasped for air as he staggered about camp. "Goddamn-it," he muttered as he looked into the grub box. "Key-*ryst*, I'll lose another day getting supplies." He dragged a wet cloth across his face, brewed a pot of coffee and made a breakfast of crackers and cheese. Tottering about, he broke up the camp and drove home.

A couple days of rest on the farm didn't restore his strength. It's just a bad cold, he told himself. That's all. Another night's sleep, and then I'll finish the survey. Though tired, he rose in the morning and stopped in Featherstone to buy groceries on his way to the Oxbow. He recalled nothing after wheeling a cart along the aisles of the IGA. When he woke up later, he lay in the same hospital bed he had before. Harald sat at his feet.

"What… what happened?" Leif asked.

"You collapsed in the canned goods aisle. That was yesterday. I'm glad you're alive. Double pneumonia. It could kill you. I told you camping was a bad idea at your age, especially at this time of year. In fact, living alone on the farm is risky. You could die out there, and no one would know."

"Hell, I'm going to die somewhere. So will you. We all will," he growled. "The farm's a good place to die. Where do you want to die—here in your hospital?"

"Think of Karla and Ted," Harald said, ignoring the question. "It'd be hard on them if you died out there all alone. No one would know it for days. Maybe weeks."

"Wouldn't bother me. I'd be dead."

"I'm your doctor. Your brother. When I release you, I want you to stay at a care facility or my guest house. You choose."

"*No!* You're not my keeper." Leif wheezed and then started coughing. "I'm not going to your goddamned guest house. It's my life. I'll live and die as I damn well please." He felt the anger burning on his cheeks.

"Just for a little while," Harald pleaded softly, backing down a bit. "It's my place or a care facility. And just until spring, and you're out of danger."

"Danger, *danger*? For Christ's sake, *what* are you talking about?"

"You nearly died. Another attack and I might not be able to save you."

"Oh, cut the bullshit," Leif laughed until he coughed again. "You can't save anyone, and you can't lose anyone. You don't control life and death. Babies are born when they're ready... people die when they're ready. Living and dying aren't in your power. All you do is fix a few things in between birthing and burial. You're not a god—you're a mechanic."

"What do you mean?" Harald whined, stung by the put-down. "I just saved you from meeting your maker. Another day and we would have buried you."

"You didn't save me from anything," he said, enjoying an argument he felt he was winning. "Dying is the last act of living. And unless we're killed suddenly, it's something we do naturally. I've seen people die—sometimes horribly, sometimes peaceably. When they go, it's because they're ready. Sometimes, the bodies are ready, but not the spirit. Or sometimes it's the other way around. When the moment is right, when body and spirit agree, it's like flipping a switch. Those most willing go easiest. There's dignity in it. I'll be willing when my time comes."

Harald stared at him, his guts tumbling in confusion, unable to understand his brother's opinion. He stood up, jammed his hands in the pockets of his coat and walked out without a word. Leif chuckled.

The doctor returned the next morning, hoping to find his brother in better humor. "I hope you've thought about the will I gave you," Harald said and sat on the bed.

"Well, yes, I have. Thanks." Leif lay propped on a pillow and studied his brother through half-closed eyes. "It was really helpful."

"Good. You can sign it here. I'll get witnesses, and Sam can file it."

"It's already signed and filed."

"Really? I talked to him this morning. He didn't mention it."

"Morrie Isaacs filed it for me."

"*Isaacs. That Jew!*" Harald jumped off the bed. "Sam wouldn't charge you."

"Morrie's my friend, Jew or not. And on this deal, I want my own lawyer," he said, biting off his words. "Don't worry, he just took what I gave him and filed it. Morrie didn't change a thing."

47

"Oh."

"Yeah," he explained. "Karla will get money and family things—just like you suggested. I left in the power of attorney."

"Oh, okay," Harald said, relaxing a little. "Well, I got to do my rounds. I'll drop by later."

Leif lay back after Harald left, closed his eyes and considered their conversation. We're not close the way brothers should be. It's likely we'll never be close. We might be if it weren't for Regina. Without her, I might have taught him about life—life as it really is. But as it is, he's never tasted the real sweetness of life. Or ever will.

CHAPTER 10

Harald tried not to let Leif's choice of Isaacs bother him. But it did because he didn't know Isaacs personally, only that he had been a deputy attorney general who retired to Featherstone. If Isaacs didn't change anything, does it matter who filed the will, he wondered. As long as I have power of attorney, I can do what's best for him. He looks awful. Another bout of pneumonia will kill him. If he dies at the farm, people might blame me for not taking care of him. It's better if he lives in town. Once he's at the guest house, I can sell the farm to pay for his care and give Karla her share.

Harald returned home frustrated with Leif's refusal to move into the guest house. We're different men, he thought, but I am his brother, his doctor and his guardian. It's my duty to look after him. He's quiet now, but once his strength returns, there will be a new showdown over returning to the farm.

"I don't know what to do with him once he's in the guest house," Harald blurted to Regina over a plate of ravioli. "He's recovering so fast I'll have to discharge him in a day or two. He's got his back up. Insists on going back to the farm."

"Well, let him go," she said, throwing down her napkin. "Let nature take its course. It's what he wants. Once it happens, we can sell the farm." She stared into his eyes until he looked away.

"I can't do that. He's my brother. I'd blame myself if he died out there alone. A lot of others would blame me, too. If he dies, I want him to die in comfort."

"Oh, Harald," she said, throwing up her hands. "He'll hate the guest house. And we'll hate having him there. Then we'll have this conversation every day. Is that what you want?"

"No, but... the guest house is the best way. The hardest part is keeping him there," he said, pushing back from the table. "He'll break out once he feels stronger. If he goes to the farm—and he will—I'll lose control of him. I don't want to do that."

"Well, dear," she smiled, "you must have something that will keep him quiet, you know, something you can give him as part of his treatment?"

"No, that's... oh, I suppose it won't hurt," he conceded, though her hint was contrary to practice. That's the problem, he thought. I can't out-argue her. She's got a talent for putting things, so it's a choice between her judgment and mine. On the other hand, her ideas have always played out as she said they would. So, no reason to worry. He nodded. "I guess keeping him calm enough to stay put is good for him, too."

"Of course it is," she said. "Everyone knows you're a fine doctor."

He swallowed against a queasy stomach, disgusted with himself. Why can't I say no and make it stick, he wondered. It's her idea, but it's my neck if I'm caught. I could lose my license. He dabbed his mouth with the napkin. "I told Meade he couldn't visit Leif—"

"—Good. He's the kind of reporter who grabs a thread and unravels everything. Look at what happened to the Ferrall's last year."

Right again, he thought, but Meade did the right thing by exposing the Ferralls. They had murder on their hands. Nevertheless, Meade has a talent for digging that makes trouble. I wish I hadn't been so free with the names of people close to Leif, Harald thought as he got up from the table. If Regina knew, she'd rip me a new asshole.

"I talked to Sam today about exercising the power of attorney," she said in an off-hand way. "He said we should wait until we're certain Leif will stay put. After that, we can go to court. Once we do, we can start negotiating with the Wingspan Associates and get the township to zone the farm for development. If the good weather holds, they might get the access roads in this fall." She rose from the table. "Well, I've got some reading to do, then I'm off to bed."

The antibiotics did their work. Leif's lungs cleared, but he remained too lethargic to resist the move to the guest house. Harald suppressed a sigh of loss as he helped his brother into the car. He understood so little about the once robust forester he had idolized as a boy. Too late now. He had shriveled into a feeble patient awaiting his end.

Harald hired a stout matron with a toothy smile as Leif's companion and daytime caregiver. She was to cook his meals, do his laundry and make certain he took his medicine. No one cooked homestyle dishes like Mabel, he said. And he thought no one could accuse him of neglecting his brother while in the care of someone like her.

Mabel Lund was waiting to greet them at the guest house door. "Doctor Harald told me a lot about you," she said cheerily. "I'm sure we'll be great friends."

Leif looked at her with a dull eye but didn't reply.

"Those are for you," Harald said and pointed to a pile of new clothes from the Sears store. Flannel pajamas, a terry robe, slippers, wash-and-wear shirts and slacks with an elastic waist, a cardigan and slippers. "You'll be more comfortable in them than your work clothes."

Leif glanced at them in disgust. Not the proper garb of a forester.

"Mabel's got supper ready," Harald said. "You're in good hands. See you tomorrow."

"Eat as much as you like," she urged. "It'll build up your strength. Now, take your medicine," she coaxed and gave him two white tablets and a glass of water.

He grumbled but took them and looked around in the guest house. The oiled pine cupboards, simple kitchen table and matching chairs were better than he had expected. He liked the fieldstone fireplace but thought the gas insert spoiled it. Decorative hunting horns, quirts and spurs reminded him of Regina—inauthentic and pretentious. He gazed at a print of men on horseback chasing a fox and wheezed with mirth, imaging his portly brother in a red jacket riding to the hounds.

Leif's mental fog persisted, and Mabel's daily routine ordered his days. She arrived daily at 7:30 a.m. sharp and cooked his breakfast. After he dressed, she made his bed, cleaned the bathroom and washed the dishes. At the same time, regardless of the task, she gabbled on about her children, the grandchildren, her sisters, what the neighbors were doing and the gossip she overheard at Zion Lutheran Church. While she chattered, he watched the television, doing his best to ignore her. He watched black-and-white movies that reminded him of a world the way he remembered it, the way he wanted it to be, even if it had never been so. After lunch, he retreated to his bedroom for a two-hour nap. He thought his mind seemed clearest in the hours just before supper when Mabel made certain he took the medicine. She left him each day at 5:30 p.m.

From the bedroom in the back corner, Leif could look into a grove of hackberry trees. When his mind was clearest, he tried to estimate the volume of lumber in a tree. It was hard because he couldn't do the math in his head. At other times, he picked out trees that needed pruning to create the straight trunk prized by lumbermen. He noticed his van parked behind the house. It sat at the end of an abandoned driveway that ran through the trees to a back road. Turning from the window, he wished he had the energy to get away and finish the survey.

Ginger told Boston when she heard that Leif had collapsed in the IGA and was in the hospital. The news filled him with a surprising sense of loss, almost like a death in the family. He had taken a personal liking to the old ranger because his shaggy tales revealed a refined moral compass of simple but cardinal values. He had a sick feeling the opportunity to write the profile had just slipped away.

Then Daniels called with more details. "This worries me for a lot of reasons. I value Leif's friendship. He's the only one I trust to survey the Oxbow. If he's out of commission, I don't know… I'm going to delay my announcement."

"I'll call Harald and…" but he heard Daniels make a noise like a cough or a snort. "If I learn anything from him, I'll give you a call."

"Good. Stay in touch. Your view of things is important to me."

Boston hung up, feeling Daniels's call was more than news. It was an opening to draw him into something beyond the Oxbow story. As usual, the codger was playing it close to his vest. He waited a day to phone Harald, asked about Leif's health and when he could see him for an interview.

"Oh, I'm afraid that's impossible," the doctor said. "The pneumonia has affected him, you know. Especially his mind. He doesn't know what day it is or where he is. He needs rest. Talking about his career isn't advisable. I doubt he could give you anything useful. I'm afraid the answer is no."

"Why?" Boston pushed back. "Isn't that up to him?"

"No. I'm his doctor and his legal guardian."

"Where is he?"

"I just moved him to my guest house because he thought it was too risky to live alone at the farm. It will be good to have his company. Maybe I can arrange a visit later on when he's stronger."

"What about his Oxbow contract? He still has to write the management plan."

"Oh, his working days are over. That's one of several loose ends I'm tying up. I told the parks department to cancel the contract. Someone on the staff can finish it."

Boston hung up. "What the hell," he whispered. "Something he just said is a lie." But finding the lie was like swatting at a mosquito in the dark when all he heard was its whine. He didn't lie about pneumonia. Maybe it's what he said about being too old to live alone. Or maybe the guest house or the end of his working days. No, it's saying he's Leif's legal guardian. That doesn't square with what Leif told me.

CHAPTER 11

When Boston hired Ginger, she insisted he keep his father's office as the *Statesman*'s publisher. Though he worked from home most of the time, it remained unchanged. The wall behind the desk had a photo of London and Cincinnatus Meade next to framed awards and editorials. These were the paper's touchstones. The desk had a new IBM word processor, but Boston preferred to write on the Remington portable his father gave him at graduation. He used the office as a convenience when in town. Today, he used it to make a phone call.

"You look down in the dumps," Ginger said, leaning against the doorway. "Anything wrong?"

"Oh, nothing really," he sighed. "Not with me, anyway. But my story about the Oxbow isn't going anywhere. Neither is the story about Leif."

"Tell me what you mean." She sat facing him.

"He's out of circulation indefinitely. I can't interview him," he said, scratching his head. "The Oxbow story is going nowhere. Both stories are dead in the water."

"Maybe they weren't meant to be," she said, wrinkling her brow in sympathy. She often said that when things lay beyond her control. It was another version of the serenity prayer about accepting the things she couldn't change. Or, in his case, things he couldn't bend to his will.

"Maybe, but I doubt it. Here's the rub. Leif likes to talk about his farm and tell tales of his ranger days but avoids talking about himself. Okay, so chalk some up to modesty, except the stories reveal him.

Harald hasn't told me anything useful but goes on and on about what he's done. And yesterday, when I asked when I could see Leif, the bastard flat-out lied to me."

"Yeah, well, I know how sweet you are when lied to." She put two fingers under his chin and kissed him. "I've got a meeting. See you later."

Lucky me, he thought. She's sweet when it counts. Then he went for a brisk walk around the Green to clear his mind. The Oxbow story is rained out, and the principal player is benched if not out of the game. Daniels is in a jam. No survey, no management plan, no ordinance and no donation. And until there is a plan, he's stuck with two thousand acres he can't use. That makes my problem a small one. If I can't interview Leif, I might as well interview those who know him.

He returned to the *Statesman*, called Seabury College and asked for Professor Brewster. The operator put him on hold, and after a series of clicks, a woman answered.

"Professor Brewster, please."

"He's not here now. I'm Sophia Colombo. Who's calling?"

"Boston Meade from Featherstone. When will he return?"

"Not for at least an hour."

"Please ask him to call when he returns. My number is—"

"—I'm a *professor*, not a secretary," she said and hung up.

Boy, academics are a prickly bunch, he thought. An hour and a half later, a man answered his call. Boston introduced himself and said he was writing a piece about Leif Nielsen. "I understand you know him well. If you're willing, I'd like to meet you and ask some questions."

"What kind of questions? Does he know about this?"

"Yes. I've done two interviews with him. He mentioned you as someone I should talk to. I'm interested in his life as a forester and woodsman."

"He's practically one of my family, so I don't care to reveal anything that he wouldn't want known. As it is, I've got a full schedule this semester. You will have to see me on campus. The only free slots are ten-fifteen to eleven on Monday, Wednesday, Friday, and two-fifteen to three on Tuesday and Thursday."

"Well, can we meet after classes, say over dinner—on me, of course?"

"That's better. Thursday evening is open. Come to my office at 301 Milton Hall. Say, five-fifteen. We can go from there."

Boston walked to the Carnegie Library through the damp air. The building was more impressive for its architecture than the reference collection. The *Directory of American Private Colleges* listed more than twenty private colleges in Minnesota. Most were affiliated with a founding religious denomination. The directory displayed statistics about curricula, students, student-faculty ratios and graduation rates but nothing about individual professors. The Seabury catalog for 1980 said Brewster graduated from Seabury and earned a PhD at Yale. He was an associate professor of history and married. His first book, *The Lion and the Fox in Colonial Virginia*, received a national award. The college's 1985 catalog didn't mention he was married.

Returning home, Boston cooked *ratatouille* and baked French bread. The yeasty aroma of baguettes raised his spirits and made the big house cozy against the misty rain spattering the windows. Then Jester dashed to the front door just as it slammed open.

"What a day," Ginger moaned as she hung her damp jacket in the foyer.

"Tell me all about it, starting with Mama."

"She's still Mama. I talked, and she stared out the window. Then we recited the rosary." Mama had made the children recite it daily, and it was the only activity that seemed to bring her out of dementia, however briefly.

"How was your day?" she kissed Boston on the mouth.

"Quiet. I went over the notes on Leif and made an appointment with a Professor Brewster at Seabury College. Harald said he's Leif's protégé. We're meeting over dinner on Thursday, so you're on your own."

"That works. Robin and I are having a girls' night out in Rochester for dinner and community theater."

Perfect on several fronts. He respected Robin Jensen, the Bohemian front-page editor, and he liked her as Ginger's alter-ego, gal-pal and confidant. The divorced mother of three had a laid-back manner that could cool Ginger's hot temper.

"I've got my doubts about this interview," he said and set the tureen and the baguettes on the table beside the tossed salad.

"Why?"

"When I called, a colleague answered. She refused to take my number. Real snippy. Said she was a professor, not a secretary and hung up."

"Yeah, well, you're still that high-pressure Chicago reporter." She giggled.

"Oh, thanks. When I did connect, he seemed wary, protective of Leif. It wasn't an easy conversation."

"Don't be too hard on yourself. You've cracked tougher nuts." She ate a spoonful of *ratatouille* and then dipped the bread into it. "Say, this is perfect on a rainy day. Every woman should have a kept man like you."

CHAPTER 12

It was an hour's drive from Featherstone to Seabury College in Wacouta. Boston followed the valley road along the Wacouta River through a block of state forest where the maples were showing color. The town seemed largely unchanged from its heyday as a steamboat landing where the Wacouta River joined the Mississippi. Its core of antebellum brick commercial buildings and houses now catered to tourists.

The wealthy Episcopalians who founded Seabury College established it on a natural terrace below the bluffs. The design and brickwork in Old Main, St. Michael's Chapel and the original classroom buildings around the quad reminded Boston of New England universities. He stopped a student who pointed him toward Milton Hall. Three flights of wooden stairs brought him to the floor's only office: 301.

"Mister Meade, I'm Sandy Brewster," said the lean, blue-eyed man in a tattersall shirt and sport coat who extended his hand. His thick, light hair covered his ears, making him look younger than his years. "Thank you for coming. This is my colleague, Sophia Colombo." He turned to the taut-faced woman who stood behind him. "Do you mind if she joins us?"

"No, not at all. I'm happy to meet you both," Boston said, struck by the woman's dark eyes, arched brows and olive complexion. With glossy black hair piled atop her head she seemed taller than Brewster. She would have struck him as exotic but for the plain dark skirt and jacket that suggested the habit of a nun.

"We can walk to the Lion's Den," Sandy said. "The linguini is the best ever."

He walked behind the professors and looked for clues to their relationship as they walked. Their body language didn't suggest lovers, but he sensed a current between them, but it wasn't the spark of romance, it seemed more like the kind to blow a fuse.

The tightly packed café throbbed with a Bohemian vibe that reminded Boston of the off-campus holes-in-the-wall he knew at Columbia. Some of the waitstaff greeted the professors familiarly as they took a booth.

"Forgive me. I was short on the phone," Sophia said in a broad Bostonian accent that changed the "are" sound to an "ah." "You caught me at a bad moment."

"All is forgiven," Boston said and smiled. She relaxed, and he noticed the beauty of her full lips, high cheekbones and white teeth. He guessed the pair were about the same age, but something about her persona, her energy, overshadowed Sandy. As the professors sat together, he noticed they were careful with each other. Maybe they were becoming a couple but still unaware of something going on between them. Ginger and I did that dance a year ago.

A young woman in a Gurrl Power! T-shirt greeted Sophia by her given name. She responded, "Right-on, sistah," and urged her to keep wearing the T-shirt. The student smiled and put down three menus and three glasses of water.

Boston told them a little about himself as a Featherstone native, a journalist and a columnist. Both professors were familiar with *American Outlook*. Sandy said he grew up in Waterford, his mother subscribed to the *Statesman*, and he remembered reading about the Ferrall case. After that, Boston sensed he had rapport with Sandy, at least.

Over the beer, linguini and salad, he outlined his idea of a story. As it had evolved in his mind, he wanted to use the Oxbow survey as a present-day event to illuminate the way Leif embodied scientific forestry and the arts of the woodsman. Anything he quoted, he would let Sandy and Leif review before publication.

"That's fair enough," Sandy said. "Leif was my father's hunting and fishing buddy. I was just starting my adolescent rebellion when Dad died. Leif stepped in when I was more than Mom could handle."

"You—a problem," Sophia interjected. "*Ha!*"

"I often spent weeks at Leif's farm—have you been there?" Sandy asked. "He showed me that plants and animals existed in a mutual web of life. He said all life was connected. He gave me hard chores. It was his way of instilling a sense of honor and keeping promises. He said an honest man's word was all he needed to get ahead. It's old-fashioned, but I tried to be like him. He was severe and sometimes harsh when I got out of line but never cruel or disrespectful. There were two ways to do things on his farm—his way and the wrong way."

"Typical men," Sophia muttered under her breath.

"Can you give me an example?" Boston asked, ignoring her.

"He said you can't learn anything until you admit you don't know it. I once told him I knew how to paddle a canoe. 'Show me,' he said and sat in the bow facing me. I paddled and paddled, but the canoe went in circles. When I fessed up after my excuses, he showed me how to flick the paddle to correct the torque. Then, he made me paddle until I could drive the canoe in a straight line. It wore me out."

Boston noticed the protégé's face shone as he talked while Sophia rolled dark, skeptical glances from the corners of her eyes.

"There are better ways to teach," she said crisply.

"No there aren't. I learned humility. That's the door to learning. You know that."

"I think there're better methods."

"Not if you're a boy of thirteen. Earning respect made me try harder."

"*Hmm.*"

"Good linguini," Boston said, thinking the interview was going better than expected. Sandy was a fountain of one-liners, episodes and adages he ascribed to Leif. While he ate, he studied the silent struggle beneath the professors' outward cordiality. He was easy-going and tolerant, but she was sarcastic about men and their behavior. Well, that's not important. Their relations aren't my concern. "Tell me more about Leif's farm," he coaxed.

"I worry what will happen after he's gone," Sandy said. "As far as I know, he doesn't have a plan. He acts like he'll live forever."

"It came up in our first conversation," Boston said. "He told me he didn't have a plan. Then, after the hospital, he said he had a plan to protect it, but he said it in a way that didn't invite questions."

"I hope that's true. No one in his family loves it the way he does. His daughter can't afford it. There's Harald, but Leif knows he'd sell it in a heartbeat."

"You know his daughter?"

"I've met Karla a few times. She's a little older than I am. Divorced. Lives with her teenage son in the Twin Cities. I can't say we're real friends. I know Harald because he and my dad were colleagues for a time. He's nothing like Leif."

"That's my impression. He told me more about his life than about Leif's."

"That's him. He wouldn't be where he is if it weren't for his wife. She has pretty much directed his career."

"How so?" Sophia asked, suddenly interested.

"Well, she's a very political lawyer who likes to work behind the scenes. You know, the hidden hand. She knows who has power, and others look to her for critical support and direction. That's why she's a Republican powerhouse in the first congressional district. She calls the shots. Several would-be candidates who bucked her learned the hard way."

"Yeah, women have to be invisible to get anywhere," she interjected.

Boston caught the annoyed narrowing of Sandy's eyes and wondered why he invited her. So far, she hasn't added anything to the interview.

"Leif thinks a man's integrity is worth more than any other quality—including love," he continued. "He has his flaws—God knows—but he puts stock in being truthful. He's got a rare integrity. You hear it in his talk. It clings to him like pipe smoke. It's not showy, but it's there. He'd risk his life to keep his word."

"You make him into a paragon," she said, pursing her lips.

"In his way, an old-fashioned paladin. He regards contracts as an insult to a man's character. An honest man needs only his word and a handshake. Contracts are necessary only to keep shysters in line."

"That's awfully simplistic," she said and laughed.

"Simplistic or not, it's how he lives. He comes from an older, simpler time. Many times, he told me that a man is rich if he has one true friend. And to be his friend, you have to clear a high bar. A man who does a purely unselfish act is a man of integrity. I want to be that true friend. As for unselfish… Well, another time he said a man's character doesn't show until he is willing to give his prized possession to another."

They talked until Boston noticed most of the restaurant tables were empty. In the background, he heard a 1970s band singing about checking out but never leaving the Hotel California. Time to go, he told himself. "It's getting late," he said. "Thank you, Sandy. Professor Colombo, a pleasure to meet you."

"Please call me Sophia," she said, and her smile replaced the dark mien that had clouded her beauty for most of the evening.

"All right, Sophia. Thank you. Sandy, I hope to visit Leif soon. Then I'd like to follow up with you."

"Call any time."

It was late when he returned home but Ginger was still out with Robin. He made some tea and jotted further thoughts and observations on what he had learned. The professor had revealed so much about Leif that he had filled two reporter's notebooks. Sandy's an academic, but he has an eye or an ear for limning character and telling a story, he thought. He admires Leif but didn't white-wash him. On that basis, I can probably trust his candor. Sophia is something else, however. Innately beautiful, even exotic, but she deflects attention away from her figure with shapeless clothing and a massive chip on her shoulder. He is a self-deprecating Minnesotan. She is neither.

Midnight came and went before Ginger returned. "You asleep?" she whispered as she crawled under the blankets next to him.

"Not anymore," he murmured. "Your feet are cold."

"Sorry. I overheard something that might interest you."

"Can it wait until tomorrow?"

"No. I might forget."

She sat up, and he admired her figure under the nightgown.

"We ate at the Palladian—you know, the fancy-schmancy place. We just sat down when Harald and another man came in. They sat behind us, and he did the talking. The other man, he called him Sam, talked carefully, you know, like a lawyer."

"All right," he said and yawned. "Give it to me."

"They talked about a farm—mentioned Tarn Lake. He said Leif signed the will that Sam-man drafted. Someone named Isaacs filed it but didn't change a word. They had drinks and talked louder. He wants to use the power of attorney now. It sounds like he has a project ready to go. If he acts now, they can start development before winter. Sam-man said don't rush things. Robin and I hardly said a word to each other at dinner."

"Harald is up to something," Boston said. "Leif said he would never give him the farm. Never. Anything more?"

"No. Their dinner arrived. After that, they talked about playing golf next week." Then she kissed him and drifted into slumber.

He lay beside her and stared at the ceiling.

CHAPTER 13

Sandy and Sophia remained in the café for a few minutes after Boston left. "Thanks for sitting through the interview," he said. He valued her as a critical listener and judge of character despite her barbed asides. She might have picked up on something he missed. If Meade was a phony, he counted on her bullshit meter to detect it. Yes, he thought, she's too critical sometimes but rarely off the mark. "Give me your impression of him."

"I think he's deadass on the up-and-up," she said, reverting to Bostonian slang.

"What's that mean?"

"You can trust him. Absolutely. That's more than I'll say for most male reporters. His project sounds more like scholarship than news. Besides that, I didn't detect an outsized male ego."

"Thanks, that helps," he said with a smile. "That's my impression, too."

They walked back to campus and stopped at the corner where their paths diverged and talked a few minutes longer. Then she said good night, and he watched her vanish into the darkness. He thought this evening was the easiest time they had spent together. Certainly a far cry from their rocky start on the day they moved into 301 Milton. What a disaster that was.

The renovation of the humanities building forced the history and American studies faculty to share remote offices. Except for tenured faculty, office assignments were the luck of the draw. He and Sophia shared a third-floor garret under the mansard roof of Milton Hall, where the low ceiling sloped to the half walls and a filthy dormer window admitted dim light. As a candidate for tenure, he had expected better quarters or shared space with someone he knew well. Instead, his partner was a near stranger with whom he had scarcely had a personal conversation in the three years since she joined the faculty. So far, the pairing reminded him of a blind date gone bad. I should've known that when we met to inspect our space, he reminded himself.

As he recalled it, Sophia took one look at the garret and said, "What a frickin' shithole! *Ya huh*, this is what admin thinks of women. You know that, don't you?" When I said, "No, I don't," she roared back with, "Well, *wake up*. Women get the shaft at Seabury. Only forty-eight women in a faculty of two hundred. Only ten of them have tenure compared to thirty-six men. That says women aren't valued. I get this hovel because I'm a woman. What's your sin?" He recalled agreeing it was a dump but said the assignment was the luck of the draw, not a conspiracy. She countered with a stink eye and said, "You think so? *Ha!* You don't see it because you're part of it." Then he ignored her jibes because she whined like a spoiled brat.

They had agreed on a time to meet and move in, but he arrived late, and in the scrum of professors, he didn't immediately recognize Sophia as the curvy woman in baggy jeans with a heavy braid down her back. Then she nailed him with a sarcastic, "Nice you could make it." He apologized for being late and picked up a box of her books. "I don't need your help," she barked. "Women are strong." He pointed out that it was a narrow stairway and suggested moving her things first, and then she could help him with his. "*Fine!*" she snapped as he started up the stairs with the box.

They pushed the desks to face the opposite walls and stacked the four folding chairs by the door for student visitors. He watched covertly as she arranged well-worn copies of *Feminine Mystique*, *Sexual Politics* and *The Second Sex* next to *The Golden Notebook*, *The Women's Room* and other titles in the feminist canon. As she worked, she sputtered about the differential status of male and female faculty. "Well, tenure will give you a passkey to the patriarchy," she taunted.

What a bitch, he thought, tempted to lash back. It would feel good but would make enforced cohabitation worse. Instead, he covered his anger with a cheery silence and hoped it annoyed her.

The explosion he anticipated came several days later when Sophia asked about his sabbatical. After he described it, he asked about her summer, and she recounted visiting her family in North End Boston. He said spending time with the family sounded like a pleasant vacation. She scowled and said, "No, not at all. I had to put up with Papa. He still thinks he's in Italy—in the sixteenth century." He said he was sorry to hear it and turned back to the papers on the desk. A moment later, she stood over him with anger coloring her face. "You're just like him. You don't like what I say, so you turn your back and ignore me."

Sandy slammed his fist on the desk. "I don't know your father—but at least you have one! I don't know your family, and I don't know you. So, don't blame me if I have nothing to say."

She didn't back off. "You're like the rest of them… it's, it's what men do to keep us down. You shut your ears so you won't hear what women suffer—"

"—Don't hand me that crap!" He felt anger warm his face. "I know what women face every day. My wife was as militant as you, but—"

"—but she gave up independence to have your child instead—"

"—That's enough! Becky is *dead*!" he cried, bolting from the chair. "Our marriage is private… sacred. It's none of your goddamned business! You didn't know her, so don't presume you do." When he saw her face pale, he realized he was yelling. Hating her would be easy, but he was stuck with her and knew one of them had to make peace. "Look, this is a small space," he said, lowering his voice. "You hardly know me. I hardly know you. We're together for a semester… at least. So, let's set aside our personal lives and opinions long enough to get to know each other."

"I'm sorry for… about your wife," she said as tears welled in her eyes. "A shitty thing to say."

"Yes, it was all of that!"

That was a month ago, he recalled. Despite her prickliness, I feel outclassed in her presence. Tonight, she revealed another side, and maybe she saw another side of me. Maybe that will soften her edges and make for an easier co-existence. He entered his house, suspecting there was more to Sophia than he had seen and hoped to know her better.

Boston called Karla the evening after Sandy's interview, hoping she would be as forthcoming as Sandy. She answered with a crisp "hello," followed by silence until he introduced himself.

"Yes. Do I know you, Mister Meade?" she asked in the guarded voice of a housewife dealing with a door-to-door salesman.

"No. We haven't met. Your father gave me this number. I'm working on an article about him and would like to talk to you, if you're willing."

"Talk about what?"

"His life as a forester, as a woodsman, as a man."

"I'd rather not, if you don't mind. He and I have been through a lot, and I don't want to upset that. Now that he's ill, talking about him would feel…" she paused and clicked her tongue, "…feel macabre."

"I understand. I did two interviews with him and promised him I wouldn't quote anything he didn't approve of. I'll give you the same promise."

"Well… all right, but you'll have to come to the Twin Cities."

"That's fine. Whenever it's convenient for you."

That was two days ago. Now, as he arrived at her townhouse in the suburb of Bloomington, he considered her caution on the phone. She had questioned everything and asked for proof. Maybe it was because she worked in a law office. Or maybe she had been betrayed and hurt. She left no doubt about protecting Leif. On the drive up, he thought about how to build trust. Maybe that was expecting too much. Maybe it wouldn't be worth the effort. Won't know unless I try.

Karla's townhouse was at the end of a *cul-de-sac* in a quiet neighborhood, except for the occasional plane on its approach to the airport. She seated him in her living room, offered coffee and they made small talk.

"I'm sorry I was short with you," she said. "I'm worried about Dad. Harald updates me almost every day. I dread each call."

"I understand. Your uncle says he's too feeble for an interview. I find that hard to believe."

"I know. Me, too. Harald's worried about his reputation. He's afraid it will suffer if Dad dies at the farm. Of course, he dreams of dying there. That's where he's most alive. I'm sure he hates being cooped up in the guest house. I don't know what I can tell you that Dad hasn't already told you."

"Let's start out with a little biography, mine and yours," Boston suggested, noting how she radiated anxiety like heat from a stove. He told her about growing up in Featherstone, recapped his career in Chicago and resettling in Featherstone a year and a half ago.

Karla nodded. "I remember you now," she said and smiled. "You discovered the money laundering. I was fascinated by the articles in the *Statesman*. I know who you are." Then she smiled, and it was as warm and radiant as the rising sun. She told him about raising seventeen-year-old Ted and working as a paralegal. Getting Ted into a good college was her immediate goal. After that, she wanted to finish law school. "Of course, I'll have to win the lottery to pull it off."

Feeling they had a rapport, he said Leif was fascinating for his duality as a scientific forester and old-time woodsman. "I'm interested in him and what makes him tick. Tell me about your memories of the farm," he coaxed. "I can see your dad is deeply attached to it."

"Yes, but I have mixed feelings. I loved it when he took me out to see things like bird nests or flowers. That's when I was about ten or eleven. But it was lonely without other kids. My parents argued a lot over money until it got bitter. Mom and I left when I was fourteen."

"He told me about that," he said. "Is your son attached to the farm?"

"Oh, Ted loves it," she said and seemed to melt. "Dad taught him so much he wants to study ecology. You should talk to him. He may have a different view than I do."

"Tell me what you think is the farm's future."

"I wish I knew," she said and heaved a sigh. "Dad promised to make his will. I doubt he'd leave the farm to Harald. And I hope he doesn't leave it to me."

"Why?"

"Harald would sell it for real estate. Regina would make him do it even if he didn't want to. And I don't want it because I can't afford to keep it as it is. It would kill me to sell it. That would be like selling him. Or killing him."

"Is there a solution?" he asked.

"I wish there were, but I can't think of any he would approve of."

"He told me he filed his will so the farm wouldn't be developed."

"Well, that's a relief," she said, brightening. He hasn't said anything to me."

Karla smiled now and then as they talked, and he found her attractive when she did. After several hours, he felt she had given him more than he expected—especially her candor about Leif, Harald and Regina. Like Sandy, he felt she was a truth-teller he could trust. He thought some of Leif's grit lay hidden beneath her caution. Despite all that she told him, he sensed she was holding back. Maybe it was turmoil over the farm. In any case, he felt she trusted him if only because they cared about her father and the farm.

CHAPTER 14

News that Leif was settled in Harald's guest house bothered Abigail Brewster. She didn't know what to think, except he was in poor health. At least Harald is looking after him, she thought. But she knew Leif was a proud man who hated to be dependent on anyone, even Harald. Or particularly Harald. Giving him cheer, if not hope, is the least I can do, she told herself as she brushed her gray hair and put on lipstick.

Her friendship with Leif didn't extend to Harald, whom she also knew. The doctor tried to discourage a visit when she called to arrange it. "Visitors aren't a good idea right now. He needs rest," he told her but gave in after a brief argument. "Make it a short visit," he said.

Abigail forced a smile to cover the shock of seeing Leif in the leather recliner, wrapped in a robe and watching television. He appeared thinner, and his skin seemed slack and translucent as parchment.

"Hi, Abby," he croaked with a weak smile. "Seeing you makes me feel better already. Sit here." He waved vaguely at a chair next to him.

She asked how he was feeling, and they talked briefly about his health before he asked about hers and then Saginaw's. After that, he asked about what she was doing and told her his yarn about the time he cut down a bee tree. He turned so he could look at her. Next to Lilja, he had long admired her as the finest woman he had ever known. She was in her late thirties when her husband died, and leaving her with two adolescent boys. He respected her grit for picking herself up and finding work as a high school French teacher. More than once, he thought of courting her but didn't. Abby was a realist, and he knew she recognized his failings. Instead, he steered Sandy away from trouble and later gave her a shoulder to grieve on when Paul died in Vietnam. When Becky died, he took Sandy timber-cruising on snowshoes to work some of the sorrow out of him. He understood survivor guilt. Three men on his forestry crew died in the fire that he survived. Abby's friendship meant more than a romance, and her presence excited him.

She held his hand as they talked until she sensed he was tired. "It's getting late. I'll come again in a few days. I'll tell Sandy. He'll come on Saturday if he can."

"Oh, don't bother him," he yawned and then coughed. "He has a lot to do. Tell him to see me at the farm when I'm better."

"When are you going to the farm?"

"Soon. It won't be long. A week or two."

"Tell me if you need anything," she said and rose to leave.

"Sneak me in some whiskey and tobacco," he said in a hoarse whisper.

"You know I can't," she replied with a light laugh.

"I know… but it's a lovely thought," and grinned.

Mabel closed the door after Abigail left and turned to Leif. "I overheard you, Mister Nielsen. You know what Doctor Harald said. You're staying here all winter."

"Mind your own goddamn business," he snarled. "I'll leave when I'm ready."

"*Oh*," Mabel cried and scuttled into the kitchen. An hour later, she called him to supper and watched him take his medicines. Then she left for the day.

From the front window, he watched Mabel's car stop at the chateau. "She'll tell him about Abby's visit," he muttered. "She's spying on me and spilling it." He turned away, feeling betrayed and alone, as if the universe were conspiring against him with Harald and Mabel as its agents.

It was Harald's habit to visit Leif every other evening, and he was usually cheerful. When he stopped the next evening, he asked Leif how he was feeling.

"Fine. When can I get out of here?"

"Spring. In the spring—if you're well enough."

"Hell, I can't stay. I've got to finish the Oxbow."

"Don't worry," Harald said. "I explained it to the parks people. They'll cancel the contract but pay for what you've done. Someone will finish in the spring."

"You sonofabitch!" he yelled. Leif shot out of the recliner, grabbed Harald by the lapels and shoved him against the wall so hard it knocked a picture askew. "You little shit, you've got no right to—"

"—It's for your own good," Harald squeaked. "You can't work."

"The hell I can't. My work is none of your goddamn business." He tightened his grip. "I've never welshed on a contract. I won't start now."

"You'll get paid. That's all that matters."

"You little shit!" Leif bellowed and then coughed as bile seared his throat. He gripped Harald by the throat and closed his hand, choking him. Then he let go and shoved him to the door. "Get out. Get the hell out—and don't come back!" Suddenly, he felt energetic and relished seeing fear in his brother's eyes as he crawled away. He slammed the door and sat down, his body trembling. "By God, I'll meet my obligations."

CHAPTER 15

Leif noticed the autumn sky had a milky haze and an ashy sunset. Opening a window, he smelled the smoke from western forest fires. He watched a CBS television reporter say the mega-fires came from fuel left by eighty years of fire suppression. Then the camera cut to a ranger in a hard hat who said that setting fires under certain conditions was a safer, cheaper and more natural way to manage large forests.

"*Key*-ryst. You don't know what you're talking about," he sputtered and lunged out of the recliner. "You can't control a fire. It cost me an eye, you sonofabitch!"

"Are you all right, Mister Nielsen?" Mabel asked in alarm.

"Fine. Just leave me alone."

"*Jeez*-zus, they forgot everything we learned," he grumbled. "Get on a fire by ten in the morning and stop it before it burns ten acres." The news triggered memories of *that wildfire*—the 1936 blaze that still happened yesterday in his mind. Sometimes, he smelled it in his sleep. On that day, smoke blocked the dawn, and the air felt viscous as he and his crew hacked a fire break with shovels and Pulaski's. Sparks rode the wind and set new fires behind their lines. Then came a deep roar as embers fell like hail and flames raced through the pine tops faster than they could run to the river. He was carrying a fallen man when he collapsed on the riverbank, and others dragged them into the water. The man he carried was already dead. Two others got lost and died. He blamed himself. A prescribed fire spit on their graves and those of every other dead firefighter.

He felt low. The Forest Service had turned its back on the hard-won lessons of his youth. Then Harald, the highfalutin' commissioner, told him his services weren't needed and canceled the contract. He steeped himself in resentments, dwelt on each thing he disliked in his brother and savored the tang of righteous anger that raised his pulse and cleared his head. "Goddamn him. I'll finish the job," he said, pounding the chair's arm. "I'll finish it if it's the last thing I do."

Then he snapped off the television and leaned back. Saginaw's coming later today, he thought. It won't do to be upset. He got up, went to the bedroom, changed from pajamas to clothes and sat to wait for his visitor. Sandy arrived, happy and full of energy.

"Hullo Saginaw," he called in a raspy voice. "So, tell me, how's the professor business is coming along?"

"I'm teaching three sections of U.S. history, working on a book and the faculty votes on my tenure in December. Otherwise, I don't have much to do." They laughed, and he saw a flicker of the ranger's old fire in his good eye.

"I'm sure they'll give you tenure. Hell. That's a lifetime appointment. Never have to look for another job. Nothing at all like being a ranger." He struggled to adjust the recliner until he sat upright.

"It's good to see you," Sandy said. "I hope you're getting better."

"I feel like a goddamned vegetable rotting on the vine. I'd get out of here if I had the energy."

Sandy asked for one of his old ranger stories, but Leif turned serious. "My brother, the big shot doctor, thinks I'm going to die any day now. I know Regina hopes so. But when my time comes, I want my ashes buried by the pink boulder. And I want you to nail my corked boots to that oak."

"Thanks. I'd be honored, but not too soon, I hope."

"No, no rush. I've still got some kick left." After that, he pumped Sandy for details of his sabbatical, the book he was working on and his plans for the future. Then, they skewed off to reminiscence about the days they spent fishing and working in the woods. Then Leif asked,

"Say, did I ever tell you about the time a moose wrecked my camp on the Canadian border?"

Sandy had heard the tale so many times he could repeat it verbatim, but he shook his head because Leif liked to tell it.

"*Jeez*-zus! What a mess that was." With eyes bright, he drew an excited breath, wiped his mustache with a thumb and forefinger and began. "Let's see, that was in October of twenty-nine—me, Packer Williams and Three-Finger Bjornson went cruising timber along the border lakes."

His voice rose, describing the wall tent with a kerosene lantern for heat, the northern lights blazing across the sky, wolves howling across the lake and the rutting moose rattling its horns in the woods. He said they woke when the tent collapsed on them. He paused, wheezed and caught his breath. "*Jeez*-zus, what a mess!" The panicky bull bucked and bawled with ripped canvas hanging from the antlers and the tent ropes tangled around his front legs. Before the moose broke loose, it smashed the lantern and set some small fir trees on fire. "*Key*-ryst, we had to put out the fire. Then we sat up all night wrapped in sougans covered with soot. Goddamn, but that was cold."

Mabel entered from the kitchen and smoothed the apron over her broad belly. "I have to leave early. It's my grandson's birthday. Supper is ready when you are, Mister Nielsen. It's in the oven. Doctor Brewster, will you see that Mister Nielsen takes his pills. They're on the counter."

"Glad to," Sandy said as Mabel scooted out the door. He got up and found the covered dish inside the oven wrapped in a towel. A small tray on the counter held a vial of antibiotics and a bottle of Bayer aspirin. Mabel left a note on the doses. When he shook out an aspirin, he noticed it lacked the Bayer trademark. In fact, it had no trademark. He sniffed it. Then he licked it. A chill of recognition ran down his spine.

"It'll be a minute, Leif," he called. Alarmed by his suspicion, he opened the cupboard doors and searched the stacks of plates, cups and bowls. Standing on the step stool, he found a prescription vial of benzodiazepine behind some salad plates on the top shelf. He shook one into his hand, sniffed and then licked it. Identical to those in the Bayer bottle. He knew what it was. As the campus nurse, Becky had trained the faculty to recognize drugs and the signs of abuse.

No wonder he's lethargic, he thought. This could be lethal for an old man with pneumonia. Harald's too well-trained. It's not a mistake. It's intentional. "Damn you," he whispered. "Well, Harald, this is going to cost you."

"Leif, listen, this is important," he said, making certain the ranger was alert. The ranger had a right to know what he was taking. "Those aspirins are really a sedative dispensed from a Bayer bottle."

"*What!*" He fixed him with his good eye, keenly alert.

"They're tranquilizers. That's why you're drowsy. That's why you're confused."

"You mean, that stuff is, is dope? What is he…? Jeez-*zus,* I'm a prisoner guarded by Mabel. God-*damn* him," he exploded, and color flushed his cheeks.

"That's why I told you. What do you want to do?"

"That bitch made him do it. I can just hear her hinting at what to do until I die. He's so pussy-whipped he'll do anything she says." Leif rose from the recliner. "I won't take any more dope. But if he finds out, he'll think of something else. You think I'll feel okay in a couple days?"

"Yeah, I think you will. We've had overdosed students. Most were fine after a week. You haven't OD-ed so, it might not take that long."

"I'm leaving once I get this out of my system. Of course, the little shit might notice and up the dose if I'm too alert. Mabel makes sure I take it."

"I've got an idea," Sandy said. He went to the half-bath off the kitchen that Mabel used. As he hoped, its medicine cabinet had a Bayer bottle. He tasted a tablet. Aspirin. Then, he transferred the sedatives from the Bayer bottle to the prescription vial and replaced them with aspirin. One a day would be benign. "I'll have the sedatives tested."

"Good. Call Morrie Isaacs about it. He's my lawyer. I don't think Mabel will notice. I'll pretend to be dopey until I leave. By God, I'll show that shifty sonofabitch."

They laughed together like adolescents pulling a prank but Sandy worried that Leif might recover too quickly and suffer withdrawal. It was a chance they had to take.

"Well, there's something I haven't told you," Sandy said.

"So, shoot," Leif said, now enthusiastic.

"I'm sharing an office with an interesting woman while ours are renovated."

"Well, it's about time, boy. You've been a widowed man far too long. I was starting to worry. What's she like?"

"Oh, just your type—you know, dark, full-figured, Italian and a women's-libber."

Leif made a noise in his throat—whether a cough or a laugh, he couldn't tell. "Well, bring your new woman around," he said, taking Saginaw's hand as he stood to leave. "I want to meet someone who's finally got you excited."

CHAPTER 16

Sandy left the guest house fearing for Leif. He had always seemed to be as timeless and as indestructible as the pink boulder. Now, his gaunt face and feeble voice belonged to a shadow. It was worse than seeing him dead. Sandy drove home wondering why Harald disguised downers as aspirin. His treatment of Leif violated several oaths. He was risking his medical license, so it had to be a good reason or a desperate one.

He entered his house in Wacouta so enraged at Harald he wanted to smash something—anything—just to release the pressure in his chest. Opening the hutch, he poured a shot of brandy, downed it and then remembered that revenge was best served cold. He brewed a pot of chamomile tea and called Isaacs.

"Leif asked me to call you," Sandy said as an introduction. "His brother is treating his pneumonia with benzodiazepine." He heard the attorney draw a deep breath. Then he told Isaacs about how they were dispensed from an aspirin bottle while the prescription vial was hidden in the cupboard. "I told Leif, and he refuses to take any more. I substituted aspirin for the sedatives and have the drugs with me. I hope there's a way to get an analysis."

"You did what? You're not a doctor," Isaacs scolded. "Maybe Harald had a good reason to prescribe them."

"He does. They keep Leif groggy enough to manage. There's a woman there all day who watches him and sees that he takes his meds. He told me he felt like a prisoner. My wife was a nurse and taught the faculty to spot drug use among students. Harald did it deliberately because he disguised it as aspirin. It's malpractice, at the—"

"—You don't know that," he replied in a sharp voice.

"I know this. They're habit-forming. They'll depress his breathing. He'll never recover. The drugs are chemical handcuffs to hold him captive. That's illegal."

"Don't try to practice law, either. You don't have the training," Isaacs barked and then drew a long breath. "All right, bring me the pills tomorrow. After that, let's figure out what's happening and what we can do."

Vestiges of anger still lingered in the morning when Sandy passed the drugs to Isaacs. Worries shadowed him, and his Monday classes passed like out-of-body experiences. While his lips lectured on the Lincoln-Douglas debates, his mind dug for the motive behind drugging Leif. It wasn't for his health. If Isaacs knew something, he didn't let on. And if he called Harald on it, he would deny it or say sedation prevented over-exertion or the pharmacist made a mistake. No, the reason must be a hidden one.

When his afternoon classes ended, he gathered his notes and climbed the stairs to Milton 301. Today, mounting the three flights took as much energy as scaling a mountain. He mumbled a greeting to Sophia and sat down. She looked up from a monograph, smiled and returned to her book. He let out his breath in a long exhalation as he began grading essays on the Kansas-Nebraska Act.

"Are you okay?" she asked a few minutes later and shut the book with a snap. Then she swiveled the chair to face him.

"Yeah, fine. Why?" he replied, still looking at his papers.

"You're sighing—like you're depressed, like something awful happened. That's not like you," she said quietly and waited for his answer, but he didn't reply. "I'm sorry. I didn't mean to pry. But I meant—"

"—No, it's all right," he said and marked the paper with a "B-" and a comment. Then he swiveled to face her. "Leif is in a bad way."

"I'm sorry. Maybe you'd like to talk. It sounds like you're holding in something …oh, I didn't mean to—"

"—Yeah. I feel like talking," he said, seeing something like compassion in her eyes that he hadn't noticed before. "Let's go out for a drink."

"*Ya huh*, good idea," she said, grabbing her purse.

They walked to The Landing, an antebellum brick hole-in-the-wall on a side street fronting the Mississippi River. He chose a booth among the plants suspended on macrame cords. Hidden speakers oozed James Taylor singing about fire and rain and sunny days that would never end. He ordered a carafe of red wine, poured some and then told her about visiting Leif at the guest house.

"Tell me more about him," she asked. "It's hard to match someone as kind as you are to a mentor who is a crusty old forest ranger."

He laughed quietly at her words. "Leif can be crotchety, old fashioned, bull-headed, irascible and opinionated. He's lived alone most of his life. It goes with that."

"Charming," she said with a wry smile and sipped wine.

"I worshipped him because he was good at the things most important to me—camping, hunting, fishing and woodcraft. After Dad died, he made sure that I spent time with men."

She smiled indulgently.

"I was a handful for Mom," he continued. "He instilled discipline the same way he ran a crew of lumberjacks. Tough but fair."

"My father is tough but not fair. Does Leif have a softer side?"

"No," he said. "I did as he said because I wanted his respect. That was important. He spent time with me because he wanted to, so I owed him obedience."

"He loves you, doesn't he," she said, not really as a question.

He shrugged. "I guess, but he's never said so. He respects and trusts me. It's not the same as love. Love isn't a word he uses with men. Respect is more to him than love."

"That's so… so frickin' patriarchal," she said, wrinkling her nose.

"*Shut up!*" he snapped and saw her flinch. "He means everything to me. You aren't listening. You're just sitting there, smug, looking down your nose, judging him. It's what you do in meetings, too. Leif is who he is—he's not a type."

She looked down. Her lower lip trembled. "Sorry, it's a habit."

"Yeah, I know. A bad one. I'm touchy and angry about where he is."

"I'm… ashamed," she said, touching his hand. "I'll listen. I promise."

"All right," he exhaled. "I didn't mean to take it out on you. But if you want to understand him, then listen to the stories. Don't judge, don't analyze. Just listen, and you'll understand." Then he ordered some grilled cheese and more wine.

He told her about some of their adventures. She laughed at the story about the time a bear swam to their island camp and the silver-haired forester dashing from the tent in long johns waving an axe at a bear and shouting, "Git you son-of-a-bitch." The bear ate all the bread, so Leif cooked pancakes to make sandwiches. On another trip, the ranger baked him a twenty-first birthday cake in a reflector oven.

Sandy wanted to stop talking, but she begged for more. The hours slipped away as he told her about learning to carve decoys, tie fishing flies and cultivate patience. She heard of Leif's rigid adherence to commitments regardless of their personal cost. He said he was saddened at the sight of this once vital mentor laid low. Then he told her about replacing the tranquilizers with aspirin.

"You should report that," she urged, wide-eyed.

"I did. I gave the pills to his attorney. He used to work in the attorney general's office. He'll take it from there." Then he rubbed his hands together nervously. "Leif's brother is also his doctor."

"That's awful. He's lucky to have you as a friend. I want to be your friend, too."

"Of course you are," he said and meant it. "Thank you for listening. That's what a friend does. I've got to find a way to bust him out of Harald's grip, if that's what it is."

"Any time you need to talk, I'm here," she said and briefly put her hand over his.

He liked her touch and didn't move his hand. Later, he touched her fingers as they talked intently on the slow walk to the place where their routes parted. There, they stopped and talked for another half-hour. On the way to his house, he wondered why he had told Leif about Sophia. She *is* an interesting woman, he told himself. We're friendly, but we've only known each other for a month. He knew he liked and respected her as a professor, but until now, he was careful about what he said and how he said it. Still, depending on the moment, his feelings about her shifted from admiration to fascination to irritation to curiosity. He covertly admired her curvy figure and occasionally wondered what she would be like in bed. We're temporarily sharing a space, but we're not in a relationship, are we, he wondered as he entered his house. That would never work. She's a cactus.

He entered the living room where Becky's gaze met him from the framed photo on the mantle. He had placed it there and put her photo in strategic spots in the other rooms so her eyes were the first thing he saw when he entered. As Becky gazed at him, he felt a mix of sorrow and guilt because he couldn't shake his thoughts of Sophia.

"You're gone," he whispered to the photo as he removed it from the mantle. "You're gone, and it's time I let you go. It's time to stop living in your shrine." With great care, he gathered the photos from all the rooms and put them in a closet. He kept a snapshot of her on the nightstand. "Good night," he whispered.

CHAPTER 17

The sedatives wore off quickly, and Leif soon felt like himself. As his mind cleared, he pieced together what had happened. The realization gave him acute chest pain. *I didn't tell Harald I changed the will, so he thinks he's my legal guardian. He's holding me so he can sell the farm! Goddamn him!* What a mess. The realization upped his desire to leave at once, but he tamped down the temptation. *When I go, I'll go to the Oxbow, but I need to build up my stamina. Mabel probably won't see a change in me because she's always talking. But Harald might. So, I better put on a dopey act.*

After Mabel left for the day, he looked at himself in the bathroom mirror—an old man with pouchy eyes, bristly cheeks and a ragged mustache. "You… look… like… shit," he said in disgust. He splashed cold water on his face and blinked. A hot shower and a brisk toweling restored some pep. He combed back his hair, shaved the white bristle and trimmed the tips of the mustache. The sting of Aqua Velva made him feel as good as new.

Seated at the kitchen table with a notepad, he worked through the steps of an escape plan. It began with the goal of arriving at the Oxbow in the early morning of D-day. He would escape the night before that. Though the van was packed, he couldn't go directly from the guest house. He needed a couple things from the farm. From now on, he would use the afternoon naptime for two hours of stretches, push-ups, squats and knee bends to rebuild his strength. He needed three days of fair weather to finish the Oxbow after a night when Harald would be too busy to follow him to the farm.

Leif waited until dusk, left the guest house by the back door and checked the van. He remembered he had filled the tank. Then he walked along the unused driveway and moved aside a couple downed limbs. After that, he walked for an hour in the dark along a gravel road that climbed out of the Wacouta Valley. For the next four nights, despite light rain, he walked longer distances until he could hike up and out of the valley without stopping to catch his breath. He felt ready, but timing was everything, and he watched the forecasts and prayed for another streak of fair weather.

Mabel arrived on Tuesday morning aflutter over the party Harald and Regina were hosting on Thursday. "Like nothing you ever heard of," she babbled. "Mayo Clinic doctors. A catered banquet… string orchestra… high school girls serving the guests and boys parking cars. They asked me to oversee the kitchen. I'm *so* excited. You must be proud of your brother."

"Oh, I am," he agreed. "Yeah, that party is a real big deal," he added, realizing he now had the perfect alignment. After today's rain, there would be four days of good weather, and the party would tie down his brother for the evening. It was all he could do to contain his excitement. He ate supper and then went for a walk after Mabel left. Afterward, he cleaned the soil from his boots and ran his damp clothes through the dryer to hide any trace of his outings.

Mabel prepared supper early on Thursday afternoon and watched Leif take his medicine. "I might be a little late in the morning," she said as she left. "There are cinnamon rolls for breakfast." She left at 4:00 p.m. to assume her duties at the party.

After she left, he put the cinnamon rolls in a paper sack and raided the pantry and refrigerator for groceries. He soon had two shopping bags filled with bacon, eggs, bread, butter, ring sausages, potatoes, apples and cheese—grub for the Oxbow. Turning off all but the kitchen lights, he watched as headlights cut through the dusk and swung up to the chateau, where light glowed from every window. It was past dark at 7:30 p.m., and he felt it was time to go. He had liked Mabel's home cooking but not her mindless chatter. It's not her fault, he admitted. She doesn't see her part in Harald's scheme. I'm a cross she's being paid to bear. He wrote a short message on the kitchen notepad, folded it into an envelope with two twenties and propped it against the coffeemaker. Then he went out the back door with the sacks of groceries. A barred owl hooted in the trees as he waited for his eyes to adjust to the darkness. Another owl answered, and their hooting mingled with the muted violin music from the party.

He lifted the van's hood, retrieved a spare key and started the engine. With headlights off, he drove the lane to the county road and turned west toward the farm. *You're free*, he thought, exhaling. An hour later, he saw the lights at the Plowboy Bar and the only place to buy two other essentials at this hour—whiskey and tobacco.

"Hey Leif, long time no see," the owner called. "Heard you were in hospital." The wiry tavern keeper shook the forester's hand. "Glad you're cured."

"Good to see you, Fred," he said, smoothing his mustache. "I stayed at my brother's place 'til I got on my feet. Good as new."

"You're here to celebrate your recovery, I guess. Name it. It's on the house."

He ordered Jim Beam, and Fred poured. They touched glasses, but the old man sipped because he didn't want to get a snoot full. However, he enjoyed the flavor, and talking to another man was a tonic.

"I'm heading north tomorrow," he told Fred. "Time to fix a deer hunting shack. Haven't used it in a couple years. It needs some glazing and shingles, then."

"You're in luck," Fred said. "The weather guy promises a week of good weather."

Leif nodded, finished his drink and bought a fifth of Jim Beam and a can of tobacco. "I'll be back in a couple days," he said on his way out the door.

He got out of the van behind his house and took a deep breath. The cool air smelled damp, the stars seemed lower and larger than usual and muted quacks and splashes reached him from the lake. A sudden sense of gratitude overwhelmed him. Thanks to Saginaw, you're a free man on your own soil. Entering the kitchen, he detected faint aromas of bread, fried bacon, pipe smoke and onions. A new fire in the cast-iron stove drove off the chill. He poured a finger of whiskey into a jelly glass and set about finishing his preparations for tomorrow's start.

The tent, Coleman stove, kettles, Hudson Bay blankets and other camping gear were already in the van. He put the groceries he stole from the guest house into the grub box and added a can of Hills Brothers coffee and tins of sardines, peaches and tomatoes. Then he stuffed union suits, wool socks and a Pendleton shirt in a satchel. Then he added his woolen cruiser's jacket, a stained felt hat and knee-high rubber boots.

He checked the thin, leather field desk to see that it had topographic maps, graph paper, colored pencils and a straightedge. Then he set it in the van next to the portable typewriter. It was after 10:00 p.m. when he tossed off the last of his drink, banked the fire and fell asleep to the ping of hot metal in the stove.

Leif woke in the dark and sat on the edge of the bed. The alarm clock read 5:15 a.m. He breathed deeply, reassured that his lungs were clear of phlegm. Then he padded into the kitchen, revived the fire and made coffee. While it cooked, he put on canvas pants and a wool shirt and felt ready for anything. Nothing revived him like starting a trip. Neither its length, duration, nor its destination mattered, only that the journey started. Life is a series of journeys, he thought.

Lighting the day's first pipe, he drank coffee and listened to the early news on WCCO. Fred was right; five days of fair weather ahead. Good. You can finish the Oxbow in three. Satisfied, he cooked a pot of oatmeal seasoned with maple syrup and ate it with a cinnamon bun and jam. Afterward, he stood outside under the morning star and huffed a lungful of frosty air to clear his head. It was still dark at 6:15 a.m., so he drank coffee on the porch and watched the dawn bloom along the horizon. As the light grew, the lake's glassy surface reflected the wispy, pastel clouds above it until a squadron of ducks cut dark wakes through it.

Let's have a little fun, he thought with a snort before he put the key in the ignition. He brought a shotgun from the house and put it in the van. Then he dragged his duck boat, oars and a half-a-dozen decoys from the barn to the lake. Paddling beyond the reeds, he anchored the decoys in open water. Returning to shore, he rolled the boat until it was half full of water. Then he shoved it into the lake, and it coasted to a stop near the decoys. Then he hurled the oars and floating cushion after it.

Laughing, he got behind the wheel and drove north past the Plowboy Bar. Though it was early, Fred might see him. He continued north another mile and then turned east onto an asphalt road. After several miles, he angled south and east toward the Oxbow on the vacant gravel roads.

Mabel might arrive late, he thought. She'll find the note, squawk like a chicken and call Harald. He'll read the note, shit his pants and go to the farm. When he sees the duck boat, he'll call the sheriff. They'll have a mystery. Maybe I drowned hunting ducks. Except, where's my van? Maybe I was kidnapped. They'll have to search the lake before they look anywhere else. And if they ask Fred, he'll tell them I went north. I'll be deep in the Oxbow before they sort that out. A few minutes of laughing out loud warmed him with a sense of justice. *Jeez*-zus, I haven't felt this good in weeks. I wish I could see Harald's face.

CHAPTER 18

Harald and Regina lingered contentedly over morning coffee. "Last night was a hit, don't you think?" he said. "Thanks to you, it was an audition to join the Rochester elite. Those Mayo doctors and the IBM folks know we've got the social savvy to fit in with them. A great party," he said. "Thanks, sweetie, I'm in your debt forever."

"Yes, dear, it was great," she said, putting down her coffee cup. "I think many were quite impressed. We'll hear from them, I'm sure. They'll be all over us once they hear we are developing exclusive homes on our private lake."

He cringed at hearing her say *our* private lake, words that implied the farm she detested was now hers as much as his. She was all in now that the farm had a value she understood. That's how it has always been with her, he thought as he got up to dress. When she wants something, she moves mountains to get it. That's why we live so well.

The party was the latest of many strategic moves she had planned during a quarter century of marriage. They met while he was finishing his medical residence, and she had just passed the Minnesota bar. He was ten years older than her, but that didn't matter. They married and quickly began enjoying the good life without the complications of children. She kept her figure with diet and exercise, and he took every opportunity to enjoy good food and avoid physical exertion. Despite their seeming mismatch, he was a highly regarded internist who built a clinic in Waterford and bought into a pharmacy. Meanwhile, he served a decade as Waterford's mayor and was now a county commissioner. Their ability to accumulate wealth made it possible to build their dream house on the Wacouta River. Besides promoting Harald with the Rochester elite, she could call on their support if she ran for Congress in two years.

The phone rang at 8:30 a.m. while Harald was dressing. "Yes," he answered and listened. "*What?*" He listened a moment more. "Where? Okay, I'll be right over." He hung up. "He's gone," he cried as he rushed past Regina with the unknotted tie flapping over his shoulder.

"Who?" She put down the coffee cup.

"Leif," he said. "Mabel said he left. I'm going over."

"Big deal. He went to the farm. You've taken too much care of him. He resents it," she said, knitting her brows. "Leaving him alone is the best thing you can do... for him and us. It's what he wants. He's old. Let him go. Let nature take its course. We'll be better off when it does."

"I suppose you're right," he said as he opened the door to the garage. Mabel met him at the guesthouse with tears and trembling lips. She handed him a misspelled note:

> Dear Mable,
>
> Sorry to be a dificult patient. Please accept my apolegy. I'm away on business for a couple days. The money is for you. Treat yourself.
>
> Yours truely,
>
> Leif S. Nielsen, Consult'g forester

He read it, jammed it into his pocket, jumped into the Lincoln and sprayed gravel as he shot down the driveway onto River Street. His brother was a difficult patient, but Harald felt his obligations as brother, doctor and guardian. No matter what he did, people would talk. Wheeling onto the highway, he gunned the big car up the long grade out of the Wacouta River Valley. Hunched over the wheel, with the speedometer touching eighty, he worried about what he might find at the farm.

✲✲

Harald's Lincoln ate up fifty-one miles in forty minutes when it stopped behind the farmhouse. He got out and called "Leif" several times but heard only an echo from across the lake. Entering the kitchen, he found it was warm, with wet dishes in the sink. Well, of course, he thought. He went to town for groceries. Just like him to do things in his own stubborn way. Regina was right. A lot of fuss for nothing. Harald went to the front room to wait. We'll have a serious talk when he returns.

Meanwhile, he looked at the lake and saw a few ducks near a floating log. They might be mallards or maybe they were teal. They all looked alike at this distance. He took the binoculars from the windowsill and focused on the ducks.

"Oh my God," he groaned. The focus turned the floating log into the swamped duck boat among the decoys. "Oh, God, no!" he cried. Harald rushed to the lake as fast as his stubby legs could move and stopped at the end of the dock, panting from the exertion. "Leif," he yelled, and the name echoed back from the hills.

With leaden steps, Harald plodded slowly up the knoll to the house. "He's gone," he blubbered in a small boy's voice. "This isn't real. It's a bad dream." Of course, Regina won't care, he thought. "The farm is ours," he whispered, but the words stuck in his throat. He dialed the courthouse and said *Commissioner* Nielsen was calling to speak directly to Sheriff Meade.

"Good morning, Harald. What can I do for you?" Jack asked.

"My brother drowned in Tarn Lake. I'm calling from his place," he said and filled in brief details.

"Oh, I'm sorry. Stay put. I'll send the water rescue team."

Harald hung up. Tears welled in his eyes, and his sobs came in gulps and gasps. It's my fault he got away, he told himself. And then… *Wait*. Where's the van? Maybe he didn't drown. No one stole that old van. The realization struck like a knee to his groin. He's playing with me! Too late to cancel the deputies. They're almost here. While he waited, he thought about how to explain it without looking like a chump.

"My brother isn't well," he told them before they could ask a question. "He left my house last night and came here. The kitchen

95

stove is warm. There's a duck boat in the lake, but his van is missing. I'm afraid he wandered off. I'm afraid he's losing it," and tapped his head.

The deputy radioed the dispatcher with a description of Leif and his van. Then he walked through the house. "No sign of a struggle," he said. "Like you said, he probably wandered off. Has this happened before?"

"Well, he's independent. Stubborn. Coming here makes sense. Going off somewhere doesn't."

"We'll check the lake to be sure," the deputy said and hauled a tank and flippers to the dock. While Harald watched, the deputy vanished underwater, surfaced and dove again. After a half hour of searching the lake bottom, the diver climbed onto the dock, shedding water like a retriever. "Good news," he said, smiling, "Your brother isn't in the lake, so he's gone somewhere. Someone's sure to spot him. Maybe he'll call in with car trouble. There's nothing to do here," he added, pulling off the flippers.

Harald stopped at the Plowboy Bar on a hunch.

"Haven't seen you in a coon's age," Fred said as a greeting. "What'll it be?"

"Was Leif here last night?"

"You bet he was. Came in for a drink to celebrate. Bought whiskey and tobacco. Said he was going north to fix a hunting shack. In fact, I seen his van go by early this morning. Anything wrong?"

"I don't know," Harald said, frowning. "But you saw him pass this morning?"

"Yeah, for sure. Real early. I know the van. It was heading north up this road."

"Call me if you hear from him," Harald said, now more confused than before. He's not a looney man who wandered off, he thought. No, he planned this. The sedatives should've held him. If he dies somewhere… well, I'll have to explain what happened. People would understand if he lost his marbles. He phoned Regina from the clinic.

"So, you let him get away," she said sarcastically.

"The tranquilizers didn't do the job. And he must've had a spare key," he said, fearful her mood might last for days.

"He made a fool of you. Once he's on the farm, you'll need a court order to remove him. That will take proof. So, you better think of how to clean up your mess."

My mess, he thought and swallowed a flash of anger—and not for the first time. This isn't the moment to confront her, though, he thought. But it never is. She wants the farm more than I do. As it is, she acts like she's got the title. She wants Leif out of the way—preferably dead. Now that he's gone, why isn't she happy? Well, when things go wrong, someone has to take the blame. That's my job when no one is handy.

He wanted to snap back at her but didn't. In twenty-five years, he never learned how to challenge her and make it stick. To his disgust, he felt himself wimping out again. At moments like this, he wished he had married a woman who was loyal, unquestioning and subordinate, a woman like Mabel. However, he wouldn't be where he was if Regina had been as subordinate as he now wished. Maybe it was a fair price to pay.

For the rest of the day, he half-listened to his patient's ailments while trying to make sense of Leif's actions and what he would do when he returned—if he returned. He wrote a prescription and then double-checked his diagnosis. In his distraction, he wrote the wrong prescription.

Harald kept an ear cocked for the phone all afternoon, hoping for a call with news of the missing. He drove home and entered the house, dragging his feet. The maid looked up at him, pursed her lips and rolled her eyes toward the salon. He nodded. That's the kind of girl I should've married, he thought. Then, he braced for an explosion when he entered. Better to get it over with now than endure days of her biting reminders of how he had failed.

"Well…" she asked and pressed her lips in a hard, red line.

"I'm stumped," he said and loosened his tie. "Can't imagine where he's gone. He's left so many confusing clues." He picked up the martini she hadn't offered him and sucked the olive off the swizzle stick.

"Well, quit worrying," she said. "Stop acting like he's a baby. He's old and ornery. You're not responsible for what happens to him."

"But I'm his brother. His doctor. He was in my care. Under my roof. Don't you see… people will think—"

"—Who cares what *they* think," she sneered, drawing out the words. "Your brother is senile. He wandered off. It happens all the time. His days were numbered, anyway."

"You talk like he's already dead."

"Well, life will be simpler and richer when he is." Then she sipped from her highball, pursed her lips and forced a smile.

"But, but he's my brother… my only family," he cried and tossed off the martini. "I wish I knew him better."

"No, you don't," she said and poured a second drink. "You forget, dear, he isn't pleasant to be with. Remember the times he's embarrassed us."

"You mean embarrassed you."

Regina's eyes narrowed at his remark. She finished the martini and stalked into the kitchen to talk to the maid. As she left, he admired her derriere with a shadow of his old lust. Still trim with sexy long legs, she had poise that attracted attention. Without question, she was the classiest woman in Waterford. She embodied everything he wasn't. He wanted her as soon as he met her, was ecstatic when she accepted his proposal, but couldn't pinpoint what she saw in him. Besides beauty, she was independent and strong-willed to the point of bullying others, yet she never got the best of Leif. That infuriated her. And in moments like this, he wished he had his brother's grit.

He listened as she instructed the maid and recollected how her trouble with Leif began. She came from a monied family and, as his brother admired the big diamond on her finger, he said, "Well, I see Harald's put his end mark on you." She asked what he meant, and he laughed and said it was a brand loggers slapped onto the butt of logs. She took offense.

When Leif was newly divorced, he invited them to dinner at the farm. To make friends with her, he led Regina onto the dock to show her a marsh wren's nest. She whined about the mosquitoes. "Ignore 'em," he told her. "They gotta eat, too." Then she said, "I see why Lilja divorced you." Harald saw rage flare in Leif's eye. In a low voice, he said, "She had class, not like you, a cheap…" As Regina lunged at Leif, he side-stepped and a loud splash followed. She surfaced a moment later, flailing wildly, smeared with muck and duckweed. After that, Harald invited Leif to holiday dinners just to enjoy watching him stand up to her.

"If he's dead, do you think people will blame me?" he asked.

"Blame you—you did all you could and more. You saved him twice, put him in a better house and gave him free board and medical care. You couldn't have done more. Name one thing he ever did for us."

"Well, there'll be gossip," he said. "You know, people saying I didn't do enough. He got away from me. That sort of thing. It's bad for my practice."

"No one cares what happens to him. Nobody who matters, at any rate. And don't worry about your practice. You won't need it once we develop the farm."

CHAPTER 19

While Harald fretted, the rising sun shone on the gray Chevy van rolling along the gravel roads at forty-five miles per hour. It was more than an hour's drive from the farm to the Oxbow, but Leif saw no reason to rush through a fair October morning. It was only 7:30 a.m., too early for Harald to discover his escape. And much too early for a search.

I never had a reason to distrust him, he thought, chewing on Harald's betrayal. Not until he buried that power of attorney crap without telling me. As if I wouldn't notice. It'll hurt his ego when he finds out he's not the heir, but nothing like the beating she'll give him. She put him up to it, and he didn't have the balls to say no. Well, too bad. Then, he let go of the rancor to clear his mind for the work ahead.

The rolling upland plain gave way to ridges and wooded coulees in the county's unglaciated eastern townships. After years of buying parcels for the state forest, their winding valley roads were familiar. He entered state forest land through a wire gate, drove down a forest trail for nearly a mile, passed through a gate onto Daniels's property and went another half mile through the woods to the chasm's upper end.

It was barely 8:30 a.m. by his watch, and he guessed all hell was breaking loose at the chateau. He laughed. Harald would be in a panic and on his way to the farm. It won't be long before he sees the duck boat. After that, he cast off further thoughts of his brother.

He hid the van and pitched the tent under two large maple trees where they would be invisible from the air. Dozens of cut saplings propped up against the tent and van broke up their outline. Both were invisible from a hundred feet away. Then, he went about making a camp by the stream with the reverence of a priest conducting a rite. Freshly chopped firewood and a stone firepit would be ready for him at day's end.

Satisfied, he slung the haversack onto his shoulders and angled up the steep ridge. He stopped to rest on a ledge halfway up, breathing heavily. Slow down, you old fart, he cussed. Quit acting like a kid. Atop the ridge, it was easy walking along the chasm's rim. He estimated the gorge zigzagged three miles northeast, then south and northeast again. From geologic charts, he knew its depth was two hundred feet, but its width varied from one to three hundred feet. Counting his paces, he stopped to make notes every two hundred paces and listened to the way the chasm walls amplified the rapids of Hennessey Creek into the roar of waterfalls. The clumps of juniper hanging over the brink reminded him of gargoyles on a medieval church.

He skirted the rim for several hours, always within easy reach of tree cover. It was midday when he reached the chasm's mouth and descended the slope to the valley. Here, the creek was placid once more, and he crossed at a riffle, ate a sack lunch and smoked a pipe. After that, he climbed the slope and surveyed the chasm's other side. The maple leaves were turning color and appeared incandescent with the late afternoon sunlight behind them. He understood the process but didn't know of a scientific theory to explain how he felt to see it.

Today's work wasn't arduous, and he arrived in camp as satisfied as if he had just eaten dessert. While he pecked out a summary of the day's observations on the portable typewriter, his slow tapping merged with the rattle of a woodpecker hammering on a limb above the camp. When finished, he clipped the summary pages into the binder and locked them in the van.

The sheriff will likely start searching for me tomorrow, he thought. So, I better get well into the gorge early before the posse starts beating the bushes. Doing the gorge would be a reward. It was something he had always wanted to do. Even if it was tiring, it would climax this adventure. After that, he would write the plan and collect $20,000. That'll show my weak-kneed brother I can take care of myself, he thought.

He put a match to his pipe and then dribbled some whiskey into a cup. The first sip warmed him inside. He set the tinder ablaze, and as flames licked the kindling, he added twigs and chunks of wood. A fire must be mankind's oldest tool, he thought. It gives heat, light, security and a focus for stories and revelations. How many fires have I built in the last sixty-five years? Thousands—and no two alike. As dusk settled, he took company in the liquid spirit and the dancing shadows cast by the fire.

Good work is good medicine, he told himself as he drew on the pipe. That's when the body and the mind are focused as one. That's where satisfaction comes from. As he waited for the fire to make coals, he thought of other jobs he had liked. His favorite was a timber cruise along the border lakes separating Minnesota and Ontario. That was in October, too. *Jeez-zus—fifty-six years ago!*

Gazing into the flames, he recalled himself as a green ranger out to estimate timber with two veteran woodsmen. Packer Williams had a knack for numbers despite a sixth-grade education. In his bald head, he could estimate timber to within two percent of the volume cut. And Three-Fingers Bjornson had camp skills that could make a comfortable bed out of rocks. They were authentic and went about being woodsmen without a second thought. After the loggers left, they worked for the Forest Service. They taught me well, he thought with gratitude. Hell, best education of my life. The woods used to be full of men like them. Now, I'm the last of the breed. A goddamned shame.

After a little more whiskey, Leif took comfort in recalling how he had given Saginaw a woodsman's integrity and skill. He thought about his protégé more often these days. Sag was a quick study with an innate sense of woodcraft. Him and me won't have many more chances to cruise the woods, he thought with regret. Wish he was here by the fire to tell him so. He raised the cup. "Here's to you, Saginaw."

The first stars were out when he seared a ring sausage in the flames and simmered pieces of it in a stew of potatoes, onions, tomatoes and herbs. He toasted biscuits and smeared them with peanut butter. According to Three-Fingers, improvisation was the secret of camp cooking. He spooned the steaming stew into a bowl and began to eat. It didn't take much to please a woodsman. Then he added a slug of whiskey to his cup.

Nursing his drink, he sat by the fire and listened to an owl call "who-cooks-for-you" and another that answered in the distance. It was a barred owl, one of the seven species he had seen or heard there, including the elusive saw-whet, barn and long-eared owls. He finished the whiskey, stripped off his clothes except his union suit and crawled under the blankets. I wouldn't trade this life for any other, he thought. But Harald, you poor, dumb, son-of-a-bitch, you never discovered what life is about.

CHAPTER 20

A large, framed print of mallards landing in an autumn marsh hung behind Sheriff Meade's desk. Jack glanced at it and thought about hunting over the weekend—provided they found Nielsen. Maybe he could talk Boston into joining him. They hadn't hunted together in years, and the northern ducks were already migrating. Then, a deputy knocked and interrupted his daydream. The water safety team didn't find Nielsen in the lake. His vehicle was still missing, so it seemed likely he was with it, somewhere.

"All right, put out a bulletin on the car, contact the highway patrol and the sheriffs in the surrounding counties. Call the Civil Air Patrol, county search and rescue, and put the usual deputies on standby for early tomorrow." Another missing elder, he thought. The family doesn't notice the signs before they wander off and vanish. He called Boston and told him what he knew. "You were profiling him. Any ideas?"

"Nope. Last I heard, he was staying at his brother's guest house. I tried to see him, but Harald said he was too ill or feeble for visitors. That's all I know."

"Well, he left there last night in his van, went to his farm and then vanished. I need you in on this," he said. "Our esteemed county commissioner is giving us garbled information just when I need some truth. There's a search on tomorrow." Then he laughed. "I'll pay you my usual rate for the consultation." By that, he meant a bottle of Irish whiskey.

"Well, I don't think he wandered off," Boston said. "He was sharp when I interviewed him. Harald said the same thing a month ago. So did his friend, Professor Brewster. So, I doubt he's addled. He was surveying the Oxbow area. He might be there."

"I heard about that. Tough country to search. But I heard Harald canceled his contract because of his illness."

"Then I don't know."

Sandy strode across the Seabury commons, happily kicking at the drifts of yellow leaves. He felt more alive since he removed Becky's photos. She will always be a part of me, he thought, but it's time to move on. It was mid-afternoon when he trotted up the three flights to Milton 301. The office phone rang as he entered.

"Sandy, it's mother. Leif is gone. I just heard it." She had heard about it through the small-town grapevine of person-to-person channels. Given the sources, she wasn't certain what to believe. "It's confusing. He left the guesthouse last night and went to the farm. But he left a note saying he was traveling on business. Do you have any idea where he is or what he's doing?"

"He what... *um*, no, I don't know," he said, thinking he was probably at the Oxbow and didn't want an intrusion. "Maybe he's in town getting supplies."

"No. They found his duck boat in the lake but not his body. His van and shotgun are missing."

"*Whaa...* wait a minute. This doesn't make sense... well, maybe it does," he said. He felt he knew Leif's mind better than anyone despite the forty-year difference in their ages. "I think he wants to be away from Harald and Regina. And he's got to be with the van. You know he hates driving for more than an hour or two. So, I don't think he's gone far. Call you back," he promised, relieved Leif was out on his own. He phoned Isaacs.

"I don't know," the lawyer said. "Harald's the only source of information—for what that's worth. Leif's note to Mabel said something about business. He told a bartender he was going to fix a hunting shack… one he doesn't have. Then he—"

"—Do you think he's—"

"—No. He planned this carefully. So, no, I don't think he's nuts. Most likely, he went somewhere to be alone. All that odd stuff is just to throw us off his track."

"That's what I think, too. I'll call if I hear anything." Sandy hung up. Yes, Leif is cagey. He got away because the sedatives wore off. That proves they were handcuffs. But the escape didn't reassure him for long. The missing shotgun made him queasy. Something bad might happen. He sat at his desk, suddenly feeling less alive than before.

"You don't look so hot," Sophia said when she arrived later. "You sick?"

"No. Just… thinking. Join me for a drink?"

"*Ya huh*, thanks, I will," she said, happy he asked. Lucky me, she thought as she gathered her satchel. He still talks to me after my comments about Becky and Leif. He was right, and I was wrong. And he was clear about it. But he gave me a second chance. Maybe that's why I like him. He doesn't put me down to show he's a man.

It was nearly sundown when they entered The Landing and nabbed a cozy booth against the wall. He ordered wine and told her what little he knew about Leif's disappearance.

"Do you think he's in danger?"

"I don't know," he said slowly, thinking her concern was genuine. "He's more than able to take care of himself… But he did things that don't make sense—maybe. Or maybe they do," he said, shifting in his chair. He told her about the duck boat, the missing shotgun and the note. "He's either wily smart or the drugs made him crazy."

"Are you all right, I mean, you're upset, aren't you?" She put her hand over his.

"Yeah, I'm okay but uneasy about it."

"Tell me what you feel."

He shook his head. "Just a hunch, a gut-level thing. Leif is straightforward, but this has an element of deception. I think he's okay. It's just that I don't know exactly what he's up to." Then he changed the subject. "I just finished reading Zora Neale Hurston's *The Sanctified Church*. Great essays. I think you'd like it."

"I've read a review. Why did you read it?"

"Curiosity. I'm looking for parallel insights into questions about Puritan social norms. What are you reading?"

"*The Color Purple*. Not for the faint-hearted. A wicked pisser."

"Wicked pisser?"

"It's how we say it's awesome in Boston. I'll lend you my copy."

He ordered *brochettes* and more wine. Then they talked about the books they read as children. "My favorite was *Winnie the Pooh*," he said. "Mom read it to me. We still repeat phrases from it."

"I've never read it. What phrases?"

"Let's have a little smackeral of something.

She laughed. "I read all the *Chronicles of Narnia*. Loved them. A girl is the lead. I guess that's what started me off…"

"*Uh-huh*, I have no doubt," he smiled. They continued snacking and drinking and recounting childhood adventures. Get her away from campus, and she's refreshing company, he realized. As they walked back to campus, she slipped her arm through his and hummed softly.

"What is that you're humming?"

"*Babbo non vuole*… it's an Italian folk tune. Papa taught me. He teaches music and *loves* opera."

"Your voice is operatic. I hear many shades of emotion."

"*Grazi*. I love singing, but I don't make the time to practice."

"Sing some more, please," he begged because he heard something authentic, a *contrapunto* to her professional demeanor. Walking along, kicking at leaves and sensing her arm through his, he considered whether something was stirring between them. It might be her sensitivity to his concerns or the full lips when she smiled or her hand on his or… and… When they stopped at the corner to go their separate ways, each found something more to say. And still more until they talked a long time before saying a final good night.

*
**

He felt certain she wanted his friendship but wondered what that meant. Her militancy is admirable but irritating. We can't build a friendship on that. But it is possible with a woman who sings folk songs, touches my hand and smiles with her whole face. Admitting his interest in her shocked him. She's the first since Becky, my slender, blond, small-town girl next door. Our union felt preordained. There's nothing preordained about Sophia and me. She's a raven-haired, complex, urban woman whose authenticity conflicts with trying to prove herself. It's like we're from different planets. Is she really a woman for me?

He entered the house and turned his thoughts from Sophia to Leif. The old ranger had taught him how to vanish into the woods. But this disappearance was different because of the way he did it. Sandy went to bed, but his sleep was filled with questions as his mind sifted through the clues the old ranger left behind. He was still sifting them when he rose and took his morning jog along the Wacouta River trail. Leif left confusing clues as diversions, he thought. He's like a killdeer faking a broken wing to lure us away from the nest. No one has seen the van because he's a one-eyed driver who sticks to rural roads. Everyone is looking every place he isn't. Of course, he's sane and somewhere in the Oxbow. If anyone can find him, I can.

Maybe I should go, he thought, but Leif might be pissed. Besides, there's nothing I can do. He said he needed two days to finish the survey. He went to the farm Thursday night and would have gotten to the Oxbow yesterday morning. If all goes well, he'll finish the survey later today. So, he should be back by tomorrow night. Okay, he thought. I'll hold off calling the sheriff until then. However, his resolution wasn't reassuring.

CHAPTER 21

The old ranger rose in the night to pee and stared at the Milky Way, where billions of stars spread across the heavens like a fine mist. Pissing while stargazing, he thought. The banal with the sublime, that's life. Then he finished, shrugged his shoulders against the chill and crawled back under the blankets. He lay awake a while, troubled by his thoughts of Harald. Fulfilling the contract was a matter of honor. He wanted his brother to see what a commitment looked like. It might be the last chance to help him change course. "*Jeez*-zus, but he's gotten tricky," he whispered in disgust. He's not dishonest, just helpless. The bitch has trained him to obey. No, I can't do a damn thing about that. The truth saddened him.

In the morning, he revived the embers of last night's fire. Sitting on a log with his elbows on his knees, he basked in the sunlight while the coffee came to a boil. He drank a cupful with his first pipe. Then he ate his fill of cinnamon rolls, eggs, bacon and fried potatoes. Afterward, he packed a lunch and checked the rucksack.

The distant drone of a small plane might mean a search was on. He scattered the embers and covered them with dirt to prevent smoke. Then, he stood beneath a tree as the small plane passed low over the camp. Several minutes later, he heard it return. It seemed to be flying long patterns over the Oxbow. He waited until it passed and then rearranged the saplings against the van and the tent. When he could no longer hear the plane, he pulled on knee-high rubber boots and waded into Hennessey Creek as happy as an adolescent boy on a lark.

"By God, I did it," Leif gasped as he shambled off the ridge and into camp. It was late in the afternoon, and shadows were filling the valley. "Damned hard work. Good work. Worth the struggle." He sank onto the log and wiped a bandana across his face. His body felt played out, but his spirits soared. "I did it. End to end. Who's done that in a day?"

He glanced at the sky, wiped his mustache and smiled. At least an hour until dark. Enough time to finish putting onto paper the management plan he had already written in his head. He lit a new fire, changed his clothes and took company with a pipe and whiskey. Sitting before the blaze, he considered how to best describe the chasm. Not many people had traversed it. He had seen fishermen's tracks at the lower ends of the gorge but none in the middle. A simple narrative of the transit would make a good story.

Invigorated by the whiskey, he set the typewriter on the back of the van and pecked at the keys. He estimated Hennessey Creek dropped thirty-five feet in the three miles between its upper and lower ends. Outside the chasm, the stream was normally shallow enough to cross at the riffles in knee-high boots, but he walked with a stout sapling to probe the depth and keep his balance on slick rocks. A quarter mile into the chasm, the walls pinched in, the channel narrowed and the stream ran deeper and faster. Instead of marking trees, he built small cairns every thousand feet and made notes.

The perpetual twilight of the inner gorge gave him a sense of being swallowed deep in the belly of the earth. He knew from the state geological reports the chasm began as a series of sinkholes in the upland. As the glacier melted, its water entered the sinkholes and formed a subterranean stream that flowed from sinkhole to sinkhole. The acids in the water dissolved the limestone until it collapsed and created the chasm. In the depths, he saw the process still at work in the spring water pouring from crevices along the way.

He pecked out descriptions of hanging gardens with a few flowers, grass and ferns clinging to tiny ledges. Each fissure and shelf had a unique community of plants and insects and varied by the amount of daily sunlight. The layers of dolomite and shale contained myriad fossils of brachiopods, crinoids and cephalopods—sea creatures from a time before the advent of terrestrial life. Each thin stratum of rock read like a page from half a billion years of planetary history.

Leif poured whiskey in his cup, added water and then cranked a fresh sheet of paper into the typewriter's platen. In slow, steady taps, he described the gorge as wider at the bends but narrower on the straightaways. After wading around the first bend, he realized the stream was too deep and the current too swift to wade across. He stopped typing to consider how to describe what happened next.

He had worked his way along a submerged ledge, but it petered out just short of the second bend where the chasm turned northeast. That's when he turned around to shuffle upstream to a riffle and cross over to a wider ledge. Then he slipped, lost his balance and plunged into chest-deep water so cold it made him gasp. Holding the rucksack above his head, he drifted a few hundred feet to shallower water and staggered onto a sunny sandbar. Shivering with cold, he lit a driftwood fire among some willows. He stripped and hung the clothes over the fire on saplings and ate his lunch. As he warmed himself, he watched a pair of otters bobbing in the large pool below him. But for the plunge, he might have missed them. An hour later, he put on dried clothes and worked his way around the chasm's last bend. After that, the walls gradually opened into a valley, and the stream shoaled enough at the riffles that he crossed it in his boots.

A good story needs a climax, he thought and turned over several ideas. He had stood at the chasm's mouth in jubilation. At the same time, he had longed to follow the stream to its end. "Streams are seductive," he typed. "They are like the sirens of Greek mythology who call the voyager with a promise of something new but unseen around the bend. Or maybe around the one after that. Maybe the allure lies in the mystery of forever seeking something unknowable."

He relit the pipe and considered the management plan. It should be direct and comprehensive. As a forester, he had followed Pinchot's principle of supplying the greatest good for the greatest number for the longest time. Applied to a half-million acres of national forest, the principal made possible the integration of logging with grazing, reforestation with watershed protection and wildlife habitat with camping.

"The Oxbow is not a renewable resource," he wrote. "Once ruined, it will remain ruined. Its geology, hydrology, caves, vents and springs have much to reveal." Then, he listed the associated plant and animal life. Because it was a rare place, limiting access would keep it largely pristine. He wrote that scientific study and education were the uses that offered the greatest benefit to everyone.

For over an hour, only the tick-tock rattle of the typewriter broke the evening's silence. By lantern light, he finished in short, simple statements anyone could understand: "Use small fires on the hillside prairies to recycle nutrients and stop the invasion of weeds, red cedar and brush." He elaborated on when and how often to burn and described the desired result. "Selectively thin the floodplain forest to protect the diversity of species. Leave dead trees as habitats for bats, birds and small animals." He thought about human impacts. "Prohibit camping and all motor vehicles. Allow walking trails in the oak groves and valley forest. Restrict access to the goat prairies and the chasm. And then he summarized:

> The chasm and all land with 1000 feet of either side [see map] should receive absolute protection because the ecology is rare and fragile. Too many visitors will contaminate the caves and springs, drive out the otters, and probably interfere with the nesting bats. Complete protection is essential to allow the continuation of natural processes. Access for scientific study should be limited and supervised. Because of its uniqueness, the chasm and its surrounding land should be protected as a state Scientific and Natural Area.

The last page in the plan consisted of a single sentence: "The Oxbow Preserve survey and management plan. October 12, 1985."

Below that, he typed: "Leif Soren Nielsen, Consulting Forester," and signed his name. He put the plan, the maps and field notes in the binder and stored it in the van.

Done, he told himself, warmed and pleased and content with his accomplishment. Then he turned to the night's meal—the same as last night's, but he didn't mind as long as he had whiskey and tobacco. The fire gave warmth and mellow light. Today's feat will put an end to Regina's schemes, whatever they are, he thought. "I can't wait to see Harald's face." He chuckled. "You poor, dumb son-of-a-bitch."

He added wood to the fire, spooned the stew into a bowl and ate with gusto. Afterward, he poured a celebratory gill of whiskey into the cup and saluted the stars that had come out. The liquor gave him a buzz, and the firelight shadows danced among the trees long after Leif lost consciousness.

.

CHAPTER 22

"Tell me your plans for today," Ginger yawned on Saturday as they sat in the breakfast nook with coffee and Danish. "I've hardly seen you all week."

"I don't know," he said, raking fingers through his hair. "Leif's gone. Jack's mounting a search. He wants me on standby. Daniels wants me to stay in touch, too. I don't know what's going on with Leif or Harald. I'm pulled all over the place."

"Maybe you need to forget about it for a day."

"Oh yeah. You think that's going to happen?"

"Well, I have an idea," she said as her amber eyes sparkled with mischief.

"Good, I need one."

"Well, I'm not dressed. You're not dressed. So, let's get back into the sack and take our time getting up again. *Hmm*?"

"*Mmm*, I'd love to but—"

"—But nothing. Your morale needs stiffening—along with something else. And I know just how to raise both," she said, grabbing his hand. It was nearly noon when they returned to the kitchen, giggling and sighing.

"Thanks, I needed that. Maybe it's the solution to writer's block too."

"You're a real stud when you stop thinking. Now, let's continue the mood with a walk or a drive or a picnic. And after that, take me to dinner at the Country Club. And after that, play the piano. You haven't touched it in weeks, and I feel like singing."

"Sounds like a plan," he conceded with a grin. Later, they sat on the beach of Lake Iosco and reprised high school memories of making out there on summer nights. Then they walked the shore and threw sticks for Jester to chase. I can't help thinking about Leif," he admitted later over a walleye supper at the Country Club. "I worry whether he is all right—if anyone has heard from him or if they found him. I can't shake these questions for more than a few minutes at a time."

"I know. Your concern for him is a curse and a blessing."

Looking up, he saw Isaacs approach. "How nice to see you," the lawyer said and then introduced them to his wife. "I haven't heard anything today. Have you?"

"No. Jack would call if he did. I try not to think about it. No luck with that."

"If it's any comfort, I think Leif is safe and knows what he's doing," Isaacs said.

"What do you think that is?"

"He's somewhere in the Oxbow finishing his contract. That's what Daniels thinks. Those misleading statements, the duck boat, the deer shack, he did it to throw us off the track—especially Harald."

"The best thing I've heard all day. Have you heard from Sandy?"

"He called this afternoon. I told him what I told you. He's certain Leif is in the Oxbow. Please keep that to yourself. He has a right to solitude."

"Thanks. I hope he shows up tomorrow," Boston said.

The attorney's words bucked him up for a while before melancholy found its way back, but the cause eluded Boston when he tried to describe it to Ginger. The best he could do was to say Leif was the last of a once-large species, like the passenger pigeon. After him, his kind would be extinct.

Later, as he sat at the piano, she wrapped her arms around his shoulders. "Play it, Sam," she whispered and then nipped his ear. "Play it for old time's sake."

"All right," he laughed. His classically trained mother had taught him to play, and he had played for Ginger's rehearsals in the high school musicals. He didn't play when he lived in Chicago but resumed last summer when he returned. Playing reprised memories of his mother and gave him solace after his father's death, and now it gave them pleasure.

"Play something I can sing," she said, shuffling through the sheet music. He liked jazz and Broadway tunes, but she preferred country and folk. He played some Ellington and Gershwin interspersed with Jerry Lee Lewis and Patsy Cline. "Try this, piano man," she said and set the Billy Joel tune before him.

After Sunday Mass, Boston and Ginger walked through the woods that capped the ridge behind the house. They scuffed the leaves like children and reveled in the sunny autumnal warmth. Returning to the house, he checked his voicemail machine. No one had called. He frowned.

"What's the matter—Leif?" she asked.

"Yeah. No messages. My gut says something's odd about his disappearance."

"Like what?" She kneaded his shoulders.

"The evidence suggests he lost his marbles, but I doubt it."

"What are the other possibilities?"

"I can't shake the idea the good doctor is behind this somehow. It's counter-intuitive because there's nothing malicious about him. But there is his wife. Maybe they worked in tandem."

"Oh, like Jekyll and Hyde."

"Yeah, or like you and me."

She slapped the back of his head and then bit his ear. "Okay, enough of Leif for one weekend. I deserve some attention, too."

He took her in his arms, and then Jack called with the news. "I just notified his daughter in Minneapolis and then Harald."

"Any details."

"Nothing much until we hear from the medical examiner. He was lying by his campfire. The kids who found him panicked and ran home. The parents called us. It looks like he just keeled over. No sign of violence."

Boston exhaled. "I'm sorry to hear it. How was it you didn't find him?"

"He did a damned good job of hiding the camp. We flew over it a number of times and never saw it."

"What's next?"

"The medical examiner will decide the cause of death. If we find natural causes, then there's nothing more to do. Harald says he is Leif's executor. I'll keep you posted."

"*Uh-oh.* It's something bad, isn't it?" Ginger said as he hung up.

"Leif's dead. Guess I can put away his profile."

"Don't give up. You've got contacts with his family and friends. Go to the funeral if there is one. Schmooze a little. C'mon, you're good at it when you try."

She's right, he thought. My gut has been telling me there's more to the story than meets the eye. Maybe I can pick up hints at a memorial. It's worked before.

CHAPTER 23

The certainty that Leif was in the Oxbow didn't ease Sandy's anxiety. All day Saturday, he fought the antsy temptation to check on him. That's what a friend does, he told himself. After all, he wanted me to go with him before he got sick. But even if I found his camp, he'd be so deep in the chasm I'd never find him. But that's where he most needs help. What if he... No, don't go there. He's not crazy or depressed. He made a plan to sneak out of the guest house. Just sit tight. Honor him.

Sunday morning passed into afternoon without information. Now he checked his watch every hour, then every half-hour and thought of calling the sheriff. Waiting for the phone to ring made him edgy. His pulse quickened when it did. Sophia called mid-afternoon, and his curt words ended the call, so she didn't tie up the line. The phone rang late in the afternoon.

"Yes," he barked into the receiver.

"Sandy, it's Morrie Isaacs."

He heard the news in the tone of voice before the words reached his ears. "I just got word. Leif died."

"What... how," he moaned and sat down.

"Jack said a couple boys found him in camp at the upper end of the chasm. It appears he died suddenly of natural causes. I'm sorry. I know what he meant to you. He was my good friend, too."

"Thanks, thanks for telling me. I was right," he gasped. "The Oxbow. I should've said something. Then he might still be alive."

"No, Sandy. We both know this is the kind of end he wanted. Now I have to tell you something else… He named you his heir."

"No. He wants me to nail his boots to a tree and bury his ashes by the boulder."

"No. It's much more than that. You had better come to my office tomorrow. Harald thinks he's the executor. That's what Leif wanted him to think. You'll have a lot to learn—and quick. The county will conduct an autopsy because of how and where he died. I know the medical examiner. I'll ask him to run a tox screen for sedatives. Then, we need to get ready for what comes next. I expect Harald to call any minute now."

"Does Karla know about the will?"

"Not likely. If he didn't tell you, I doubt he told her. Please come to my office no later than eight-thirty."

"Did Leif say why he didn't want Harald to know? He won't like it. Can't say I blame him. I'd feel the same way. He deserve a heads up."

"No. Sorry. He was emphatic. Either way, there will be a challenge."

"I've got a bad feeling about how this will turn out."

"Stop worrying. It's a simple but air-tight will. As executor, you will be conducting a legal process. Don't worry, I'll guide you through it."

Sandy sat in the twilight with his eyes closed and listened to the hollow beat of his heart. The news of Leif's death seemed unreal—an intense bad dream without an end. His friend and mentor—the oak at the center of his life—had fallen. He pushed out of the chair and called his mother.

Abigail took the news in stride. After losing a husband, a son and friends, she faced grief with her native New England composure. She listened as he sobbed and spilled his guts. When he drew a breath, she recalled something silly he had done, and his sobs blubbered into laughter. She kept him laughing and crying by turns with memories of Leif until he had momentarily emptied his grief. Afterward, he washed his face and phoned Sophia.

"I'm sorry I was short on the phone," he began.

"Oh, don't apologize. You aren't rude enough for that—even on your worst day."

"I was waiting to hear about Leif. He's dead."

A long moment of faint static followed. "Oh, I'm so sorry," she whispered. "Is there anything—"

"—I'd like your company if you're not busy."

"Of course. Come to my place," she said. "I'll fix something."

Sophia hung up and put fire under the kettle for tea and arranged a plate with cheese, fruit and crackers. Then, thinking tea might not be enough, she brought out a bottle of brandy. He arrived a few minutes later, looking rumpled with tousled hair.

"He was the best man I ever knew," he said, trying to knuckle the tears back into place. "I can't imagine life without him."

"I know. You lost something of yourself, too," she said. "That's how I felt when my *nonna* died." She put her hand on his. He grasped it and gave up staunching his tears. "Have some brandy," she insisted.

Then he laughed. "I know what Leif would say if he saw me. He'd—"

"—Be touched… No, I guess he wouldn't."

"No. He'd say, '*Jeez*-zus kid, quit sniffling. You're alive, so take the brandy'." He laughed and let out his breath. "He was so matter of fact. He said everyone dies, and some do it well."

She gave him brandy and sat close to him. "I'm glad you can laugh."

He put his head back, closed his eyes and listened to her sing the *Tarantella* under her breath. "There's one other thing," he said, when she finished singing. "Let me get it off my chest." Then he told her about his hunch that Leif was at the Oxbow and his decision to say nothing.

"What's wrong with honoring his wish?"

"Nothing but… if I'd said something, he might be alive." He wiped his cheeks.

"Don't blame yourself," she said, stroking his hand. "From what you told me, this is probably the kind of death he wanted—doing something he liked."

"Yeah, you're right," he said, nodding slowly and then emphatically. "Yes. You're right. I guess I'm crying for me." He downed the brandy and they sat close together in silence. "Thank you," he said after a while and took her hand in both of his. "You're good company." Then he got up, put on his jacket and paused at the door. "Thanks again," he said and hugged her.

"Any time," she whispered, and her lips brushed his cheek.

As Sophia closed the door after him, she felt an emptiness in the apartment that hadn't been there before. Until now, it felt cozy and perfectly suited to her independent life. Now she missed him. She poured a brandy and thought about what he had lost—his father, brother, mentor and his wife. He still wore the wedding band so it must have been a strong marriage. I never knew Becky, she thought. She went on maternity leave three months after I joined the faculty. But she was popular because everyone on campus was blue when she died. And Sandy—we covered his classes for two weeks. Whenever we talk, he rubs the ring with his thumb. What can I do about that?

CHAPTER 24

The stairs creaked underfoot as Sandy ascended to Isaacs's small office. Volumes of *Minnesota Statutes*, court decisions and law books filled the shelves on the wall behind the solid wooden desk. The lawyer offered him a cup of instant coffee and then a copy of the will. He and Karla were the heirs. To Karla, Leif left an undetermined amount of cash and the family's heirlooms. To Sandy, he left the farm at Tarn Lake, personal property, and his canvas haversack and field desk.

"Nothing to Harald," he whispered. "Hard to believe."

"That's right," Isaacs said in a tone of neutral finality.

"There's going to be trouble."

"It's been known to happen."

Isaacs gave him a white envelope addressed to "Saginaw." The one-page letter typed on Leif's professional stationery and dated the day he filed the will:

> Dear Saginaw,
>
> I'm writing this in case I don't get the chance to tell you. I named you my heir and executor of my will. The farm is yours free and clear because I know you will protect it the way I would. You have grown into the man I hoped you would be. You know the woods and you know the books. That makes you

the kind of son I would have wanted. I am grateful for many years of friendship.

I have had a great life and wouldn't change much of it. And I wish the same for you. Every man should do one good thing before he dies. I had a lot of chances but didn't take them. The farm is what I value most and giving it to you is my last chance to do good. Tarn is a pristine lake. I have put the future of the lake and its creatures in your hands because I trust you to know what to do. I am also giving you a chance to do a good thing. Take care of the lake.

Ever your friend,

Leif S. Nielsen, Consult'g Forester

He read the letter a second time, unable to hold back his tears. Then he showed it to Isaacs. "This means more to me than the farm itself."

Sandy drove to Waterford at dusk, still astonished, confused and sad. He gasped and gasped again, gulping air to end the drowning sensation. Nothing had prepared him for the death and the emptiness that followed. What would Leif say if he saw me moping about, Sandy wondered. Then he heard the ranger's voice in his head saying, *Jeez-zus*. He laughed and felt better. He entered Waterford, cheered by the sight of familiar houses where light from the windows cast bright rectangles on the lawns. He turned at St. Michael's Church and parked in the driveway of the Cape Cod house.

"I'm home," he called through the unlocked front door. Abigail answered from the den. "Don't get up, Mom. I'll hang up my coat and join you." He wanted her company because she knew Leif almost as well as he did and didn't have to explain how he felt. She continued knitting as he bent down and kissed her.

"Tell me about the meeting with Morrie."

"I'm Leif's representative. He gave me the farm."

"*He what!*" she cried, dropping the knitting into her lap. "What about Karla?"

"It's mine. Free and clear. He left Karla personal items and cash."

"What are you going to do with it?"

"Mom… I have no idea. He never said a word to me. There'll be trouble with the Nielsens. I just know it."

"Well, I heard there's a memorial service on Wednesday at Zion Lutheran with a reception afterward. I suppose we should go since it's here in town."

"Leif was unknown here, but it'll make Harald look good. The county is doing an autopsy, so Leif will be happy to miss it." Sandy laughed and felt better.

Then Isaacs called. "Harald is in a hurry to execute the will. He wants to meet now. I stalled him until Thursday. I hope you will come."

He agreed and hung up. He groaned, thinking of two more days of missed classes. "And now the shit hits the fan."

The Zion Lutheran organist played *Faith of Our Fathers* as an usher seated Sandy and Abigail two rows behind Karla, Ted and the Nielsens. Most of the guests would be strangers to Leif except for Isaacs, who sat in the back. After a prayer and a passage of scripture, the pastor eulogized a man who scarcely resembled the one Sandy knew. But then, he thought, the memorial was really about Harald.

"He would have hated this," Abigail whispered in his ear.

Sandy nodded. He guessed Leif's funeral instructions would have specified a bar with a crew of rowdy woodsmen telling stories and toasting his memory until they were too drunk to walk.

"I'm sorry for your loss," he said to Karla when they met at the reception. "He was like a father to me in so many ways." He wanted her to help him with Leif's burial, but that conversation could wait until after tomorrow's meeting.

"You meant a lot to him," she said with a brave smile as she gripped his hand. "He talked about you often. Thank you for being his friend."

He thanked her, feeling out of place because he resented what Harald had done. Knowing he was the heir and not Harald added to the weight of his grief. Seeing Boston alone in a corner, he went to him. "Thank you for coming," he said, offering his hand. "It's nice to see you again."

"I'm sorry for your loss," he replied. "You gave me a good feeling for his character and what he meant to you. I didn't recognize the guy the pastor described."

"Neither did I," Sandy snickered. "I want to talk, but it may be a couple weeks."

"Whenever you're ready, I'll come. Oh, and give my regards to Sophia."

Sandy caught Isaacs's eye across the room, but the lawyer gave only a slight nod of recognition and returned to chatting with another man. Thinking Isaacs had a reason to keep his distance, Sandy stood near Harald and listened as the doctor told someone that Leif died because he ignored medical advice and went camping.

When the other man left, he asked Harald for his impression of Leif's last days.

"You saw him, he was ill. That's why he asked to stay at my place. It's anyone's guess why he went camping." Harald set his cup in its saucer. "There's no explaining the things he did, like swamping the boat or telling Mabel he was away on business and then go camping. It wasn't rational," he said, shaking his head.

"Maybe he didn't want to be bothered," Sandy said, aching to accuse Harald of… "Maybe he just wanted to finish his contract."

"The county canceled it. I told him that," the doctor continued, shaking his head. "I'm afraid he lost it up here," and tapped his temple. "He was pushing eighty, you see. I should've seen it coming. Dementia is so insidious, so subversive. But I missed it. It's the only answer I can give. Thank you for coming, Sandy," he said and offered his hand.

Harald went to stand by Regina, who was dutifully pouring coffee from a silver urn. Sandy's questions bothered him. What will the autopsy show, he wondered. I can't object, of course, not without raising questions. Leif shouldn't have recovered enough to leave, not if Mabel gave him the medicine like she said. Maybe the dose wasn't strong enough. On the other hand, it's just as well; otherwise, it might show in the autopsy. Best to let it slide. They suspect a heart attack. Maybe it will be a quick look to confirm that. No one can blame me. Another bout of pneumonia would have finished him.

Sandy and Abigail left the reception and took a long, slow drive on the winding roads. The maples had passed the peak of fall color, and the somberness gave him mental space to think. Smoking and drinking should have killed Leif years ago, but he remained physically active, sharp-witted and thin-skinned. Despite a morning cough, he was a tough old bird. Despite pneumonia, he made his body do what it shouldn't. He often said he would die only when he got damn good and ready. Well, maybe he did.

"The lies have started," Sandy said. "Harald told me Leif wandered off because he was demented—senile."

"What on earth… why would he say that?"

"It's a cover up," he said. Then he told her about finding the sedatives dispensed from the aspirin bottle and how he replaced them with aspirin. "Morrie Isaacs knows about it, but don't say anything."

"It's hard to believe he would do—"

"—I don't think it was his idea."

She gazed into the trees. "Well, dear, Leif was a great many things. I think he was ashamed to be sick and dependent. He wasn't a man to let go of his power and fade away. Maybe he knew his time was up. And knowing that, maybe he went to meet it on his terms. Meet it doing something he enjoyed. Something with a purpose consistent with his beliefs. I believe he wanted to die with self-respect. But I don't know. Sorry. It's the best I can do."

"I think you're right."

CHAPTER 25

Isaacs handed Sandy a cup of instant coffee. "I'll set the agenda and take the lead," he said. "Just follow my cues. This is a civil process. You'll do fine." They reread the will, and Isaacs listed the questions and objections that seemed most likely to arise. Then the lawyer chuckled. "You know, this is ironic. Harald had his lawyer draft an airtight will to make him the heir. He never imagined Leif would see the dodge and make a change. Now Harald's out. What goes around, comes around."

"Yeah, it is funny, all things considered," he said but didn't laugh.

"He'll be surprised and angry. Maybe Karla, too. That's normal. Just remember, their feelings aren't your fault. And you're not responsible for salving those feelings. Just remember that. One more thing… I know how you feel about Harald. Don't gloat."

"Okay," Sandy said. A moment later, he felt his stomach knotting at the sound of feet on the stairs. His stomach clenched even tighter, hearing Harald tell Karla this wouldn't take long because he already knew the terms of the will.

"Sandy… I didn't know…" Harald said, frowning as he looked him up and down. Then he offered his hand. Karla gave him a weary hello and shook his hand. Isaacs ushered them into the conference room and offered instant coffee.

"This is the will Leif signed and filed," the lawyer said a minute later and passed photocopies to each of them. "Harald, he made his will based on a draft your attorney prepared. As you see, he named Doctor Brewster his heir and executor."

"*Wait*—that's a mistake," Harald squealed. His normally pink face paled and then flushed red like an overripe tomato. "He told me I was the executor. I'm his family. I cared for him. I supported him. He told me you didn't change a thing," he shouted and rose half-way erect.

"I didn't change anything. He did," Isaacs said smoothly. "He made the changes the day after he left the hospital. I have the draft with the changes he wrote in ink. They are notarized as well."

"Well, well, I'm… I'm going to challenge that will."

"I don't see how you can do that."

"On… on medical grounds," he added hastily. "I was his doctor. His mind wasn't sound, he… he didn't know what he was doing. That's, that's why he asked me for a, a draft. All he had to do was, was sign his name and I'd, I'd take care of it. I'm in a position to judge his mind, Morrie. I say the will is invalid." Drawing a breath, he turned on Sandy. "And I know what he intended to do with *our* family's farm, that's for sure."

"Before you challenge the will, consider the unintended consequences," Isaacs warned in a soft voice. "The draft you gave him has no legal force. If the court voids this will, then your brother will have died intestate. That means the state will liquidate all the property, take a third and distribute the rest. Is that what you want?"

"My attorney drafted the will, and it named me the executor at Leif's request," he bawled. "He has copies of it. I can get sworn statements to prove that. It's his prior and true intention. I've got a Rochester law firm that'll make mincemeat of you."

The lawyer listened with a tolerant smile. "Harald, a man is allowed to change his mind—and his will. Until you can get a court to say otherwise, this will is in force. These are its provisions." Then, in a neutral tone, he listed the property Leif left to his heirs.

"This is… it's a fraud," the doctor blustered. "I can't believe you'd do this, Morrie. You leave me no choice but to challenge it."

"You do what you want," Isaacs said as if humoring a willful child. "As your brother's lawyer, I'll vigorously defend the will he filed. And until a court overturns it, and that's rare, Sandy is the heir and executor. You will abide by his decisions." The attorney paused and then shuffled the papers into a folder. "Sandy and I will inventory the property and give a list to Karla. Unless you have questions, we're finished." Isaacs's warm, tea-colored eyes peered over the rimless glasses perched on his nose.

Harald stamped down the stairs in a rage. *I should've followed my instincts,* he told himself. *I should've exercised the power of attorney before he died. But no, I let Regina and Sam talk me out of it because I'd look greedy acting before he died. Wait until his friends move on, she said. Well, for once, she was wrong. If I'd acted then, Sandy might have given up. Now, I don't have legal standing unless… unless Karla joins the challenge. She's got to believe she needs me.*

"Let's have some lunch and talk this over," Harald said as they left the building. Seeing nothing in Karla's posture or expression that showed any fight, he considered how to highlight her stake in this. *What did she expect Leif to leave her? Not the farm, but certainly cash, personal items and heirlooms. No telling how much cash he tucked away. Couldn't be much. If that and the heirlooms are enough, more power to her. But that's not likely. Even if she didn't expect to get the farm, she'd expect a share of its sale. Well, that's only fair.*

Harald's idea gelled as he parked at the Country Club. *My only niece stands to lose the most and is the one person in need of an inheritance. She must believe that. The court might give greater weight to family claims than those of an outsider. As her closest relative, I can act in her interest. But she has to agree that Leif was incompetent when he made the will.*

A couple of men in the dining room recognized Harald, and he nodded in response to their condolences. He and Karla took an isolated table where they could talk freely. "A terrible shock, wasn't it," he said while they waited for the menus.

"I'm surprised. I mean, I know Sandy meant a lot to him, but… what's he going to do with the farm? I don't understand Daddy's decision."

"There's only one thing he can do. Sell it. Farmers don't want it, but a developer would take it. That's more money than teaching history. I'm sure he knows it."

"Daddy hated the idea of development. I can't believe Sandy would do that."

"Money has a way of changing people."

"I know that. Right now, I'm focused on Daddy's burial. He wanted his ashes buried next to the big boulder where he smoked his pipe. So, I'll work that out with Sandy since Daddy specified it in his will."

"Does his burial place really matter?"

"*It does to me!*" she cried, throwing off the first sparks he had seen all morning.

"I didn't mean it that way. Of course, it matters. Just be careful around Sandy. Don't get taken in by his boyish charm. Underneath it all, he was something of a Svengali around your dad. He could do no wrong."

"I'll be careful. I'm not upset about the money or the farm. I just want to make sure that Daddy's intentions are carried out."

Their order arrived, and Karla nibbled at a salad as he tucked into the day's special of roast beef, peas and mashed potatoes with gravy. Neither said anything for a while.

"Carrying out your dad's wishes is what I want, too," he said. "He and I talked about it on the porch. He knew he couldn't hold on to it forever. That's why he asked me to draft a will. That's why he named me its executor. I was closer to your dad than Sandy. I mean, we were born on that farm. Our folks are buried there. At times like this, it's important for the family to stick together."

Karla listened but said little. "Thanks for lunch. You've been a help."

Harald went home feeling betrayed by Leif, who was made a fool of him by his deception. Then he thought of Regina's reaction. She can't wait to break ground. I'll have to tell her. Then tell the Wingspan Associates to stand down, at least for now. They won't like that, either.

Karla is essential, but she's an unsteady partner. She doesn't like Regina any more than Leif did. Somehow, I'll have to win her over. He knew it wasn't much of a plan, but it might be enough to focus her ire where it belonged—if not on Leif, then on Sandy. He entered the salon and joined her.

"Well, is it a go?" she asked, her voice rising in anticipation along with her plucked brows. "I didn't hear from you all day."

"No. We've had a setback."

"Setback, what setback?" Her face clouded.

"Leif changed his will. He named Sandy Brewster his heir. Gave him the farm."

"*What!*" she screeched and slopped gin from the pitcher. "He's not family. What are you going to do… *Harald?*"·Her dark eyes narrowed to obsidian points.

"I'm, I'm working on it. I'm working on Karla to contest the will on the grounds he was incompetent. However, an invalidated will means he died intestate. Then the state takes over, liquidates everything, keeps a third and doles out the rest. At least we'll get something."

She took two sips of her martini. "Oh, we can make intestate work in our favor," she said as her lips widened into a mirthless smile.

"How, sweetie," he shifted on his seat.

"The farm is worth maybe four hundred grand as is. The state doesn't want to sell a few acres at a time. It wants someone to buy it in one piece. Farmers aren't going to touch it. That leaves developers."

"Yeah," he said and brightened as he realized her line of thinking.

"First, we get the will invalidated, so Leif died intestate. That gets rid of Sandy. Second, we petition the court to buy the property to keep it in the family and get it ahead of anyone who might outbid us. So, we'll need four or five hundred thousand dollars."

"Easy. We can mortgage the house or the clinic."

"Good," she said, pouring him a second martini.

"I took Karla to lunch. She's not interested in the farm, but if there's money, she'll expect a share. She'll want enough to put Ted through college with maybe a little left over," he said. "Not much by our standards but a lot by hers. I think she'll do it."

"Good. Keeping her on our side is your job. Let's mortgage the house to buy the farm from the state. We'll pay the state its third, give Karla a third and we keep title to the farm. That three hundred thousand is a cost of business on the way to nine million."

Her swift thinking made his head spin. How does she do it, he wondered, imagining the expensive houses he had envisioned while sitting on the porch with Leif. One of them would be theirs, of course.

"You said he had dementia," she said, breaking into his thoughts. "The court will expect you to back it up. So, get medical records. While you're at it, get anything you can to show Brewster had undue influence on him. That will put him on the defensive—we'll make him the issue."

"I've got the medical records. They need to be brought up to date, anyway. I'm sure there are things I overlooked. As for influence… I'll need to work on that."

CHAPTER 26

Sandy retrieved a hidden key and led Isaacs into the farmhouse by the back door. He wondered if the house knew Leif was dead somehow, and the thick silence was its mode of mourning. It made him wonder if it would accept him as its new owner. A silly thought, he told himself but indulged it out of respect.

"We need to list everything he owned," Isaacs said, laying his briefcase on the kitchen table. Let's start with any money he had. I know he didn't have bank accounts, so it must be here somewhere."

Sandy laughed on his way into the bedroom. He opened a dresser drawer and pulled out a lumpy sock. "Here's some."

"I'll be damned. He really kept it in a sock."

"There and a lot of other places. He hid money the way a squirrel hides nuts."

They spent an hour going through the drawers, the mattress and cupboards, then the boxes and trunks. Sandy found a paper package marked "pork chops" in the freezer. More money. Cash turned up in an empty ammunition box and a flour canister. Beneath the cover of the toilet's reservoir, he retrieved a quart jar sealed with wax. It held thousands in $50 bills.

"Leif hasn't trusted banks since the Depression," he laughed and handed over another roll of bills.

"He was so shrewd about land and so naïve about banks," the attorney said, counting the bills and shaking his head in amused disbelief.

While Isaacs counted, Sandy found more money in a soup tureen stored in a trunk. They counted and recounted the rolls of bills in twenties, fifties and hundreds on the table's checkered oilcloth. It came to $48,860.

"I wonder if he knew how much he had," Isaacs mused. "It's ironic, but you'll have to open an account and bank the money. Use it to pay his outstanding taxes, liens or debts, including your expenses as executor. The rest goes to Karla."

"I won't charge for my expenses. I owe him that," Sandy said. "This has always fascinated me." He lifted the lid on the brass-bound pine trunk Thor Nielsen brought from Norway. A velvet-lined case held heavy silver brooches, pins, rings and bracelets, ivory hair combs and mother-of-pearl shirt studs. A flat wooden case held a few settings of bone china, sterling flatware and table linen. Wrapped in a blanket were photos of Leif, Harald, their sisters and parents. "All this goes to Karla."

The old man's personal effects included two out-of-style woolen suits—one brown, one gray, a pair of oxford shoes, four ties, three starched shirts and a newly cleaned Stetson. The dresser held socks, underwear, wool and flannel shirts, canvas and whipcord pants and a woolen vest. They added bamboo rods and reels, boxes of flies, a double-barreled shotgun, a Savage deer rifle, a .22 rifle and two revolvers with ammunition for each to the list. They listed the furniture.

They entered the barn and added to the list a small Ford-Ferguson tractor with a plow and disk, a large riding mower, two chain saws, a two-wheeled cart, the duck boat, a cedar strip canoe, tool chest, surveyor's transit, and chains and scaling tools for measuring logs. On the walls hung a Trapper Nelson pack frame, bears paw snowshoes, axes, pitch forks and pruning shears. In the attached lean-to were ladders, decoys, a cant hook, several shovels, rakes, hoes and an auger. He knew that if Leif were there, he would tell stories about each item—artifacts of a full life.

"In addition to this stuff," Isaacs said, "there is the van and camping gear at the sheriff's office."

"I know," Sandy said, dreading the prospect of liquidating the material remains of his friend's life. He stood on the porch and gazed at the lake, its waters ruffled and darker than usual against the leafless trees lining the far shore. A flock of teal rose from the reeds, gathered into a vee and winged away. Leif gave me his prized possession, he thought. A moment later, he recalled how the prophet Elijah anointed his successor with his robe. The robe became a fraught gift, and he sensed the farm might be one too.

Sandy stuffed Leif's tally books into a bag and took them when he locked the house. He and Isaacs inventoried the van the sheriff had towed to the courthouse. Then he left it and the camping gear for later but took the haversack, field desk and the three-ring binder. They were too precious to leave behind.

"That's about it, and you look beat," the attorney said, laying a hand on his shoulder. "Let me buy you coffee—and I don't mean instant. I'd offer something stronger, but you've got a drive ahead of you."

"I don't know what I'm going to do with all his stuff," Sandy said when they settled into a booth at the Streamliner. "I've got no use for the guns. I'll keep a fly rod and some flies because he tied them. And the tally books. And his oldest felt hat and the cruiser's jacket. I guess I'll give the rest of it to charity except for anything Karla or Ted want in addition to the cash and the heirlooms. "Should I offer anything I don't want to Harald—you know, a gesture?"

"No. That's a dangerous idea," Isaacs said gravely. "Leif was specific about what Karla could have. He was adamant that Harald gets nothing. If you want to give something to Ted, give it to Karla or wait until after probate confirms it is rightfully yours. Then you can do as you please with it."

"Nothing for his brother."

"That's what he said. And don't ask me why."

"Oh, come on, Morrie. He's sure to ask."

"He probably will. But I don't know anything, you don't know anything, so you have nothing to tell him. It's none of his business—at least, that's how Leif saw it."

"I thought they were close," Sandy said.

"Evidently, there was a schism."

"What do we do if he challenges the will?"

"We have a signed will and his letter. Harald doesn't. Courts stick with signed documents until the challenger comes up with proof of fraud or incompetence."

"Well, Harald's going to say he was senile."

"I'll get his medical records. They're part of the estate. The privilege belongs to the patient, not the doctor. I'll get the originals so we know what we're working against. Now, stop worrying. You've got a big job disposing of a farm with a mile of valuable shoreline. Take your time to think about why Leif gave it to you."

The blustering, northerly windstorm matched Sandy's mood on the drive home. He feasted on anger toward Harald, and the miles slipped by. When the time came, he hoped to serve him a double helping of what he gave to Leif. He entered his house, and it felt cold, though the thermostat registered a comfortable temperature. Even so, his house had never had this kind of chill.

Clutching a mug of hot chocolate, he opened the haversack and removed the leather case. Opening it released the faint, nutty scent of pipe tobacco that aroused memories. He fingered the tally book and coughed a sob from his throat. Then, he leafed through the binder of field notes and hand-drawn maps. Though they weren't works of art, they were works of heart and, therefore, beautiful.

The cocoa didn't warm his body or ease his spirit, so he fixed a whiskey and water. Fortified with his mentor's drink, he read through several of Leif's small tally books for the simple pleasure of hearing the writer's voice in his head. They weren't diaries, but Leif noted events, thoughts and observations of a particular moment in abbreviated words and phrases. Then Sandy reread them with the same critical eye that had assessed thousands of historical documents for clues to the author's honesty, sanity, delusion or ignorance. He read the latest tally book and compared it to one written ten years before. Then he read them again, heartened to see no significant difference in the clarity of thought. So much for the claim of mental incompetence.

He read Leif's contract with Daniels and skimmed the usual obtuse legal garble about parties of the first and second part until he understood it. According to the terms, cancellation required two weeks' written notice. Harald said the county canceled the contract, but was he bluffing? Even if canceled, it would be like Leif to complete the survey just to make a point. Clipped to the contract, he found a typed invoice for final payment and expenses. It noted the day he began the survey and the date of its completion. He signed the management plan on the day he died. Daniels would know if the contract was still in force.

Curled up on the couch before the fire, he felt the whiskey warm him and read the management plan. Its twelve pages crackled with words the way Leif spoke—in short, declarative phrases. The ranger set out the facts and explained them so anyone could understand their meaning. He described each ecosystem, described the specific management challenges and laid out the protective measures in trenchant statements of what should be allowed or prohibited.

"This wasn't written by an addled senior!" he whispered, feeling a sense of relief run through his body. Then he turned in and slept well.

CHAPTER 27

Leif's death hit Emery Daniels hard. It was the loss of a friend, a contemporary. Not many men of his generation remained. Beyond that, whom could he trust to finish the survey in a way that would satisfy him? He was about to call Isaacs when his assistant said he had a call holding on another line.

"Doctor Brewster, what may I do for you?" Daniels asked and cleared his throat.

"I'm Leif Nielsen's heir. His personal representative," Sandy began. "I'm calling about your contract with him. I have it with me. Also, I have an invoice and the management plan. Can you tell me how to proceed?"

"First, my condolences. If he named you his heir, then he thought highly of you just as I thought highly of him. His death is a great loss. Though I knew him only briefly, I will miss him. You say you have the management plan. Is it finished?"

"Yes, he signed it the day he died. I don't know who to give it to."

"Bring it to me. Rumor has it his brother says he was demented. I don't buy it, you understand. It's just the grumbling of a sore brother."

"That's a problem. He's going to contest the will. And he claims he verbally canceled the contract with the county. As I read it, you contracted directly with Leif and used the county as a financial service provider."

"That is correct. I received no written notice of cancellation, so the contract is in force. Now, you say he finished the plan."

"Yes, sir. It's signed and dated the night he died."

"If it's convenient, come to my office on Saturday. We have much to talk over."

Sandy called Isaacs that evening and recounted the conversation with Daniels about the contract and management plan.

"Well, that's interesting," Isaacs said. "A county clerk told me Harald tried to cancel the contract. He got all huffy when she told him contracts required two weeks' written notice. He said that as Leif's personal representative and a county commissioner, his word was enough. Harald isn't popular with the county staff, so she didn't tell him the contract was with Daniels. However, she noted the date he came in. It was a day or two after Leif entered the guesthouse."

"The dots connect," Sandy said. "He wants title to the farm and had the will drafted when Leif was vulnerable. He must have counted on him to overlook the power of attorney clause. Then he drugged him, so he seemed incompetent. After that, he could exercise the power of attorney to take over the farm before his death."

"Speculating on someone's motives is dangerous," Isaacs said carefully. "It's too easy to be wrong. However, I can't argue with your recitation of the facts in sequence. I'll ask the clerk for a sworn statement. So far, there's nothing overtly criminal, but it's ethically questionable."

"I've read the management plan, and its clarity proves his mental competency."

"I would think so."

"What about Daniels?"

"By all means, talk to him. His opinion carries weight in a lot of quarters."

Sophia avoided 301 Milton when Sandy was gone. His absence had seemed ideal when they first moved in, but now the space was tolerable only when he was there. Admit it, he makes the rainy days sunny, she thought. He definitely lifts my morale when I'm cranky, doesn't reek of male privilege, doesn't annoy me and he isn't afraid to call me out, either. I miss him. So, where do things stand with us—could we be a couple? We're comfortable and… comfortable. Comfortable, *ugh*! *That's* the problem. Comfort is fine for friendship, but is something more than that possible. His loyalty to Becky's memory holds him back. That wedding band shields him the way a crucifix wards off vampires. It's like we're parked on a plateau of comfortable comradeship with nothing beyond it. At forty-one, I can't afford to wait for him to make the first move. I've got to start things rolling. Well, why the hell not? Waiting for male leadership is another patriarchal convention. She felt better when she heard him coming up the stairs.

"Ah, home sweet home," he joked as he set the briefcase on his desk. "This isn't the cave I used to think it was, it's a hide-out."

"I've tried to stay away from here when you're gone," she said, frowning. "I've missed you. Tell me about the funeral."

"Very Lutheran. Leif would have detested every minute of it," he said, wrinkling his nose and swiveling in the chair to look at her. "But his brother and daughter wanted it, so I guess that was all right." Then he heaved a huge sigh. "I'm his heir, the executor of his estate. He left me his farm."

"*Whaa…* that's a deadass pisser!" she said, her mouth open.

"Pisser?"

"It's Boston slang for incredible, awesome."

"No shit. I still can't believe it. His brother blew up when he found out. Leif let him think he was the executor. Now, he says Leif was demented, that the will is invalid and he's going to contest it. It'll be ugly."

"He trusted you a lot."

"Friends my whole life. I can't remember when he wasn't part of it."

"What are you going to do—with the farm, I mean?"

"That's just it. I don't know. It's complicated. It'll take time. Meanwhile, I've got to prep for classes and tenure."

"Well, you deserve a break from all this stress," she said and flashed a full-face smile. "Please come to dinner tomorrow night. I'll make Mama's tomato-basil salmon that will taste even better if we share it."

"All right, thank you. Let me bring something."

"Some wine, if you like, otherwise—just you and your appetite."

There—another patriarchal convention overthrown, she thought on the walk home. For once, she took pleasure in cleaning the apartment, arranging the furniture and presetting the table. *This has to get us off the platonic mesa and toward something better.*

Sophia returned home at noon the next day to prep the meal. Then she thought about Sandy while soaking in a warm, scented bath. *He is a friend but too much like a professional colleague. Well duh, sister, so am I. That's all I've shown him—or anyone else. So, it's time to do the unthinkable.* She smiled, pulled the plug and reached for a towel.

Tonight, Sophia took more time than usual applying mascara, eyeliner, blush and lipstick. Like an artist with a portrait, she worked at enhancing her natural allure while avoiding *gavoni*, appearing overdone, like a slut. Satisfied, she dabbed perfume at strategic spots. Opening the closet, she pushed aside the dark ensemble of utilitarian skirts and jackets she wore on campus and selected a flared midi skirt and a low-cut top. Slipping into seldom-worn pumps made her wince.

"You hypocrite," she scolded herself with a smile. *Is this because he expects it? No, it's because he doesn't. It's for us. We need a breakthrough, and it's up to me.* Then she combed her hair, added pendant earrings and hoped his appetite went beyond salmon.

The entrée, pasta and *hors oeuvres* were ready when the apartment buzzer went off. Sophia opened the door and leaned her hip nonchalantly against the jamb. Sandy stepped back, eyes wide and mouth open, as if she had smacked him in the face with a custard pie. *Bingo,* she thought with a warm flush.

"Is this the… I mean—"

"—Come in," she cooed and took his jacket. Then she slipped something into its pockets and hung it in the closet.

"You… you look terrific," he gushed, hoping it wouldn't trigger scolding about sexual objectification. "Those colors… they're, they're just so right for you."

"Thank you. It's been a long time since I had a reason to dress up," she said, opening the pinot noir he brought. As she bent over to pour it, she offered a clear view down the front of her top.

Oh, Jesus, he thought, excited by what he glimpsed. You aren't a shy prude. He swallowed hard. Sophia, I hardly know...

"I have one request," she said, handing him a glass. "We aren't professors tonight. So, no shop talk—*è vietato*—forbidden. We can talk about anything else. But the college, our classes and our students are off limits. Tonight, it's just between us."

"Perfect," he said, raising his glass and touching hers. They nibbled the *hors d'oeuvres* and then ate the salmon slowly while they talked. In her luminous eyes, he again saw a deeper spirit and hoped it was her true self—the one that sang. However, when he asked about her family, she deflected the questions as she had before and begged him for a memory of Leif or his mother or another episode of his life.

When they finished eating, she emptied the last of the wine into their glasses, took his hand and led him to the sofa. They sat half-facing each other with her knees touching his. For the first time, she didn't feel his defenses radiating from the wedding band. Maybe that chapter of his life is over. He's been open about it. So he trusts me. Now it's time to pose the question. The honesty of his answer will make or break our future.

"There's something I want to ask you," she said, turning serious and looking into his eyes. "I want a candid answer. A blunt one will do. It's important to me."

"Of course," he said, perplexed.

"What is it I do or say that turns off people—that makes them ignore me?"

"Nothing that I can think of," he said, letting out his breath at this abrupt change of subject. "You're well-liked by everyone."

"I didn't ask if they liked me. I asked if I turned them off. Like at the faculty senate—I feel tuned out, ignored. Be honest, is it because sometimes I'm..."

He noticed pleading in her eyes more than in her voice. She's so appealing when she's her natural self, he thought. There's vulnerability—pain or maybe sorrow—but she hides it under militancy. It was a serious question, and he couldn't duck it but feared the truth might ruin the evening.

"All right, since you asked," he said, weighing his words before he said them. "It's not what you say, it's how you say it. It's your repetitious harp on three thousand years of patriarchy. No one disputes the point. Least of all the women. But the repetition irritates them." Then he paused.

"Go on," she said, her voice shaking. "I asked for the truth."

"The faculty women agree chauvinism is a problem. In private, they say your words and actions don't match. It's your all-or-nothing approach. Instead of joining them in the one-day protest, you snubbed it as too weak. You don't walk the talk."

Tears welled in her eyes. Her lips trembled. She pressed them together and took a deep breath. "What can I do—I mean, can I do something and—"

"—It's not what you believe or say," he said. "It's how you say it. Shock gets old fast. So does scolding. But humor lasts. You've got a sense of the absurd. Use that to make your point. It's hard to disagree with a critic who makes you laugh. You can do it. That and take small steps. Weak gestures add up in time."

She leaned back and studied him for a moment without a word. "You *are* a friend," she said, putting her hand over his and covering the gold band. "Thank you."

Her sudden kiss startled him. The first kiss from a woman in years aside from his mother. He liked the softness of her lips, her scent and the touch of her body. Calm down, he cautioned. It was just an impulse, gratitude, nothing more.

"I don't know a delicate way to ask this, but…" Sophia began and took a breath. "Will you tell me about Becky—as a person, I mean? It'll help me to know you better."

"*Uh*, well," he began in surprise. "She was my world. I still feel guilty… because… because I refused to drive her to my mom's house. I didn't so I could get in more research before the baby came. If I'd driven her, she wouldn't have had the accident." He held up his hand. "The ring reminds me you pay a price for selfishness."

"I've wondered about that," she said. "Thank you for telling me. But I don't think you're selfish. Conscientious—yes. Selfish, no. You aren't omniscient and couldn't have foreseen what happened. It's more likely you'd both be dead."

"She was the light of my life," he said.

"Tell me more," Sophia asked. "How did she feel about children?

"She loved children the way a gardener loves plants," he said. "She wanted to raise daughters as strong and independent women."

"And you?"

"Boys or girls, I would have been happy either way. Thanks for asking," he said at last. "Talking helps. I've been carrying it around. Guess it's time to stop living in a past I can't change."

She leaned forward and cupped his face between her hands. "I've never met a man who's so open, so genuinely vulnerable."

"It was a relief to tell you."

"Talking—that's how we heal," she said."

"It's getting late. I better go," he said, wishing he could stay. He felt her trust and loyalty. They had an intimacy he had missed since Becky's death. He wanted more of it with her but feared that if he didn't leave now, he would do something foolish. "This was lovely. Thank you."

"It was," she said, removing his jacket from the closet and holding it out. "I don't want you to go."

"Well, let's do it again. I'll cook next time." He shoved his hands into the jacket pockets and felt something small. "What's...?" He removed his hands and stared at two foil-wrapped Hershey's kisses.

"Some kisses are even better chocolate," she said and pressed against him.

He looked into her eyes and then, throwing caution aside, folded her into his arms, still clenching a chocolate in each fist. Once started, they couldn't stop kissing their lips, necks, cheeks and chins.

"Where did you learn to kiss like that?" she whispered.

"French class!" He laughed and then realized the chocolates had melted into a gooey mess in each hand. "Now, I really better go."

"Go? Go? No. I don't want you to go, I want you to come—"

"—You think it's a good idea to—"

"—There's one way to find out," she said, licking his sticky hand.

CHAPTER 28

The autopsy report arrived at Brewster's house by registered mail. He read it, and his fury returned. Leif died of a heart attack caused by over-exertion and complicated by sedatives that hindered his recovery from pneumonia. Well, you've got medical evidence against Harald, he thought, savoring it until he felt disgusted with himself. When he called Karla that evening, he wished he knew her well enough to read her mood over the phone, but he couldn't.

"Hello, Sandy. How nice to hear from you."

"I'm calling about your dad's burial." He couldn't tell if her cool civility came from passive hostility or mourning or both. "I want it to respect your wishes. He was my friend, but I had no idea he named me an heir. Of course, I understand if you feel left out, disappointed, angry or confused. I would. You are his daughter, and my regard for him extends to you."

"Thank you. I understand," she said. "I'm confused, but I'm not angry with you. I believe you."

"Thank you. I just received the autopsy. He died of a heart attack from over-exertion and an incomplete recovery from pneumonia. For what it's worth as consolation, he died suddenly."

"I'm glad he didn't suffer. Over-exertion... well, that's much better than dying in that guest house. Daddy died in the woods. He wanted something like that."

"He asked me to nail his corked boots to a tree. Beyond that, he didn't give me instructions. I want to honor your ideas about a burial at the farm."

She laughed. "Nailing his boots, *ha!*... that sounds like him. I favor cremation. Will you please make the arrangements? I'd like to bury him next to the pink boulder with the kind of informal ceremony he would have liked."

"Perfect. I know he'd want a ceremony with whiskey and tall tales. I know a few of his friends. Maybe you know others to invite. Let's talk again soon." He hung up, relieved they agreed on that much.

Harald called two nights later while he and Sophia were eating supper at his house. He answered, glanced at her and mouthed, "Harald." The doctor sounded chipper as if his rage had never happened. Then, he got down to business.

"You know, our family burial plot is going to be a headache for whoever owns that property," he said. "So, here's an idea. I have a cemetery lot in Waterford. If we bury Leif there, we can put my sister and parents next to him later on. At this point, it doesn't matter where he lies."

"It matters a lot!" Sandy said. "He wanted to be buried on the farm. I won't go against that."

"But what will happen to the graves and our rights to visit them when you sell?"

"You'll have the same rights as now."

"A new owner might change his mind."

"It'll be a condition of the sale. A perpetual easement. Besides that, there are state laws to protect your rights."

"Come on. That won't work."

"It will if the property isn't developed. He wanted to be buried at the farm, so that's where he'll be buried."

"He's dead. It doesn't matter where his ashes rest."

"It mattered to him, and it matters a great deal to me. I gave my word."

"Your word... your word. You're not family. I am. So is Karla. I say—"

"—You have no say, *doctor*. You're not in—"... a click... "—the will."

*
**

The night with Sophia had shoved them off the comfortable plateau with a passion. Now each was making up for years without sex. Sharing his bed with her and listening to her breathing made him feel alive again. As good as it was, he resisted the temptation to imagine, assume, or discuss a future. Enjoying the moment was enough for now.

"I've got to get the farm ready for Leif's burial," he told her one afternoon. "Will you come with me? We can stay with my mother this weekend."

"*Ya huh*. I'd love to meet your mother."

He called his mother that evening to arrange the weekend visit. "Mom, do you have room for another guest?"

"Of course, dear, I have lots of room. What is her name?"

Mothers! He coughed as a warm flush rose up his neck and spread across his cheeks. How did she know? Did I let something slip? Oh well… On the drive to Waterford, he told Sophia his mother guessed he was bringing a woman with him.

"You see, we women have superpowers you men lack," she laughed.

He let it go because he didn't have a come-back and told her how his mother returned to teaching after his father died. Even while working full-time, she chaired the town library board, read to children and led the sacristans at St. Michael's Episcopal Church. Each morning, she walked with a younger woman and spent the month of April in southern France. A side-long glance told him Sophia was hanging on every word.

"You'll have to sleep alone this weekend," he said as they entered Waterford.

She laughed. "Oh, you mean we can't…" and her eyes grew round and then squinted in mirth. "Of course, but later on couldn't we—"

"—Nope," and shook his head. "The guest room is on the first floor. Mine is on second. The stairs creak and so does my bed."

The highway from Wacouta to Waterford followed the river through a forest. Most of the trees were bare except for some oaks holding onto a few rusty leaves. He told her about canoeing the river with Leif, fishing for bass and cruising timber on the bluffs. They broke out of the forest near Waterford.

"See that," he said as they passed a stone manse. "That's Nielsen's house."

"My God! It's a frickin' chateau."

"Yup. That's what I'm up against. A rich bastard with a well-connected wife."

"People with that kind of money give me the creeps."

"Now you know." After that, he drove around Waterford on a tour of his high school, the library, city hall and the coffee shops where he used to hang out. Abigail's house had lights in the windows, and the front door wore a wreath of grape and bittersweet vines tied with a calico ribbon.

"We're *here*," he called as they entered. Abigail kissed his cheek, greeted them and swept them into the living room. Over supper, she focused her attention on Sophia until Sandy suspected her of cultivating a potential daughter-in-law. He knew she would never admit it, nor was he ready for the altar. But all the same, he was happy the two women seemed to like each other. One thing at a time.

The day broke chilly but clear, and Sophia appeared for breakfast in baggy jeans, a Seabury sweatshirt and her hair bound in a single braid. The professor in dark suits had made herself into something of a small-town woman. She and Abigail lingered over coffee while he packed the car with mops, brooms, pails and liquid cleansers. When she peppered him with questions about Leif on the drive to the farm, he thought it odd but marvelous that the old ranger had taken root in her imagination.

"I used to spend weekends there when I was a kid," he said. "Slept on the couch under a quilt and woke to the smell of bacon. Leif always cooked lots of it with eggs, hashed potatoes, sourdough bread and strong coffee. His meals were hearty lumber camp fare, but he was a chef with the Dutch oven. Nothing topped his beef pot roast with rich, silky gravy and biscuits followed by deep-dish apple pie or a peach cobbler."

"Stop. I can almost taste it. I'm hungry already."

"Then you should've eaten more breakfast," he scolded. "Leif usually told tales at mealtimes because I suspect he was lonely and wanted attention. Someone to let him know he'd been heard. Especially as the men of his stamp died out."

"Tell me one of his tales," she begged like a kid who wanted a bedtime story.

"Sure, but why?"

"You shine when you tell them. Now that I know your... I want to know the other parts of you, too."

He blushed and laughed. "Well, his stories usually began as a comment on something someone said. Then he'd say, 'That reminds me of the time...'" He glanced at her and then, in his best imitation of Leif's voice, told her the story about Tanner Bill's arrest for moonshining during prohibition in the Superior National Forest. "Everyone knew Tanner made hooch for the money. He hid the still in the horse barn at an abandoned logging camp." Sandy side-glanced and saw her watching him intently. "As I was saying," he continued, repeating another of the ranger's phrases. "As I was saying... we didn't allow moonshining on national forest land, so I told Tanner to get rid of it. He didn't. One day, my crew stopped there and came back soused. So, I rounded up a sober crew, armed them with axes and drove over in a couple one-ton trucks."

"Go on," she urged. "Don't stop."

"Well, as I was saying, when Tanner came out of his shack, he looked at the crew and said, 'I guess you're here about the still.' And I said, 'Sorry, Tanner, I warned you. We mean it.' He held out his wrists so I could cuff him, but I said, 'Get in the truck.' Then I told the crew to get rid of the Who-Hit-John and bust up the still. Meanwhile, I drove Tanner to the ranger station. The crew came in hours later. They got rid of the hooch all right—and were hung over for the next two days. Tanner signed up for fire duty and never went back to moonshining. That's how we took care of people then."

She laughed and clapped her hands. "Wonderful. That helps."

CHAPTER 29

Evenly spaced survey stakes curved gracefully across the hayfield from the gravel road to the farmhouse. From there, another line of stakes paralleled the lakeshore eighty feet from the water. Seeing a yellow bulldozer next to the barn made Sandy's breakfast churn in his belly. He swallowed hard to keep it down.

"What the *fuck*!" he screamed. "They're going to cut a road! Ruin it. It's Harald. His way of saying it's his. It's pressure. Sell to a developer or else." He parked by the house, spattering curses like bullets. "I'll beat you, you sonofabitch! I'll shove the stakes up your fat ass. I'll… Oh, sorry."

"I've heard worse, just not from you—not until now." She touched his arm. "Let it all out."

"Goddamn motherfucking asshole! I'll…" Then he took a couple deep breaths. "Okay," he gasped. "Let's dig the grave… I'd like to dig one for… then we'll deal with the stakes. C'mon," he said, grabbing her hand and hauling her around the house to the porch.

She gasped in surprise. "It's, it's deadass beautiful! I had no idea."

"Yeah. And I've got a fight on my hands because of it." He rolled aside the barn door and returned with a spade, a posthole auger, a board and a piece of canvas. "Follow me," he ordered and led her through the ankle-high grass to the pink boulder. She perched on it with her arms around her knees while he dug the grave. Turing the auger, he understood anew how this stony soil had defied the plow. His shoulders and arms soon ached as the aggregate resisted.

Putting his anger into digging, he kept on until he bored a hole four feet deep. He covered the soil with the canvas and put a board over the hole.

"Let's walk along the lake. We'll pick up the trash as we go," he said, yanking out a survey stake and sticking it under his arm.

"My turn," she called and pulled the next one.

They walked the shoreline and took turns pulling stakes with righteous zeal until each carried a thick bundle. As they crossed the hayfield, a pheasant burst from underfoot in an explosion of bronze feathers. Sophia shrieked and dropped the stakes. The cackling rooster launched itself airborne and quickly vanished into a thicket.

He laughed. "That reminds me of the time—"

"—I hear a story."

"Leif and I hunted pheasants here many times. His dog had a good nose—"

"—You shot them?"

"Yes, of course. Boys don't have a conscience at fourteen. That comes later—"

"—If it does at all," she said under her breath. "Blood sport rituals—"

"—Hunting isn't about blood and death. It's relationships. It's social."

"Can't you make friendships without killing something to prove your manhood?"

"Aw, drop it!"

"*Ha-ha*, I said it to goad you."

"Well, it worked. Now—as I was *trying* to tell you, six of us were walking abreast on this field when a rooster got up just about where that one did. It flew across the front of us, shoulder-high at point-blank range. We each yelled, 'I got 'em, I got 'em' and shot as it passed. After eight or ten shots, the bird vanished untouched," he laughed. "We stood there with our mouths open. No one said a word. How could all of us miss? Leif gave a whinny and said, 'Jeez-*zus Key*-ryst.' Then we all laughed. The bird made fools of us, and we never forgot it. That's what binds us together."

"I love hearing your voice when you tell those stories," she said, holding his hand. "You loved him."

"More than loved," he said softly. "Worshipped him. He was there for the big moments of my life—as if he were my father."

She squeezed his hand between hers. Then they returned to the house and dumped the stakes in a pile.

"Now we've got to mow the grass. Wait here." He entered the barn and appeared a moment later on a riding lawnmower. After cutting a swath around the house, he stopped where Sophia sat on the porch. "Think you can drive this?"

"Is that a requirement for being your woman?"

"One of many. Especially here. You say women are equal. Well, show me."

"Oh, and I suppose you'll sit on the porch and drink while I do it."

"That's an idea. Thanks."

"I've never done this," she said, sitting uneasily on the mower. "But I'm ready."

He showed her the gears, the clutch and the throttle. "Ease the clutch out," he said, now all business. "Overlap the cut a couple inches and watch out making turns. Never put your hand under the deck or you'll be known as Three-Fingers Colombo. Stick to the lawn around the yard. If you have trouble, shut it down."

"Okay," she said and kissed him. She popped the clutch, the mower lurched forward and she quickly disappeared around the side of the house.

Sandy honed his anger as he filed a keener edge to the scythe's steel blade. "You're a dead man, Harald," he said. "Sooner or later... You're dead. You jumped my claim. There'll be a reckoning," he said as the blade slashed swathes through the tall grass.

He cut the grass around the boulder and then over the Nielsen graves. They lay on the gentle slope facing the lake, and he wondered if that was so they could see it on resurrection day. Judgment comes before the resurrection, he thought. Judgment is coming for you, Harald, but your resurrection isn't guaranteed.

Sandy returned to the house and saw the mowed area was wider now. Then Sophia passed him on the mower, beaming in triumph and blew a kiss. He entered the kitchen and poured whiskey into a jelly glass. Seated on the porch with his feet on the rail, he raised his glass as she passed. Sophia returned the salute with her middle finger. Then she shut off the mower and joined him on the porch.

"Are you better now?" she asked. "I didn't think you capable of rage."

"I'm under control," he said and offered her whiskey.

"*Mmm*. It's a little early for me."

"Never too early for a snort out here." He stretched his arms to loosen them, and she held his glass. "Let's eat lunch. Then I've got to disable that 'dozer."

Sandy went to the barn and returned with an axe. While he busted up the lathes, Sophia unpacked a basket of sandwiches. He was about to light a fire when she pointed toward the road where a pickup drove toward them across the hayfield. It stopped by the bulldozer, and two muscular men in coveralls got out.

"Hey, what in hell are you doing?" the red-faced driver yelled as he approached. The second man held a crowbar and began to circle around Sandy.

"What are you doing on my property?" Sandy said as he brought the axe across his chest in a position to swing it. He knew he couldn't take both of them. Maybe not even one. "Who the hell are you?"

"Your property? I'm Pete Larson. Damson Construction. We're putting in the access road. Did you pull our stakes?"

"Your stakes?" Sandy spat. "Yes. You're trespassing."

"The hell I am."

"Get this straight, Larson," Sandy said, lowering his voice and unlimbering the axe as his rage returned. "This is my property. I never heard of you. Didn't order a survey. And you're trespassing. So yeah, I pulled the stakes."

"Trespassing? This is the Nielsen farm, isn't it?"

"No. It used to be. Now it's mine. I'm Sanford Brewster."

"Well… *uh*… Wingspan told us to… *uh*…" Larson glanced at his partner and shifted on his feet. "They… *uh*, contracted us to get started."

"Well, Leif Nielsen died and left the farm to me. So, you get your bulldozer out of here today. If you don't, I'll call the sheriff and file a complaint."

Larson and his partner looked at each other in silence for a moment. Then Larson shrugged. "Jeez, mister. Don't blame us. Wingspan hired us to do it. If it's not Nielsen's place then… well, I'm sorry we troubled you." He shrugged again. "We'll be back with a trailer for the 'dozer tomorrow." The men got into the pickup and bounced away.

"*Goddamn*, that felt good!" Sandy exulted despite the tremor in his knees. "I felt like I was channeling Leif."

"I'm shaking," Sophia said. "What if… you were crazy fearless. *Tu se pazzo*. A real man."

"You see, testosterone has its uses."

"*Ya huh*, if it's the good kind. Now, let's eat."

The stakes made a fast, crackling fire that held the afternoon chill at bay. He set camp chairs in front of the fire and retrieved the whiskey and two jelly glasses from the kitchen. They ate before the fire, warmed by the flames, the whiskey and affection.

"It's so beautiful here," she sighed. "I wish you didn't have to sell it."

"Me, too. I can't afford to keep it, so I want to get it into the hands of an organization that will protect it. That's the only way to save it. But I'm stuck."

"What about Seabury?" she asked.

"Seabury… what about Seabury?"

"The environmental studies program needs a field station. Why not this?"

"Oh! I never thought of that. But the program doesn't have money to buy property."

"At the moment, it doesn't. I'll look into that while you slay the dragons," she said. "I'm on the scholarship committee. The fundraising staff has donor contacts. So, maybe there's someone out there who wants immortality."

"I'll be right back," he said and entered the barn. Then he returned with a small tarp and spread it by the fire.

"What's that for?"

"To lie on—in case we're overcome with passion."

Sophia spent Sunday morning with Abigail while Sandy met with Isaacs. He returned home at midday and recognized the kitchen aroma as Leif's recipe for chicken pot pie with biscuits. The open wine bottle on the counter and the burst of laughter from the living room told him all was well. He poured a glass and joined them. Seeing the women at ease with each other told him Sophia would be welcome again. Later, when they returned to Wacouta, he went the long way on winding roads over the ridges and down the valleys. Then he stopped and got out at the edge of a bluff so she could look at the countryside spread out like a quilt.

"I see a lot of your mother in you," she said, grasping his hand.

"Yeah, and I see that you like her. The two of you seem *simpatico*."

"Oh. I adore her. She's composed and independent. It comes from inside her. She doesn't beat you over the head with what she believes—like *someone* you know." She elbowed him.

"How are we alike?"

"It's your sensitivity when you meet with students. You're direct but not confrontational—unlike *someone* you know." She laughed and squeezed his hand. "Tell me about your father."

He paused a moment. "Dad was an outgoing guy. Patient with Paul and me. He tanned our hides when we sassed Mom. We could sass him, but not her."

"Did he put her on a pedestal?"

"Not exactly. But he respected her judgment. When dealing with someone difficult, like another doctor or a nurse, he asked her for advice. Dad had a temper a lot like mine and deferred to her. She kept him in check and saved him from big mistakes."

"I think you're like your mother. If you weren't, I don't think we'd be together."

He wanted to ask about her family, but she usually changed the subject. We can't go on being one-sided about family, he thought and asked about her parents.

She sucked in her breath. "There's really not much to tell," she began without enthusiasm. "They came from Italy in the 1930s. We four were born in North End Boston, and Papa tried to run the family like his father did." She said Enrico Colombo was a concertmaster who taught violin at a small conservatory. Her mother was a ballet dancer and gave private lessons. Sophia was the oldest child, followed by two sisters and Martin.

"You're graceful. Did you dance when you were younger?" he asked.

"Yes, until I got these," she said, cupping her breasts. "Then I quit. There's only one place to dance with a set like this," she giggled.

"Well, I like them."

"So I've noticed. Anyway, my sisters are married, but not Tino. He's gay. Papa doesn't know it, but Mama and I do."

"Why not your father and sisters?"

"It would kill Papa, but he'd kill Tino first because he's counting on him to perpetuate the family line." She snorted derisively. "We're Catholic, you know. He spent a lot on my sisters' church weddings but next to nothing on my doctoral party. He's disappointed, says we're selfish for staying single and not doing our duty to bring children into the world."

"I take it he doesn't respect your achievements."

"He's never said so. I know he loves me, but... I think he's resigned..."

Seeing his questions snuff the sparkle from her eyes and hearing an undertone of bitterness, he changed the subject.

CHAPTER 30

November opened with low clouds riding on a raw northeast wind that promised cold rain by nightfall. Sandy and Karla chose November 2 for Leif's burial out of convenience and not for the religious significance of All Souls Day. He and Sophia arrived at the farm first and built a fire in the stove so that the kitchen was toasty when Karla and Ted arrived. The other guests would be along in an hour. While the four drank coffee, Sandy said Harald wasn't coming because Regina was ill. From Karla's "*uh huh*," he surmised she doubted the illness as much as he did. Her eyes flashed anger when he told her about the survey stakes. She said it was just like Regina to force Harald into doing it.

Karla seemed composed and gracious, but he sensed an invisible tension that kept her buttoned up. He didn't feel he knew her well enough yet to talk about the future of the farm. One thing at a time. While they discussed each step of the ceremony, Sandy overheard snippets of conversation from the front room, where Sophia and Ted talked about his academic interests.

"Thank you for coming," Karla said with a bright smile at the arrival of Isaacs, Abigail, Daniels, Boston, Fred from the Plow Boy tavern, the renter and several others. She gave them coffee and cookies, then gathered them in the front room. "This will be an unorthodox burial, but I hope you will agree it's in keeping with Dad and the man he was." She paused, then said, "Sandy."

On cue, he held up a pair of leather boots with spiked soles. He handed them to Ted and picked up a hammer and several spikes.

Buttoning their coats against the wind, they followed Karla with the urn of ashes down the knoll to the pink boulder.

Sandy held up the boots. "Leif wore these in the late twenties working on Minnesota's last big log drive. The fringe on the tongue is the badge of a whitewater man. Now, imagine a river full of pine logs, bank-to-bank and as far as you can see. Picture all of them going down the Little Fork River on the spring flood." He paused. "Imagine him with a long pike pole, hopping from log to log, pushing and shunting the trunks to prevent jamming in the rapids. Men were often crushed or drowned doing that. He had only the spikes and his balance for safety. Log drives didn't stop when a man died. Instead, a couple comrades buried him on the bank and nailed his boots to a tree to mark the grave. Leif wanted his grave marked according to this tradition."

He nodded to Ted, who held a boot against the oak as he drove a spike through it. "Ted, you do the other one," he said, giving him the hammer. The lanky youth smiled at his mother and drove the nail home.

Then Karla knelt at the hole with the urn. "Goodbye, Daddy," she whispered as tears rolled down her cheeks. As she poured the ashes into the hole, a sudden gust lifted some of the finer particles into the air. Sandy saw it as a sign that something of Leif would linger in the air above the farm as a blessing. Then Karla sifted a handful of gravelly earth into the hole. Ted followed, and then the other friends in succession, with Sandy last of all.

"Daddy didn't want a tombstone," she said, patting the pink boulder. "But every morning, he sat here and smoked his pipe. This is his marker. His monument." As the guests followed her to the house, each patted the granite in passing. They were almost at the house when a flock of migrating snow geese, as pale as ghosts, flew low over the lake. Who knows, Sandy thought, Leif's soul may well be traveling with them.

Karla gathered them around a small table in the front room, and Sandy poured slugs of Leif's favorite whiskey into a dozen plastic cups—including one for Ted. And then, one by one, each recounted a favorite memory or story. At the end of each tale, the teller raised the cup, saluted Leif and downed the shot.

166

"Thank you for giving Ted a part in this," she said softly, laying a hand on Sandy's arm. "He's going to miss Daddy terribly. This will mean a lot to him."

"I know. It means a lot to me, too. Ted can call me any time he wants to hear your dad's tales. I've memorized a lot of them. It's something of a heritage. He should learn them, too. It's up to me to pass them on. They'll bring Leif back if he knows them."

The friends left the house, and the four hosts stood about the front room, warmed by the stove and fresh cups of coffee. Karla stood close to Sandy and quietly asked if there was a way the estate could support Ted's college education.

He felt for her as he listened. It was a reasonable request. Leif would have helped her as much as possible, of that he was certain. But the question had a double edge. The will specified what he wanted her to have. And he needed her support to undercut the challenge. But Isaacs warned against a deviation that could give Harald's lawyer an opening to exploit. He must not promise anything.

"Tell me what support looks like to you," he said.

"Fifty or sixty thousand. I assume you'll sell the place eventually."

He drew a breath. "I hear you, and I understand you, but... *uh*... right now, I don't understand what your dad handed me. Or why. So, I don't know what to do with it. Please, give me time to get my arms around it and find a way forward. I can't promise you anything because I don't know anything. But I promise we'll talk again before any decisions are made."

She nodded, patted his arm and left him to gather her things for the drive home. He liked her. And not only because she was Leif's daughter but because he sensed her loneliness as an only child whose homestead was leaving the family. She's got the gut—the grace—not to blame me. At least not yet. That's something she got from him. That's a part of him, too. And she's beautiful when she smiles.

After Karla and Ted left, he and Sophia stood on the porch out of the wind. A flurry of early snow swept the lake and veiled the trees along the far shore. "This place is magical," she said. "Have you thought more about what you will do with it?"

"That's the sixty-four-thousand-dollar question," he said, shrugging. "Leif left it to me. I can keep it, sell it or give it away as I please."

"Tell me what you please."

"I want to do what it takes to keep it as it is. What he would have done if he had known what it was. Right now, I don't know what my options are." He poured the rest of the whiskey into two cups and handed one to her. "Here's to what he would have done."

"Are we bookin' it to get back to your house?" she asked.

"No, not especially."

"Good. Let's go inside, build up the fire. I want to stay a little longer."

CHAPTER 31

Harald looked out the dining room window at the wind lashing the dark treetops along the river. "Maybe we should have gone to his burial," he said as they sat down to eat lunch. "We probably looked spiteful for bailing out. Sore loser and all that."

"We're not sore losers. We've been cheated. And stop worrying about what others think. Leif had no influential friends. You had a higher duty to stand by your ailing wife."

"Yes, but... you weren't—"

"—No yes-buts," Regina said and dabbed her lips. "The ceremonies are over. Now we need to make certain Brewster can't interfere with our plans. Wills are challenged—"

"—Sure, and most challengers lose. Then they have to pay the costs," Harald said.

"We'll win this one. Isaacs is a night-school lawyer. He's no match for Sam." She got up from the table and walked to the foyer. "C'mon, dear. Let's go for a walk."

"In this wind?"

"Yes, in this wind." Regina walked nearly every day except in rain or snow and usually dragged him with her. A brisk walk cleared her mind, and, while walking, she talked to him about the things she wanted done. The walks often affected his mood, too, and he usually agreed to do what she had in mind. Sometimes, he thought the idea had been his own.

It was nearly dusk when they left the house, crossed the road to the Wacouta River path and into the teeth of the cold east wind. Regina looked chic striding in a wolf-skin parka as he lumbered along like the Pillsbury Doughboy in his puffy down coat.

She put her arm through his as they walked. "You've been so busy with Leif's affairs you haven't had time to think about what we need to do," she began in a soothing voice. "What we need to do is pretty straightforward."

"How's that, sweetie?"

"Our challenge hinges on his state of mind when he signed the will."

"Yes, we've been over that. He did some bizarre things after he escaped—"

"—Don't say escaped, dear. Escape has horrible connotations."

"Oh, you're right… I mean, after he wandered off."

"Yes. He wandered off in a fog like so many of the elderly do. His bizarre note to Mabel, fixing a hunting shack and sinking the boat are powerful and unrefuted facts that suggest mental decline. I assume the medical records will back that up."

"That depends. They're ambiguous enough for wide interpretation. I'll need to bring them up to date."

"Good. Anything we need to worry about?"

"I don't think so. I wasn't going to let Sandy visit him, but I'm glad I did. If Sam put him on the stand, he'd have to admit to Leif's foggy state of mind." His face broke into his Porky Pig grin.

"Isaacs would object, and the judge might agree. Or worse, he might not say what you want him to. It's better that he's not on the stand at all."

The river path threaded a twilight world of deep shadows slit by pewter highlights off the river's inky flow. Chest deep and eighty feet across, the stream glided silently beneath the footbridge to a deep pool under a log jam at the bend downstream. They stopped at the footbridge, and Regina left Harald on the bank in the wind while she walked to the center of the span. Gripping the railing, she gazed into the dark currents for a long time. Then she returned and took his arm.

"You need to call in some political favors before we go to court," she said. They walked back to the house, feeling the wind at their backs.

It wasn't long before Sophia spent every weekend at Sandy's house. He didn't mind that; week by week, she moved a few more clothes into his closet. They were energetic but gentle lovers, and the pleasures of sex didn't fade after forty. *Al contario.* She told him the struggle to save the farm was as important to her as anything she had ever tackled. Unlike her other causes, the farm was tangible and didn't benefit her personally. And best of all, he and she were pulling together as one pair and not as academic colleagues.

"You know, it's strange I haven't heard from Harald lately," Sandy said over supper at his house. "He must have heard we pulled the stakes. This silence is creepy. I wonder what else he is cooking up behind the scenes."

"What do you think it is?"

"With their connections, the possibilities are infinite and—" he got up to answer the phone.

"Sandy, it's Harald. I'm sorry for my outburst over the will. Leif didn't tell me he changed executors. Naturally, I've been upset. I hope you understand."

"Of course. That's wholly understandable," he said and waited. "He didn't tell me, either."

"I've been thinking of ways to help you see that Karla is taken care of."

"I'm listening," he said. He glanced at Sophia and mouthed, "Harald." Then he stuck a finger down his throat.

"Your dad and I were colleagues, as you know. He doctored my folks before I started a practice. I miss him, especially when I have to diagnose a difficult case. He was quick to get to the heart of the matter. You remind me of him."

"Oh yeah, I forgot. You worked together," Sandy lied and tried to guess at why this trip down memory lane. He circled his ear with a finger for her to see.

"Our families have been involved for years. I hope you'll take it into account."

"Of course."

"I know you're busy at college and all," he continued. "So, here's a simple idea to help you with the farm."

"And that is—"

"—A group in Rochester called Wingspan Associates. One of their principals is a patient of mine. He and his colleagues want to buy the farm. In fact, I think they approached Leif a couple of years ago. I gave them your name."

"I know. I pulled up the survey stakes and ran off the bulldozer driver before they did anything," he said, biting off his words.

"Oh? I don't know any—"

"—Of course, you know. You told Wingspan you owned the farm and wanted to start the development."

"I never said—"

"—Don't lie to me. You're the only one who could do that. I'm not ready to make a decision. So don't push me!"

"I… I'm not. It's a… a misunderstanding," Harald said. "Don't let it prejudice you. Wingspan has won environmental awards. It could be a win-win for the farm."

"Or a win for you—"

"I'm just trying to make sure Karla gets all she's entitled to. I think Wingspan will be generous. They'll give her what she deserves—and pay you well, too."

"*Uh, huh*," he said and hung up. "Goddamned liar."

"What was that?" Sophia asked.

"He denied sending the survey crew. Called it a 'misunderstanding.' He claims he's trying to help me so Karla is well taken care of. He gave my name and number to Wingspan—high-end developers out of Rochester. They'd ruin everything."

"He has no feeling for the land."

"None. It's money, money, money," Sandy whispered, rubbing his thumb across his fingers. "He's probably shilling for Wingspan and stands to gain from it."

"You *are* wicked-wise for a stuffy old professor," Sophia teased.

"And you're uncommonly sexy for a—"

"—You're going to do something about Harald—"

"—Yeah, string Wingspan along. Find out what he's up to. Who's involved."

"And then?"

"And then I'll say it's no deal. He'll get pissed and challenge the will. But he's going to do that anyway. He's got a year to do it. My guess is that he and his lawyer will claim he had dementia when he made the will.

"He'll fight. What's the danger to you?"

"None. Nothing physical, at least. I worry about pressure from Karla. She hasn't said where she stands. He might claim I'm merely a steward for the family, that I'm incompetent because I won't sell to the highest bidder and give them the money. People might buy that. Families pass farms through generations. Letting it out of the family is a source of shame. Farmers who lose their land sometimes kill themselves over it. But not Harald. He isn't bold, but I'm told his wife has a mean streak."

"Can you trust Karla?"

"Is she honest? Yes. I think so. She's torn between letting me do what he wanted and getting something for Ted. I'm sympathetic, but at some level, I suspect she resents the fact that I'm the heir."

"You need to find middle ground."

"I'm working on it," he said. "I need a buyer who'll preserve the property. I saw Boston Meade at the funeral. I need to talk to him. This might be a good time."

CHAPTER 32

The phone rang a few nights later as Sandy and Sophia cuddled on the couch before the fire. He ignored it at first but it kept ringing, and she nudged him to answer it. "I'll keep your place warm," she said as he set down his glass of after-dinner wine.

"This is Reid Johnson from Rochester," the caller said. "I would like an appointment with *Doctor* Brewster."

"What can I do for you, Mister Johnson?" He glanced at her and rolled his eyes. Johnson had the avuncular sincerity of a funeral director. Here we go, he thought. "Do you have a son or daughter at Seabury?"

"*Uh*, no. I'd like to see you about the Nielsen property. I just learned you own it. We were under the impression that Doctor Nielsen owned it."

"Who's *we*?" Sandy asked sharply. "And how did you come by that information?"

"Oh, sorry," he said. "I represent Wingspan Associates. We watch probate filings. We specialize in discrete, ecologically sensitive residential projects. Ours have won a number of awards. The Tarn Lake property has been on our radar for years. Perhaps you might be interested in selling all or part of it."

There's no probate filing yet, he thought. "Tell me what it is you'd like to cover. I have a full schedule," he said evenly, bridling an instinct to cut him off because Johnson might spill something useful.

"I want to show you some ideas for the farm. I'll meet you in Wacouta, of course. Working together, you can settle the estate on good terms for all concerned. We talked to Mister Nielsen a couple years ago, but, for one reason and another, he wasn't ready to make an agreement."

Another lie. "I'm available at eleven on Thursday. Let's meet at the Happy Chef on the Great River Road." Johnson agreed and ended the call. "Well, the vultures are circling," Sandy said after he hung up. Then he called Isaacs and asked him to join the meeting.

"I've heard of them," the lawyer said. "They develop the kind of homes most of us could never afford. Six figures stuff. I'll ask my colleagues what they know."

"Thanks for coming," Sandy said when Isaacs joined him in the campus coffee shop on Thursday. "Johnson never mentioned Harald, and I think that's a tip-off," he said.

"Yep. My Rochester colleagues didn't have anything definite on Wingspan. It's privately held and buys the choicest real estate. Then, it partners with developers for a significant share. My friends say there's a whiff of something questionable about them but... I'm surprised we're meeting him—you must have something up your sleeve."

"I want to string them along. Act like I'm interested to get their site plans, an audit statement and any other information in due diligence."

"And then?"

"I think Harald suggested them because he stands to gain from it. If I play along, he might leave me alone until I can get a buyer."

Isaacs chuckled. "Son, for a non-lawyer, you have an enviable devious streak. Let's go meet the man."

They sat in a Happy Chef booth and watched the parking lot. "There he is," Isaacs said as a balding man got out of a dark Cadillac and entered the restaurant. His Glen plaid suit stood out against the logo wear of the sales reps, technicians and long-haul truckers. Johnson smiled as he approached them. The waitress poured coffee, and the agent laid out glossy folders of Wingspan projects, including the Nielsen's house. All of them reflected classic architectural designs set in manicured landscapes with shrubs, flower beds, walkways and ponds. Isaacs and Sandy poured over them with noises of admiration.

"Now, let me show you a sketch for the farm," Johnson said, unfolding the prospectus for "The Preserve on Tarn Lake." An artistic rendering showed twenty houses on lots, each with one hundred and fifty to three hundred feet of lakeshore. There was a gated access road along the back of the lots and a common "natural area" with walking paths. Parts of the prairie would be planted with pine and spruce trees. Other parts would be fairways and greens. The farmhouse and barn would be removed, a small marina would replace the dock and some of the reed beds would be cleared for a swimming beach. The knoll with its gravesite and bolder would be reserved as a "heritage center" with a kiosk to honor the pioneer family buried there.

"I hope you like the concept," Johnson said. "What do you think?"

"You've given this a lot of thought," Sandy said in what he hoped sounded like appreciation despite an overwhelming urge to puke on Johnson's tailored suit.

"It will be a showcase," the agent continued smoothly. "The Preserve will set the gold standard for environmentally sound development. A demonstration that you can preserve nature while adding social and economic value that is a benefit to both. We'll protect the lake by restricting access. The houses will generate a lot of local taxes."

"Tell us about your environmental awards," Sandy said.

"Thank you for asking," he said with a smile. "The state realtor's association recognized us for outstanding environmental planning three years in a row. And the homebuilder's association just chose us as its environmentalist of the year."

"And what do you need from us?" Sandy asked.

"I'd like to option or initiate a purchase agreement—after probate, of course."

"For how much?"

"We are prepared to offer up-front cash for the property. Or, if you prefer, a share of the Wingspan project in return for the property."

"What is your cash offer, and what's a share worth?"

"The estimated development value is more than nine million over five years. The farm's appraised value is four hundred thousand, but we're willing to offer four hundred and eighty in cash or one hundred thousand now and a share in the project. One share is worth at least four hundred and eighty thousand. That doesn't include residual income from developing a marina, a putting green and maintenance fees. Of course, taking a share includes accepting proportional risk, you understand. Either way, you will get more from Wingspan than trying to sell it locally or piecemeal." Johnson smiled.

"I think you're right about that. It's tempting, don't you think, Morrie," Sandy said, trying to sound enthusiastic while his guts churned with fear. He hadn't felt this uneasy since college when three toughs chased him down a dark alley.

"Absolutely tempting," the lawyer agreed. "Mister Johnson—"

"—Please call me Reid."

"Before we go any further, Reid, we need information about your company, its officers and stockholders. As custodians of the estate, we need a current annual report and a financial audit for our due diligence. With such a valuable offer, we naturally want to confirm your company's *bona fides.* You understand, *caveat emptor.*"

The agent nodded and promised to send the information. Then he shook their hands enthusiastically and left.

Sandy and Isaacs stayed in the booth and ordered more coffee. "I smell Harald behind this," Sandy said as he picked up the tab.

"Of course. He tipped his hand sending the survey crew. We need to know everyone who is involved with Wingspan. I'll make more calls."

"I'm nervous, Morrie. I need advice on how to go ahead."

"Nervous is good. Trust your instincts. Act interested like you planned. Get all the information you can. As it is, neither you nor anyone else can do anything until probate. There's a lot of money behind his proposal."

"Nine million for a hundred-eighty acres of rocks. Unbelievable."

"Where there's that kind of money, there's power to go with it. And where there's power and money, there's pressure. Lots of it. So, get ready. It's headed your way. We're up against real players."

CHAPTER 33

Sandy's slumbers were filled with dreams of Harald running over him on a yellow bulldozer and hiring dozens of lawyers to sue him for malfeasance. Worrying about the farm drained him of all desire but a restful sleep. Preparation for teaching and tenure took time away from Sophia. They still interacted professionally on campus, but keeping their affair secret added another layer of stress. Then he agreed to meet with Daniels on Saturday, though it meant another day away from her.

"Thank you for coming," the banker said. "I don't travel far at my age. May I offer you coffee or water?"

He declined both and sat facing Daniels, who was seated behind his huge desk. He didn't find the old man intentionally intimidating, but his bushy eyebrows and pale eyes created a naturally fierce appearance.

"I understand you knew Leif well," Daniels said, peering through large lenses. "Did you see him during or after he was in the hospital?"

"Yes, once, at the Nielsen's guest house."

"How did he seem?"

"Unhappy. Lethargic." He thought about the sedatives but said nothing. Not until he knew where Daniels was headed.

"That concerns me a great deal," the banker said. "Not only because I thought highly of him but because I heard gossip he wasn't mentally competent. That his actions before he died were caused by dementia. What's your opinion?"

"The rumors are lies. He was fully competent. I know for a fact that certain medications made him lethargic. But as you know, he had enough wit and energy to finish the survey. His report is so lucid I can't see how anyone can say otherwise."

"Good, we agree," he said, pounding the desk. "I'm glad we see alike. Now, here's my concern. Commissioner Nielsen might convince the county board that Leif was impaired and claim the management plan is unreliable. That would give Commissioner Jorgenson his excuse to back out of our agreement on the donation."

"Doctor Nielsen is going to contest the will because it leaves him nothing. Now I'm feeling pressure to sell the farm to developers."

"*Hmm...* that figures. The county board and the economic development department tell me Jorgensen and some others are against taking property off the tax rolls. They want more development."

"I meant to tell you Morris Isaacs is my attorney."

"Good man. I know him well. Now, give the county the invoice for work and expenses. I'll take the management plan to them myself. May I call you Sanford?"

"Call me Sandy."

"All right, Sandy. We have a lot riding on this. Let's talk soon."

Boston rose on Monday morning feeling grumpy with congestion and a headache. He had a cup of coffee with Ginger before she left for work. Still in pajamas and bathrobe, he peered at the steady November rain. The thermometer outside the kitchen window registered 38 degrees. A good day to stay in PJs and shake off the miserable cold. His business phone rang as he started up the stairs to bed. He answered it, though he wasn't in the mood for conversation.

"Do you have a minute?" Daniels rumbled. "I would like your view of some recent developments."

"What developments?" Boston asked, wiping his nose.

"Leif Nielsen's state of mind before he died. It may affect what the county does with the Oxbow. And it certainly could affect the farm on Tarn Lake."

"What do you want me to do?"

"Meet with me tomorrow along with Professor Brewster and Morrie Isaacs."

Boston knew the old banker didn't gossip or air his suspicions. Instead, he laid out what he knew were facts, raised questions based on the facts and left Boston to pursue the leads. This has to be something big, he thought, and agreed to meet.

So, Leif's state of mind is the issue, Boston thought. The interviews with him might be relevant to whatever Daniels has in mind. He read the notes while propped up in bed. Then he added details he recalled but hadn't written down. By the time he re-read the notes, he had most of them committed to memory. The day slipped away, and with it, the headache and congestion.

Ginger's singsong, "I'm *ho-ome*," filled the foyer as Jester galloped to meet her. She kicked off her wet shoes, hung up her coat and padded down the hall to the den. "Well, you look better," she said, hugging him from behind and then nipped his ear. "I'll kiss you when you're over the bug. What are you working on?"

"Checking the interviews with Leif. Daniels set up a meeting tomorrow with Isaacs and Brewster. He wants to discuss his state of mind."

"Jack said something about that to me in passing. He also said Harald has been visiting county departments when he's not at the hospital."

"Did he say why?"

"No. We were both in a hurry. Call him. He's your brother."

Jack tried to avoid the phone—except emergencies—for the first hour of the day. That gave him a window for thought over a cup of coffee. He had scarcely entered his office when the front desk put a call through to his phone. He grumbled and picked it up. "Hey brother, what's up?" Jack asked. "Sounds like you got a cold."

"Yeah, but I'm better," Boston said and then sniffled. "Ginger said Harald has been buzzing about the county offices. Any idea why?"

"I can tell you've got something in mind."

"Daniels worries the rumors about Leif's mental state will cause the county to back out of the Oxbow donation. I don't think that's the only target. It might have something to do with forcing Leif's heir to sell his farm to a developer."

"That fits," Jack said. "I've seen him in and out of zoning and economic development. I hear he's got the Chamber of Commerce on board, too. And Jorgenson is dead set against taking land off the tax rolls."

"Daniels, Isaacs, Brewster and I are meeting tomorrow morning."

"I'll keep my ear to the ground. Let you know what I hear."

Daniels welcomed the men into his dimly lit office. Boston accepted a cup of coffee and took a chair with Brewster and Isaacs.

"I think we agree that Leif was mentally sound," Daniels began and cleared his throat. "However, this canard of incompetence threatens the future of the Oxbow and Sandy's farm. Boston, you've got a nose for what's hiding under a rock. What does your nose tell you about this matter?"

"Something is rotten in the state of Denmark."

"Well spoken," Daniels rumbled with a hearty laugh. "I wanted the donation to be a quiet transfer of title. Now, to squelch this rumor, I'll have to reveal it sooner than I wanted. Boston, you were going to write a piece. Can you write it focused on the preserve so the public will know what it's about to receive?"

"Not a problem. It's news."

"Good. I've got a copy of the management plan for you. Sandy and I have read it, and it leaves no doubt he was lucid when he wrote it."

"I think the *Statesman* could do an article or an editorial or both."

"Good. I trust you can do that."

"Yeah, but Ginger has the last word."

"This will help my case, too," Sandy added.

"I agree," Daniels said. "I have no personal stake in the farm, but Leif was a friend. I won't be silent while he is defamed."

"Jorgenson will be a problem," Sandy said. I ran into him at the courthouse. He made it brutally clear he won't let the farm leave the tax rolls. If I try to sell or give it to a tax-exempt group, the commission will block it."

"That sounds like him," Boston said.

"Yes. He said, 'I already gave away too much with that Oxbow deal. I'm not going to shrink the tax base.' I asked if that was a threat. He said, 'No, it's a fact of life.'"

"A lot of people might agree with that," Daniels muttered.

"Jorgenson said it's my duty to develop the farm to benefit the Nielsen family. Besides that, the Tarn Lake project will offset taxes lost from the Oxbow donation."

There was a stir among the four of them. "Now we know," Boston said. "Jorgenson is backing Harald because he's up for re-election next spring. Regina has the power to boost or kill his GOP endorsement."

"Where does that leave us?" Daniels asked.

"An article with excerpts from the management plan would undercut the incompetence rumors. Let me do that. As for Jorgenson—"

"—I know something that might influence him," Isaacs said, speaking for the first time while quietly taking notes.

"What is that, Morrie?"

"Our commissioner made creative but *sub rosa* use of tax increment financing to lower his business taxes. It looks a little shady from the outside. Maybe a conflict of interest or even self-dealing. Now, if it came to light in, say the *Statesman*—"

"—Morrie, you haven't lost your fang for the jugular," Daniels hooted.

"I'll get someone on it," Boston said. "Get me the details."

CHAPTER 34

Sandy went away from Daniels's office knowing he faced a two-front war. The immediate one was Harald's challenge to the will. Even if the doctor lost that in court, he could win by mustering the county board to block all but commercial use of the farm. He already had the Chamber of Commerce, zoning and economic development agencies behind him. They had the political and legal clout to wear him down. The pressure to develop wasn't going away. Even with Isaacs's skill, he knew they couldn't defeat Harald single-handedly. He needed an ally that had the legal and financial muscle to match the county.

Together, the farm, the wildlife department and the Nature Conservancy protected the Tarn Lake watershed. The wildlife department was a passive ally and not inclined to tangle with county government. The Nature Conservancy protected endangered ecosystems by owning and managing tracts like its preserve on the lake. Sometimes, it bought the development rights on private property and let the owners keep the title. Buying development rights might ease the pressure, but Sandy couldn't afford to own the farm. The only solution was persuading the Conservancy to buy it.

Sandy called the Conservancy's director, hoping he would be interested in adding to the existing preserve. Barry Putnam said he knew about the farm but seemed non-committal about buying it. Nevertheless, he suggested they meet at the farm on Saturday.

Sandy had hoped for fair weather to pitch the farm, but today's steely clouds cast the land and water with twilight shades of pearl, pewter, slate and charcoal. The moaning of the wind about the eaves upped his anxiety. He waited by the stove with his stomach as full of butterflies as a man about to propose marriage. Then Putnam arrived, and Sandy welcomed him inside as the director shrugged his shoulders against the chill.

"Good of you to come, Barry," Sandy said, offering coffee to the thin-haired man in his mid-fifties. "Sorry about the weather."

"It's out of our reach," he laughed. "Part of a larger continental system." Putnam turned and looked out the front windows at the spumy waves lunging down the lake like a pack of hungry dogs. "After your call, I checked our files and saw I was here a few years ago," Putnam said. "It's a priceless remnant of Minnesota before the invasion of corn and soybeans."

"That's why I called you. Leif left me the farm, free and clear. He knew I wouldn't develop it. My task is to keep it consistent with his values."

"And you think there is something the Conservancy can do to help you," Putnam said as if he didn't understand.

"That's what I want to explore. The lake is undeveloped, the water quality is pristine. The waterfowl nesting here are rarely seen anywhere else in the region. That's why you own the land at the far end of the lake." He refilled Putnam's coffee cup and then his own.

"He was a good neighbor," Putnam said. "Tell me what you have in mind."

"The situation is this—I can't afford to own the property long-term. Leif's brother was not his heir, but he and the county commissioners are leaning on me to develop it with second homes. Ever hear of Wingspan in Rochester?"

Putnam grimaced as if he had tasted vinegar. "Wolves in sheep's clothing," he said. "They don't walk their talk of environmental sensitivity. What are they offering?" he asked, no longer sounding noncommittal.

"Four hundred eighty thousand for the farm as is. Or... I could be a shareholder in the development for a lot more down the road."

"Four hundred eighty grand. What's their plan... as if I couldn't guess."

"I'm sure you guessed it. The county chair opposes taking property off the tax rolls. Wingspan envisions twenty exclusive homes worth ten million that will boost the tax base. That's the pressure I'm under."

Putnam whistled. "I'm sorry, but we can't match ten million," he said, turning away from the window. "Not even close. Wish I could."

"You don't have to. I'm not in it for the money. Let's take a walk if you're up to it. I want to show you a few things."

Sandy led Putnam to the knoll and paused at the pink boulder and saw him glance at the boots nailed to the tree. Then he pointed out the location of the lots along the shore, the access road and the reeds that would be ripped out for a marina. He doubted the horned grebes would continue nesting once there was boat traffic.

As they turned back, Sandy shouted to be heard above the wind. "All this land from here to that line of trees is virgin prairie," he hollered. "It's bluestem and needlegrass. A neighbor cuts it once a year for hay. There are over two hundred species of flowers and dozens of nesting birds like the horned lark, loggerhead shrike and butterflies, including painted lady and several swallowtails. Wingspan proposes planting the prairie with spruces and building a golf course." Putnam shook his head.

They angled east down the lake toward the outlet. On the way, he pointed to where the swimming beach would clear out the bulrushes, wild rice and arrowroot that ducks and muskrats depended on. They stopped at the outlet and then walked back to the house.

Putnam stood at the window, picked up the binoculars and studied the ducks coasting in the shelter of the reeds. "Mergansers, buffleheads, redheads and scaup," he said. "Northerners in migration."

"Now that you've seen the farm, you can imagine what I'm up against. If they win, it will destroy the lake. Foul the water. Drive off wildlife. They'll probably trample your preserve. If we work together, we can protect the entire lake and its whole watershed. If you buy the farm, its prairie will complete the protection of a mixed ecosystem of woods, marsh, lake, prairie and hardwood forest. It'll be a microcosm of a once vast biome. The Conservancy is my first choice, but my window for a decision is small. There must be a reasonable financial transaction."

"What's reasonable?" Putnam asked without taking his eyes off the lake.

"Reasonable isn't a fixed price. Reasonable is whatever it takes to protect the shores of a deep, spring-fed lake and its watershed. Reasonable is what it costs to keep the nesting swans and horned grebes. Reasonable is making sure no homes, motorboats and septic systems devalue what the Conservancy has already invested in its preserve."

"You know how to push my buttons!" Putnam laughed with a sidelong glance.

"That's what they're for."

"I see you've thought it through," Putnam said, and Sandy could see his tongue moving around under his lips while he thought. Finally, he looked him in the eye. "I can't commit on my own. All I can do is recommend its purchase. The board meets next week. I'll write a proposal and recommend an option to buy. If they agree, we can meet the Wingspan price of four hundred eighty thousand. Once approved, we can draw up a purchase agreement if you're willing to take the payments in several installments."

"That's fine," he said. "But there's one other request. I noticed you lease some preserves to other organizations for scientific and educational uses. I want you to consider leasing it to Seabury College. It has an environmental studies program and a curriculum for managing ecosystems. Maybe the students could help you as hands-on training for burning the prairie or rooting out invasive species in the woods."

"That's an interesting idea. We would have to negotiate directly with Seabury."

"That's all right, so long as it is Seabury. That's my only condition."

They shook hands, and Sandy felt as if he had slipped a diamond ring on his true love's finger. He returned home, relieved and wondered what Leif would make of this arrangement. I'll never know, he thought. That's why he gave me the farm—he trusted me to make the right decision. He garaged his car, entered the house and called Isaacs.

"I'm glad you called," Isaacs said. "Harald just filed a challenge to the will on the grounds that Leif was *non compos mentis*. He claims you exercised undue influence over a vulnerable elder and stole the farm from his daughter and brother."

Sandy swallowed hard against an onset of nausea. "Oh *shit*," he cried. "I didn't know about the will… I was out of state all year. What can I—"

"—Calm down. We can prove that. Harald is desperate."

CHAPTER 35

Sophia entered 301, saw Sandy at his desk and peered over his shoulder at the elaborately interwoven doodle he was drawing. It had no beginning and no end. It reminded her of an ancient Celtic design. "What's going on?"

"Trying to figure out what to do. It reminds me of a—"

"—Leif story," she said, bouncing lightly in her chair.

"Yeah," he said without a trace of glee. "When he was stumped, he'd say it reminded him of the time Hunk Backstrom logged Buster Lake north of Duluth. He started cutting after deep snow covered everything. His crew banked 300,000 feet of pine logs on the lake's shore, expecting to float them downriver in the spring. Once the snow melted, Hunk discovered Buster Lake didn't have an outlet. The logs went nowhere. That's how I feel."

"But that's not what's really bugging you."

"No," he sighed, and his shoulders dropped. "What bothers me are the rumors saying I took advantage of Leif to steal the farm from Karla. Of course, this will get back to Mom. It'll make her life miserable. That's the point, of course. It's a Hail Mary pass to pressure me. I know what I want to do about the farm. The question is what to do about Harald."

"It's time you do something for Karla. Leif gave you so much of himself. I think she deserves something from him, too."

He swiveled his chair to face her, his face screwed tight in frustration. "Is that a question of equity for a woman or a strategy to take her away from Harald?"

191

"A bit of both!" she snapped in her strident tone. "Why is that hard for you?"

"Leif specified what he wanted her to have. He gave *me* the rest because he trusted *me* to make a decision." Then he shot a thick rubber band at the wall. "Now everyone thinks they know the answer. I wish to hell I knew."

"You'll follow your conscience," she whispered. "You'll make the right choice."

"Thanks for your vote. I'm not against helping Karla," he said, jumping up and pacing the room. "She's torn. The Nielsens need her support and promise her a ton of money for Ted's education—if they win. But I can't promise her anything directly without violating the will. That would only strengthen their challenge. On the other hand, if I can get her to back the will, the challenge has no legal standing."

"How much does she want for Ted?"

"At the burial, she said enough to send him to a private college. We never finished the conversation, but I promised to talk about it later. I know Seabury costs fourteen thousand a year. Even with four-point grades, most scholarships are two to five thousand. Not enough to outbid Harald's promises."

"Is Ted a good student?"

"You talked to him. What do you think? Please tell me you have an idea."

"I'm vice chair of the scholarship committee," she said, knotting a multi-colored silk scarf around her neck. "Let me explore that end of things. A multi-talented student might qualify for several scholarships."

"You're beautiful," he said, kissing her. "What a great idea. I'll call you tonight," he said, grabbing his briefcase. He rushed from Milton to the environmental studies department across the campus and talked his way into the director's office. After an hour of intense conversation, he went home feeling his hopes coalescing into a plan. Putnam's call in the late afternoon came like sunlight breaking through the November gloom. The directors approved a $480,000 purchase option on the farm and agreed to approach Seabury about leasing it to the environmental studies program.

*
**

Sandy relaxed on the couch. *The worst is over. Everything is in place. All I have to do is keep Karla on my side of the table.* He picked up the phone and called Isaacs. "I've got the ducks lined up," he said. "The Conservancy will pay the asking price for the property. I'll donate four hundred thousand to the Seabury environmental program. Then I'll set up a sixty-thousand-dollar fund for Ted's education at Seabury. I'll hold the other twenty grand for other uses."

"All right, Sandy," Isaacs said with a note of caution. "Giving Karla an incentive to support us is fine, but be careful how you do it. No *quid pro quo*. Don't promise her something conditioned on her support. Otherwise, it will bolster the claims about your Rasputin-like influence over vulnerable adults. Instead of giving her the funds, it's better if the scholarship is an anonymous gift with criteria tailored to Ted."

"Oh. So, she'll have to trust me to do the right—"

"—That's about the size of it."

Sophia arrived for supper, and he outlined the plan for Ted.

"Mister Isaacs is right. You need to be at arm's length. The college will want to handle the money anyway and set the criteria. So, leave that to me."

"It has to look fair, but make certain Ted comes out on top," he said and grimaced. "Putting it that way makes me feel—"

"—like losing your virginity... you'll get over it," she quipped. "Now, how about this... Ted's in band, sports and has high grades in AP classes. Environmental studies is interdisciplinary. So, the application could require a thousand-word essay on the connections between the natural environment and healthy social, cultural and emotional development. It could be judged on its content and style. A lot of science students hate writing essays. So that naturally narrows the pool of applicants."

"Ingenious. It narrows but doesn't eliminate—"

"—It will. I have a reputation for favoring women applicants over men, so my ardent support for Ted will carry extra weight. Then there's the other twenty thousand—"

"—I have plans for that, but not for myself."

"Tell me how you see this from Karla's perspective," she said, finishing her salad.

"She wanted something for Ted. This should do it, but let's find out. I promised to resume the conversation, anyway." He got up and dialed Karla's number. Her phone rang and rang until he was about to hang up.

"Oh, hi, Sandy," she said, still formal—and distant.

After brief pleasantries, he makes his pitch. "I'd like to resume the conversation about Ted's education if you're still interested."

"I wondered if you meant it," she said. "What do you have in mind?"

"There may be a way to help Ted without violating your dad's will. Describe his college plans and where he's applied."

"He's been accepted at the University of Minnesota. But then, so is almost everyone. He's got good grades—ranks twenty-third in a class of three-hundred-twenty. National Honor Society, AP classes in English and biology, school jazz band and letters in track and basketball. He even had essays published in the Minneapolis paper."

"Have you thought of Seabury College or any of the private schools?"

"Yeah—in my dreams. Like I could afford to send him there."

"What does he want to study?"

"Environmental science. Daddy turned him on to it."

"I'm negotiating with a conservation buyer for the farm. I can't tell you who it is yet, but it won't develop the property."

"Well, what happens to it?"

"It'll remain pretty much as it is now—protected and undeveloped—except it may lease the farm to the Seabury environmental studies program for practical conservation education. Once the purchase is inked, I can tell you the buyer."

"How much are they paying *you* for the farm?" she asked.

"Four hundred eighty thousand," he said and heard her gasp.

"Four-hun-dred-eight-ty-thou-sand-dol-lars," she repeated slowly. "And how much of that do you get?"

"In the end, nothing," he said and waited.

"Well, who gets all that money?"

"The estate will donate most of it to support the Seabury program."

"But we talked about sixty thousand for Ted's education."

"I remember. Sophia's working to make that possible, but no details yet."

"I'm not sure that would be enough. Can't you make it—"

"—Karla, sixty thousand will cover four years of Seabury's tuition, room and board with some left over. Besides that, your dad left you cash, to which I added the money from the Oxbow contract. Once I've paid his taxes and bills, there will be nearly sixty thousand for you."

"Oh, I didn't realize that."

"Your dad gave me a difficult job to do that I'm trying to do what he wanted. I want to help you, but—you understand—your uncle's challenge complicates this."

"I know. He promised cash for Ted's college if the challenge succeeds. What can you promise?"

"Let me be clear. I can't promise *quid pro quo*. So, I can't promise anything in return for anything. If I did, it would violate the terms of the will and undermine our defense of it. So, I'm not offering a bribe to gain your support. You must follow your conscience. However, once I sell to this buyer, the college will have funds for a scholarship to support a qualified student majoring in environmental studies. Ted could apply. However, I'm not on the scholarship committee." He raised his eyebrows and looked at Sophia as he waited for Karla's response.

"How big is the scholarship?"

"A four-year ride."

"So, that means I wouldn't see any money."

"Correct. And no tax liabilities." He held his breath while she said nothing.

"But you can't guarantee Ted will be chosen, can you?"

He paused to choose his words. "Like I said, I'm not on the committee, so I can't guarantee anything but... I know his grades and the courses he's taken more than meet the criteria for several scholarships. And, I know the number of eligible applicants will be in the single digits."

"*Sooo…*" she said and clicked her tongue during the pause. "*Sooo…* my options are to trust you in hopes Ted receives a scholarship to Seabury or support the challenge that tarnishes Daddy's memory. And I know how rarely the challengers win. Either way, I'm taking a chance."

"You understand the situation perfectly."

"Okay, it *sounds* good," she said with more energy than when she answered. "I want to see the purchase agreement first."

"The only detail I'm withholding is the name of the buyer—by mutual agreement."

"I understand. I'll go along, provided I see the agreement."

"Thank you. We'll talk again." He hung up and let out his breath.

"Boy… are you a smoothie," she said with a smile.

"That was the easy part. There's still probate. Karla is on board in principle, but it's not what she expected. I can't blame her when she is promised cash."

CHAPTER 36

Harald's pulse quickened when he recognized her voice on the phone and asked Karla how she was feeling. As he listened, his high forehead furrowed, and his lips puckered. "I don't think that's a good idea," he said. "A big mistake. We'll lose if you do that. You're better off sticking with me." He listened for a moment. "Look, look," he said, now rattled, "Look, Karla, don't agree to anything until you talk to my attorney, please. You'll lose everything. I think we should... don't do anything until we can bring in our attorney." He ended the call and noticed Regina standing in the doorway dressed in a silk robe with a towel wrapped around her wet hair.

She gave him a dark scowl, and he knew she felt peeved. "Now what?" she demanded, folding her arms across her breasts.

"Karla is siding with Sandy. He offered her a deal. He's got a verbal agreement with some buyer. She doesn't know who. It's four hundred eighty grand. Same as Wingspan offered."

"*What?*" she screeched. "That stupid piece of... *trash!* What else did she say?"

"He didn't offer her any money but said Ted might qualify for a special four-year scholarship to Seabury. That's all she wants." He fell silent in defeat, violently sick to his stomach as he waited for what he feared would follow.

"I don't like this. I don't like it at all."

"I don't, either. Karla is next of kin. If she sticks with Sandy, I can't lay claim to the farm," he whined.

"You can't do anything, Harald—and never could. Well, I'll just have to figure out something—*as usual*. We'll have to offer more than he can." She left the room and went to the kitchen to check on the maid, who was making dinner. He could hear her fix martinis. Tonight, he thought two might not be enough.

"We can't just let ten million slip through our fingers," she said, now composed. "The question is… how to make certain we are a party to the estate."

Harald scratched his chin. "I don't know. I'll talk to Sam. Maybe he can think of something. Sandy is the problem. We may have to cut him in on part of the deal."

"You tried that. He's a Boy Scout. All he wants is a merit badge for good behavior," she sneered and pursed her lips. "We'll have to remove him."

"Remove him? What do you mean remove him?"

"Well. You said he's up for tenure. Let him choose between tenure or the farm."

He looked at the pattern in the Persian rug and recalled a couple of Republican candidates who had bucked her. Both went down the hard way. Regina played for keeps. No holds barred.

"What do you have in mind?" He picked up a martini.

"When caught in a squeeze, you cut your losses. Take the easy way out."

"I don't see where you are headed, sweetie."

"His mother lives here. What do you think she'll do when people hear that Sandy-boy bilked you and Karla out of their inheritance? His Mama will pressure him, and he'll do what he has to do to protect her. And think how the Seabury trustees will react when they hear one of their professors is a fraudster. That hoity-toity college won't grant tenure after he took advantage of a vulnerable adult."

"Jesus Christ, Regina!"

The Meade and Kaminski clans gathered at Jack's house for Thanksgiving dinner. Kris Kaminski and Jack married despite her parents' resistance. Stan and Olga were slow to accept a man of mixed races, even if he was a Catholic. Their acceptance began when the children were born fair-skinned like their mother and blossomed after tasting Jack's Creole barbecue. Kris and Ginger had also forged a bond of sisterhood, confiding in each other when annoyed or frustrated with their respective man. Olga, the *babcia*, shooed the men out of the kitchen and blocked the doorway with her ample figure. "You go watch the football now," she ordered. "Let us *matkas* show Lily how the turkey cooks."

"C'mon, Pa, Boston, Ben… let's see what games are on," Jack said, leading the way to the downstairs rec room. "Okay, men, choose your drinks. There's beer, whiskey, vodka, gin and sodas."

The men made their drinks. Jack muted the television, and the men discussed whatever was on their minds—the Featherstone high school football games, rising crop and livestock prices, and Reagan's meeting with Gorbachev in Iceland. As the men talked and drank, the muted television flickered with game plays as the aroma of roasting turkey seeped into the rec room. It seemed an eternity before Olga called them to a dinner of her pierogis, turkey, mashed potatoes, cranberries and pie. The women retired to the living room, where Ginger gave them a needlepoint lesson, and the men went downstairs to watch the Chicago Bears play the Detroit Lions. With the pre-game sports chatter muted, Boston briefed Jack on the Oxbow donation.

"I've heard about that," Jack said. "There's a rumor that Brewster defrauded Nielsen's brother and daughter out of the farm. I don't believe it. There's no evidence, but you know how small-town folks like a scandal."

"That worries me. Few people knew Leif, but everyone knows Harald. All they hear is that a feeble old man gave his farm to a shyster professor. That kind of tar doesn't wash off easily—if ever."

"You mentioned a war council," Jack said. "Tell me about it."

"The *Statesman* will publish a piece about the Oxbow based on interviews with Leif and the others. It'll reference the management plan, which I've read. Maybe print some excerpts. We hope it will sink the incompetence rumor. If people see that Leif was sane, it will undercut the rumor that Brewster finagled his property."

"Keep me in the loop," Jack said. "Oh, they're about to kick off," he said and turned up the volume.

Waterford's residents had delicious gossip to spice up their Thanksgiving turkeys. The rumor of fraud evolved and metastasized with each phone call, coffee klatch and church supper until everyone heard a hometown son defrauded the Nielsen's out of nine million dollars. Abigail heard about it before the anonymous notes appeared in her mail. All had a Waterford postmark. Sandy blew his top when she told him.

"Don't worry about me," she told him. "I'm fine. Our friends are behind you."

"God-*damnit*!" Sandy slammed the phone into its cradle.

"What?" Sophia had heard him swear, but rarely in the office.

"They're spreading rumors about me. Making Mom's life miserable. It's pressure on me through Mom. She's tougher than them, but it's ugly."

"That's not all," Sophia said. "One of my students works in the admin office. There's a memo going out that suspends your tenure vote."

"What! First I've heard of it."

"What can we do? The faculty supports you," she said and stroked his hair.

"I don't know. It's more pressure to sell the farm." He also knew, as she did, that if denied tenure, he would have to leave Seabury after a year. Spurned by his alma mater, tarred as a con man, eight years of hard work—gone. Self-pity beckoned, but she gripped his hand before he gave into it.

"Whatever it is, I'm behind you. All the way."

The college provost called Sandy later that day and asked him to stop at his office. As Sandy walked to the ivied Old Main building, he imagined how innocent men felt when condemned to death. The provost's secretary told him to sit, knocked on the frosted glass door, then motioned him in.

"Please close the door and sit down," the provost said without warmth or collegiality. "It is my duty to tell you that several regents are seriously concerned about granting you tenure."

"I'm aware of it. What are their grounds?"

"It's your moral character," he said, steepling his fingers. "They received information from a credible outside source that you induced a vulnerable elder to give you his farm instead of his daughter and brother. I understand it is worth ten million dollars. If true, granting tenure would reflect poorly on the college."

"Well, it's not true!" he shot back.

"We intend to find out. Students look up to you as a professor, but we don't know about your outside activities. The tenure vote is suspended for whatever time it takes to investigate. That means it may not happen this year. Or not at all if the regents aren't satisfied. We take this seriously because it comes from well-respected attorneys."

"Attorneys aren't immune to lies or to lying," Sandy blurted before reminding himself the provost wasn't his enemy. At least, not yet. "I was on sabbatical... in Massachusetts. I last saw Mister Nielsen in October—and *that* was after he made his will. He didn't tell me I was the heir. I learned it the day he died. His attorney will verify it."

"Give me his name and number. I'll call him. Now, tell me about the property and your relations with this man's family."

"I've known him all my life. He was a father to me after mine died. For reasons I'm not privy to, he and his brother had a falling out over the farm. My friend was a retired forest ranger. His daughter lives in Minneapolis. His brother is a wealthy doctor in Waterford, and the doctor's wife is a well-connected attorney. The will provided his daughter with cash and personal and family items. He left me the farm."

"So, he left you ten million dollars in property, and you are stiffing the family?"

"No. It's worth ten million only if it's developed. He left it to me because he didn't want it developed. He knew I wouldn't do that. The brother is connected to a development firm and contesting the will."

"What are you going to do with the farm?" the provost asked, knitting his brow as if he didn't believe him.

"I'm negotiating with a conservation organization for five percent of its development value with the condition that the organization negotiates a lease with Seabury's environmental studies program for a field station. Proceeds from the sale will go to the program. I don't get a cent out of it. All I get is grief like this. I hope *that* answers your question!" Only when the provost flinched did he realize he was shouting.

"I need to know the buyer."

"I can't tell you until I've signed an agreement. When I do, you'll recognize the name. Meanwhile, here are the names and numbers of a banker, a lawyer and the newspaper owner in Featherstone. They knew Nielsen and are familiar with the issue."

"I will follow up, but you're not off the hook."

He left the provost's office too furious for self-pity, at least for the moment. If they want war, they'll get it. Fight fire with fire, he seethed on the way to the library. He went through the Seabury catalog for the names of the regents. The provost mentioned lawyers, and the board had two attorneys, both Harvard graduates. One practiced in Minneapolis, and the other in St. Paul. Regina probably knew them. The state bar association directory yielded their firms and phone numbers. Still steaming, he returned to 301 and called Isaacs.

"All right, Sandy," Isaacs said. "Keep your shirt on. Don't level charges. Give me their names. I'll call them. A little chat between comrades of the bar may end the rumor."

"Thanks, Morrie. You'll get a call from the provost, too. So will Mister Daniels and Boston."

"I'll wait for the provost to call. Meanwhile, focus on our rendezvous with Harald and company the day after tomorrow. They have another proposal. I don't like it, but the final decision is yours."

CHAPTER 37

As the heir and executor, Sandy felt as if he were riding a log rushing toward the rapids. Worry had taken a heavy toll even before he entered Isaacs's conference room where the Nielsen's waited. Willard greeted Sandy and shook his hand, but the Nielsens merely nodded in his direction. The attorneys took chairs at opposite ends of the table, with Sandy facing the challengers. Harald glared at him, and Regina looked over his head. A David versus Goliath match, Isaacs thought. He wasn't cowed by Willard's Georgetown credentials against his from the St. Paul College of Law. Chief Justice Burger and Justice Blackmun were only two of its many outstanding alumni. This wasn't a question of legal skill but one of enough money to continue the fight.

"We think there is an opportunity to resolve this amicably," Willard began, clasping his hands. "After we review certain facts concerning the legal validity of the will, let us explore a settlement that avoids litigation."

"The only settlement I'll accept is—"

Sandy wanted to spring at Harald's throat.

"—Harald… let's proceed in an orderly way," Willard cautioned in a stern voice. "Let's lay out our case and hear what everyone has to say."

"I was born there," Harald sputtered. "I've got its soil in my blood." Regina rolled her eyes but said nothing.

"Look, Morrie," Willard said, ignoring Harald and speaking as if they were alone. "There is a way forward without legal trouble."

"We're all ears."

"There are two ways to resolve this," Willard said dispassionately. Harald hunched forward to look at Willard on the other side of Regina. His fingers drummed lightly on the table until she covered them with her hand. "We can come to a mutual accommodation, or we can go to court. We're prepared to do either."

"Stop shadowboxing, Sam. Get to the point," Isaacs called.

"We won't challenge the validity of the will provided Mister Brewster satisfies certain family concerns regarding the disposition of the property."

Willard paused, and Sandy felt his gut pull into his throat.

"What concerns?" Isaacs asked, peering over his glasses.

"We know he has no intention of living on the farm. We know he can't afford to hold on to it for long. Therefore, he has to sell it. In fact, he is already negotiating a sale. Because the farm was my client's birthplace, family home and his parents' gravesite, he expects to have a say on any party to whom it is sold. In return, Harald and Karla will be equitably compensated." He folded his pale hands atop one another and waited.

"Sandy, your thoughts," Isaacs said, turning to him.

"Just so I understand you," he began, biting off his words. "You want me to give Doctor Nielsen a veto over any disposition of *my* property. In other words, I am an heir and executor in name only."

Willard shifted in his chair. Harald's round face flushed red. Regina's eyes narrowed to obsidian points.

"Now, Sandy—" Willard began.

"—It's *Doctor* Brewster to you," he barked.

"I'm sorry, doctor," he said, swallowing. "Please don't think of this as a veto. Think of it as seeking a mutual advantage. A resolution without litigation."

"And if I say no?"

"We're prepared to challenge you in court. We've got documents to show that Mister Nielsen was mentally incompetent when he named you the executor. We will also show that you exercised undue influence over a vulnerable adult."

As Willard talked at length, Isaacs doodled on his legal tablet as if he weren't listening. He kept on doodling for a moment after Willard finished. Then he looked up. "Just what sort of evidence do you have to prove incompetence?"

"Medical records show he had a progressive loss of mental ability due to his age and pneumonia. This is backed by Doctor Nielsen's sworn statement as the attending physician. We can present the original will that I prepared. Mabel Lund is a day-to-day witness to his mental state. All that is on top of Mister Nielsen's irrational behavior after he left the guest house." Harald smirked as Willard talked in a dry, matter-of-fact tone.

"Doctor Brewster, it's your call," Isaacs said.

He sat still for a moment, as Isaacs had coached him to do, then he looked at his hands and rubbed them together. "We'll make our case in court," he said quietly. "We have documentation, too."

"Now, Sandy, be reasonable," Harald blustered. "We'll crush you in court."

"We'll see you in court."

"Well, I think we're done for the day," Isaacs said in his mild voice and rose from the chair. "Thank you all for coming in."

Willard gathered his papers into a fine calfskin briefcase. "You know how to reach me," he said in a note of resignation. "Give it some thought."

The Nielsens drove to Waterford without speaking. *Sam is useless,* Regina thought. *Without Karla, we don't have a case.* She gazed at the countryside buried beneath the season's first heavy snowfall. Now and then, the slipstream from passing cars whipped up a cloud of loose snow that obscured the road.

As she brooded, she heard her father's voice in her head saying *you must find a way forward. You are the one with the brains and the heart to get ahead. Harald is only smart enough to take your orders, but this is no time for half-measures. You must do the thinking.* Then she remembered what Daddy taught her—*dominate those around you,* or you will end up with their foot on your neck. When in doubt, act. Those who strike first dominate. You must strike again, she thought.

Harald felt her silence and the anger radiating from it. She was seething because Sandy didn't cave in. That always happened when anyone, man or woman, stood up and didn't submit. It was her idea that he retain final approval over the farm's buyer. Surveying the access to the farm was her idea, too, though he had to give the order to do it. He also knew she enjoyed breaking people. And if it weren't for the farm, he would have admired Sandy for standing up to her.

"Let's take a walk," she said when they returned home.

He didn't want to but agreed because it might soften her anger; otherwise, its brunt would fall on him.

"I knew Sam couldn't pull it off," she said as they strolled along the river in the snow. "You saw Sandy-boy. Good deed daily and all that. Karla isn't going to help. All she wants is to get that gangly kid through college. What are you going to do, Harald?"

"I think we should stick with Sam and—"

"—Sam's a wimp with Ivy League polish. He's got no balls. Do you?"

"You're mean."

"Mean? We're in the fight of our lives—we have no choice but to be mean. Stay here!" She left him on the path and strode to the center of the footbridge. Grasping the railing, she stared for a long time into the silky, dark water that slithered silently between the ice shelves lining the banks.

Why does she do that, Harald wondered. She's afraid of the water. He stood shivering in the wind. "We've tried everything," he whined when she returned. "Let's take our chances in court."

"No, we haven't tried everything," she snapped. "Pressing his mother didn't budge him. The suspended tenure vote hasn't moved him, at least not yet. Karla is weak. She'll go with him if he throws her a crumb. If he won't quit, we'll have to invalidate the will so the property is intestate. We either win in court or we get him removed as the administrator. We'll have to play hardball."

"I thought you did."

"I haven't started yet."

CHAPTER 38

Sandy sat in Isaacs' office on the Saturday before Christmas and nursed a cup of instant coffee. It tasted almost like real coffee for once and lifted his mood as he reviewed a two-page memo that outlined the provisions for the purchase agreement. It wasn't written in legalese, but it clearly stated his intentions and terms for the use and protection of the property. He finished reading it and relaxed.

"What an ordeal," he said. "Thanks to you, the farm is close to salvation."

"Hannukah ended yesterday," Isaacs said. "My wife makes certain we observe the traditions and recite the prayers. Among other things, it celebrates a righteous rebellion to defend Jewish ways against oppression." He removed his glasses. "I mention it because you're in a righteous fight to defend Leif's values against destruction. A line from a psalm in our tradition seems to fit. 'Weeping may spend the night, but joy comes with the morning.' Remember that."

"Thanks, Morrie. I will. It's…"

"Putnam will fax the final agreement to me," Isaacs said. "If it's in good shape, you can sign and fax it from here if you want."

"Well, no. I promised Karla I'd show it to her. It's her condition for supporting us. I've got a date to see Putnam on the thirtieth and will show it to her then."

Several days later, he took Sophia to Waterford to spend Christmas with Abigail. Over the holidays, he watched how the two women, despite their age difference, shared the same vibe. That was new.

Abigail had treated Becky as if she were a daughter, but she treated Sophia as a peer. He took that as a good sign for any future for them.

Isaacs called him the day after Christmas and said the agreement was ready. It had snowed a few inches every day after Christmas, including several inches during the night of December 29. Sandy woke early on December 30, looked at Sophia and wished he didn't have to keep a date with Putnam. She got up, saw it was still snowing lightly and begged him to wait until the roads cleared.

"I can't. I promised Karla. Besides, there's too much to do before winter classes and probate. I don't want to carry it into next semester. This will nail it down. It's nearly over." He listened to the radio and heard the roads were snow-covered but passable. "I've driven in worse," he said, putting on his down coat. "I'll take the level highway along the river to Waterford. Then, it's only a few miles of hills until I hit the four-lane. Now, don't worry. The plows will be out. I'll call you when I arrive."

There were few cars on the road at 8:00 a.m., but a keen, northerly wind drifted long fingers of snow across the road. A large pickup joined him outside Wacouta, and seeing it was fitted with a snowplow, he thought it might come in handy if conditions got worse. He drove with care and felt at ease because he wasn't alone.

He thought about Leif more often these days and supposed that reliving memories was a natural part of grieving. Passing through a patch of forest, he thought of a paradox that Leif never resolved. A tree wasn't just a tree to him. It was a unique organism, an individual with its own beauty and function. He had often seen the forester look at a tree with esthetic admiration while making a hard calculation of its board feet in lumber. Americans have a peculiar split personality, he thought. It's the worship of nature coupled with a lust to rape it.

Wind gusts whipped up clouds of snow in the open countryside, but that didn't slow the on-coming semi-trailer rigs. They barreled past Sandy, churning up billowing plumes of snow that engulfed him in momentary blizzards. The slick, compacted snow forced him to slow down to avoid skidding on the curves. Fortunately, the green pickup was still behind if he needed help. He slowed even more, seeing that an on-coming rig would pass him on a curve. Its immense snow cloud swallowed him, and, in the white-out, he heard something smash into the left rear fender. Then he felt the car accelerate sideways, out of control. As the visibility cleared, he realized his car was sailing off the embankment toward some trees.

⁂

Putnam took the weather into account when Sandy didn't arrive at 10:30 a.m. Nor was he perturbed when he was an hour overdue. A boatload of year-end paperwork sat on his desk, and he welcomed an extra hour to whittle it down. It was nearly noon when he called Sandy's home number.

"He's not here. I'm his... Who's calling?" Sophia asked.

"Barry Putnam, I'm with the Conservancy. We were supposed to meet at ten-thirty. He hasn't appeared."

She gasped as if punched in the belly. "He should be there by now... he left about eight this morning. Give me your number. If he calls, I'll relay it." With trembling fingers, she went through Sandy's desk for an address book. Then she called Isaacs.

"Okay, calm down," the lawyer said. "Tell me which roads he planned to take." As she told him, he said, *uh huh, uh huh*, and wrote it down. "Now listen. I'll call my contacts in the counties along the route. And also the state patrol. They would know if he had had an accident. I'll call this number if I learn something." Then he hung up.

She called Putnam and said the attorney was searching. When she knew more, she or he would call him. Then she thought of another call and dialed Abigail.

"Yes, I know," she said. "Morrie just called me. I'll call you if I hear something. Are you all right? You can come here if you want."

"Thanks, but no. I'm shaken but okay," she lied. "Besides, I said I would stick to Sandy's phone." Afterward, she wondered how much Abigail knew about their relationship. It would be just like him to say nothing. No matter, she thought. Abigail has probably guessed we're living together. It won't upset her—*al contario*.

209

CHAPTER 39

Emil Johansson and his wife were well behind the semi's snow cloud when they saw the blue compact sedan leave the road. A second later, a General Motors pickup barreled past them and kept going. "Oh my God, did you see that?" Johansson gasped. He stopped and got out. "You go home now and call the highway patrol," he said. "I'm gonna look." Then he clambered down the embankment to the car. "Oh, no, oh no," he cried, seeing that it had plowed into an oak and was as crumpled as a beer can. A limb pierced the windshield and held the front wheels off the ground. They were still spinning.

He looked through the shattered side window and saw a man lying head down on the floor. "Hey," he yelled. "Hey, fella, you alive?" The man didn't move. He went around the car, pulling on the doors, but they were jammed. "He's a goner for sure," he mumbled as he climbed back to the road. Gudrun returned just as a highway patrolman and an ambulance arrived.

"I didn't see exactly how it happened," he told the officer. "We were coming uphill behind a semi. This car and a green pickup was coming towards us. I lost sight of 'em in that snow-cloud. He musta lost control. Guess the pickup didn't see 'em neither 'cause he kept on going. I went down. He's layin' across the seat. Nothin' you can do for him. There's a branch stuck through the windshield. That's what prob'ly killed him."

The patrolman climbed down with the EMTs, who pried open the car door with a jaws-of-life tool. Then, with cool efficiency, they lifted out the body and strapped it to a litter. "He's alive but unconscious," an EMT said as they loaded Sandy into the ambulance. "He's in shock. Might be busted up inside. We're taking him to the E.R."

"Well, he sure looked like a goner to me," Johansson said to the patrolman. "So he's alive. Must be an act of God, *huh*." He stood with the officer and talked non-stop while the tow truck winched the car to the road.

After twenty minutes in the ambulance, Sandy moaned through clenched teeth as he regained consciousness. "What... where am... where are we going?"

"We're almost to the hospital," the medic said.

"What hospital?"

"Lake City Memorial. Just lie still. You're all banged up. We'll get you checked out in the E.R."

Lake City. At least Harald wouldn't be there, he thought and drifted back into semi-consciousness. His memories of the next several hours passed as a series of blurred scenes with a gurney, bright lights, x-rays, a nurse's questions and intercom pages to doctors whose names he didn't recognize. Pain was the only clear sensation. Every joint and muscle ached, some dully, others acutely, but all of them at once. When he was fully conscious and wrapped in a hospital robe, a nurse wheeled him into a private room. His left arm was bound to his chest with a sling, and his right shoulder and side throbbed. His clothes were folded and piled on a table. The shirt was bloody, and the down jacket had a huge rip.

"How are you feeling?" the nurse asked.

"Like someone worked me over... with a baseball bat."

"You're lucky, but you've got a concussion, cracked ribs, a dislocated shoulder and lots of bruises."

He groaned. "This headache is the worst."

"We'll give you some painkillers. Before that, there's an officer who wants to ask you questions if you're up to it."

"I can do it," he said through his clenched teeth.

The highway patrol officer introduced herself and began with simple questions to confirm the information she had. Then she asked what he recalled about the accident. His words came haltingly at first. Gradually, it became easier.

"There was a pickup behind me ever since Wacouta. Nothing happened until we were in a snow cloud. Then the pickup hit me."

"Was that accidental?"

"I don't know. It hit twice. The second time, it accelerated."

"Did you get a license or anything to identify it?"

"No. It had a snowplow."

"You think the truck intended to hit you?"

"I don't know. The second time felt like it accelerated and pushed me sideways, to the right. I lost control."

"We're investigating. We have to track down the pickup. Once we do, we'll have more questions for you. After you're dressed, I'll drive you home."

The streetlights were on when Isaacs called Sophia. His contacts said there was an accident north of Waterford, but he had no details. She waited and worried. Then, a State Patrol cruiser pulled into the driveway. Bad news, she thought, trembling. Oh God. Please, no… she prayed and opened the door. There stood the officer and Sandy, his face cut, one eye swollen and his arm in a sling.

"*Oh…!*" she cried and helped the officer get him into the house, remove his coat and ease him into a chair. "Thank you, officer. I can take it from here," she said. Then she kissed him fiercely. "I want to hold you, but—"

"—Don't touch me! I hurt all over. Bring the phone. I need to make a call."

She protested but gave in. He called his mother, told her the minimum and said he was all right. No, he didn't need her to care for him. He heard her laugh and say she understood he was getting good care. Sophia overheard it and blushed. Then he called Putnam and said that, because of an accident, he couldn't make their appointment. Putnam was relieved to hear it and said he would drive to Wacouta in a few days.

Meanwhile, Sophia rushed about making him comfortable until he asked her to simply fix a quick, hot meal. Over a bowl of soup, he told her what had happened. "It wasn't an accident," he said in a raw voice. "It was deliberate. Someone tried to kill me."

"Can you prove it?"

"No, not without the driver. But consider this. I don't have a will, so I better make one. If I had died today, my property, including the farm, would be intestate. That would open the door for Harald to claim it."

"Do you think Karla's in on this?"

"No. I'm not even sure about Harald. He's gutless, but Regina, however—"

"—See, never underestimate a…" she paled. "Sorry, that isn't funny."

"No, it isn't," he barked in a harsh voice.

Then he called Isaacs and heard him let out an audible sigh of relief. "Thank God you're alive," he said with an audible tremor in his voice.

"Morrie, I don't have a will. I just realized that if I had died, my property—including the farm—would have been up for grabs. That would've opened the farm for Harald to make a claim. Can you draft one for me—just in case? It'll be provisional, but it'll leave everything to Mom."

He made *uh-huh* sounds as he listened. "I'll do it. You didn't tell the officer you thought someone tried to kill you, did you?"

"She asked if I thought it was deliberate. I said I didn't know but—"

"—Good, I'm glad you didn't guess motives. Keep that to yourself until the police investigate. You've done everything you can for now. Let the police take it. Meanwhile, get all the rest you can. Probate is January ninth, ten o'clock. Stop worrying. If Karla sticks with us, he won't have a case."

"I forgot. I need to call her," he said. "I promised to show her the agreement."

"Go ahead, but don't speculate."

CHAPTER 40

Karla moped about her townhouse kitchen, preparing supper for Ted. The snow had stopped, and a keen wind was clearing the sky but that change didn't cheer her. It was hard to accept the fact that Sandy wasn't coming. *He promised to show me the purchase agreement*, she thought. *I would have supported him if he did, but that's out of the question now that he's dead. Supporting Harald's challenge didn't appeal to her any more than the onions she was chopping. Never mind*, she told herself, *Ted deserves a chance for a good education. If Harald is my only option, well, so be it.* Her phone rang, and she wiped her hands on a towel and picked up the receiver.

"Sandy? You're... *alive!*" she gasped. "I heard you died in a car wreck."

"A slight exaggeration," he said. "A snowplow hit me. I went off an embankment and hit a tree."

"Are you hurt?"

"A concussion, dislocated shoulder, cracked ribs and a lot of bruises. Otherwise, good as new."

"Oh, thank God you're alive. I've been sick ever since Harald called me. He said he heard the news on the radio."

"On the radio? Did he know we were going to meet today?"

"Yes," she said. "He called after Thanksgiving and offered two hundred... fifty... thousand if I'd join him." She recited the amount with marked enthusiasm. "I told him I was supporting you if the purchase agreement fulfilled Daddy's intention. He asked about it. I

215

told him you were coming today to... *oh... my... God!*" she moaned. Then she repeated "Oh my God" several times, laced with guilt. "You don't think I—"

"—Of course not," he said. "Don't say anything about... Give me a few days. I'll get you a copy of the agreement."

"That's okay, Sandy. I don't need to see it. I trust you."

"Thanks, thanks a lot. By the way, the buyer is the Conservancy."

"Oh, good! What's going to happen to Uncle Harald?"

"I don't know that anything will. The police are investigating. We don't know who's involved."

"Well, I'm sure Regina is," she snapped. "She hated Daddy."

"I know. Let's let the police do their work."

"Let's get you cleaned up," Sophia said after Sandy finished talking to Karla. She ran a tub full of hot water and helped him out of his clothes. Her stomach turned at the sight of his bruises. She wiped her eyes and then eased him into the water. Then she undressed and got in with him.

"I look awful, don't I," he said as she sponged him gingerly. "But hey, I'm really better than I look. And looking at you... I'm feeling better already. Some of my vital parts are undamaged."

She took his good hand and kissed the palm. "I thank God and the Virgin Mother you are alive."

"You believe in the Virgin Mother... really?"

"Dead ass yes I do... and you should, too."

He let out his breath. "You know, there was a moment when I thought this was payback for Becky's death. Like I was going to get what she got. You know, divine retribution because I was selfish. If I had driven her—"

"—You might both be dead," she said. "I told you that. Then, where would I be?"

"That's what Leif said."

"Sandy, your marriage is none of my business. It's none of my concern until it affects us. It's time you stopped blaming yourself for something you didn't do. If you don't, it will sour things between us."

Then she noticed something else. And when she knew what it was, she hesitated to mention it.

"What is it?" he asked, catching the surprise in her eyes.

"Your ring," she said, careful to avoid saying wedding band. "It's gone."

He studied his left hand. "It must have come off in the accident." He wiggled his fingers and winced in pain. "It reminded me of what Becky and I had." He shook his head. "Maybe it's a cosmic sign to turn the page. Sounds crazy, doesn't it."

"No, it's not crazy. Now, let's get you dried off."

"What's the rush? I'm in no shape for sex, so at least let me look some more."

"*Men*," she laughed. "You never outgrow your hunger for tits and ass."

"Not when they're like yours. But when I do, you'll know I'm dead."

"I'll stay to take care of you," she said, getting out of the tub. "I'll just run home and get a change of clothes."

"You don't need anything… well, okay, a bustier and garters."

She flipped him the bird and went out the door, howling with laughter.

CHAPTER 41

There are simple cases, and then there are cases like the Nielsen's, Jack thought. This one has gotten as tangled as a fishing line ever since Isaacs brought in the sedatives. Add the autopsy, rumors about Leif's mental state, the challenge to the will and the car accident, if that's what it was, and it's another case about highly visible people. It's time Boston rode shotgun, he thought as he lifted the phone.

"Got a minute?" Jack asked. "I want an off-the-record conversation. Don't share it with Ginger just yet."

"You know I don't like keeping things from her. But if it's that sensitive…"

"Harald's challenge to his brother's will has a couple of angles that seem headed my way." Then ,he recapped what seemed to be a complex case.

"Sedatives could have a lot of side effects," Boston said. "Maybe they're part of the claim that Leif wasn't mentally sound. I hope you've got a detective on this."

"Of course, Mary Kasson. That's why I need you. You've met all the players."

"Okay, Jack. Facts first. Leif was ill—that's true. He was in Harald's guest house to recover—that might be true. Harald claims he wanted to stay there—not likely true because he went to great lengths to escape. He did crazy things—not true because they were deliberate steps to cover his tracks. And finally, he wrote a lucid ecology plan."

"Good comments—as usual. That's why I need you."

"Harald was Leif's doctor. So, that makes the medical records suspect. I talked to Leif twice in September, once before and once after the first hospital stay. He impressed me as very keen. I also talked to others. All of them—including Harald—said he was mentally sharp. I take it there's a criminal aspect to this."

"There is now. Based on the autopsy and tox screen, we're looking to see if the drugs were used to hold him against his will. We don't have all the evidence—yet."

"So, this is a criminal matter or one for the state medical board."

"It could be both. We want to interview his housekeeper about the meds. Malpractice is easier to prove than criminal intent. He could lose his license. Restraining someone against his will… well, it's still a stretch with what we have."

"But I gather there is more to come."

"Yeah. Brewster was in a bad car accident on his way to Minneapolis to sign a purchase agreement. A pickup with a snowplow followed him. He believes it pushed him over an embankment. He survived but has a bundle of injuries. Now, if we can just find *the* green pickup… For now, add that to the notes you've been keeping."

"Mind if I talk to Isaacs or Brewster?"

"No."

"The *Statesman* will publish the accident without suspicions."

"Good. Keep a lid on the drug angle and attempted murder."

Jack's information preoccupied Boston all day as he worked on his monthly column for *American Outlook*. He set it aside and realized the sun had set, and he hadn't thought about preparing supper. Ginger would arrive any minute, and there wasn't time to fix anything elaborate. She likes pancakes, he thought. I like bacon. We'll have that with applesauce.

The phone rang, and he put aside the pancake batter to answer it. "Oh, hi, Sandy. How are you? I heard about the accident."

"I'm fine, or will be, but I can't drive right now. I've got something to show you. Could you come here? It's about the challenge to Leif's will. Morrie and I are reviewing the evidence to prove his competence. We want your thoughts."

He was still on the phone when Ginger burst through the front door in her usual brash fashion to let him know she was home. "How's that column coming along," she yelled from the foyer. "Any progress?" She ducked into the den and kissed him while he was on the phone. Then she ran upstairs to change and returned in a sweat suit.

"The column stinks. That's why we're having pancakes tonight."

"I don't get the connection."

"Never mind," he said as he stirred the batter. "I wasted the whole damn day struggling with the Iran-Contra business. It's the biggest national story, but I can't see how it affects life or property in Featherstone." The batter hissed when he poured dollops on the griddle. "A Featherstone perspective was part of my deal with the *Outlook*."

"It doesn't have to be Iran-Contra. Your dad wrote great columns about ordinary things. Why not you?"

"Because I'm *not* my dad," he snapped. That comparison had always irked him. "But maybe you're right. You know Harald's challenging Leif's will, don't you?"

"Of course. I'm assigning you to cover it."

"Now that I think about it, the challenge has an element of subterfuge. At least it's got that in common with Iran-Contra."

"Explain that," she said, pouring syrup over the stack of cakes on her plate.

"It's confidential, but there are odd angles to the Nielsen case. Between September and October, Harald changed from saying Leif was mentally sharp to saying he had dementia. Daniels, Isaacs, Brewster and I know different. It is worth noting Harald was Leif's doctor."

"So, you think it's a way to invalidate the will."

"It's a possible motive. He wants the property developed in what he calls the best interest of the estate. Meaning what, he doesn't say. You can guess."

"Himself."

"And others. If the court rules Leif was incompetent, Jorgenson might use it to back out of the Oxbow donation. He told Brewster the county board would oppose removing the farm from the tax rolls. Game, set, match. On the other hand, the *Statesman* might be interested in Jorgenson's creative use of tax-increment-financing to redevelop his business property."

"I hear a hound barking on the hunt," she said. "So, starting tomorrow, you're an unpaid investigative reporter covering the Nielsen case. But that doesn't exempt you from your role as my chef. By the way, yummy pancakes."

CHAPTER 42

"There are a couple stories that might interest you," Boston said the next morning as he and Ginger met with Robin, the *Statesman*'s news editor. "They're likely to blossom in the weeks ahead. One is the challenge to Leif Nielsen's will."

"What are you getting at?" Robin asked.

"I assigned him the story," Ginger giggled. "He'll cover the probate case."

"A challenged will is usually a so-what story," he said. "It's titillating but rarely affects anyone outside the family. In this case, the challenge claims Nielsen wasn't competent to make his will. If the court agrees, it could sink the Oxbow donation and open the way to develop Nielsen's farm on Tarn Lake."

"This is the first I've heard of the Oxbow donation," Robin said, glancing at Ginger. "Fill me in."

Boston recapped Daniels's intention to donate the tract with a management plan as a county ordinance. He also recapped the struggle over the farm on Tarn Lake and how they were connected through Harald Nielsen. The fate of the Oxbow and the farm might well be determined by what the court found was Leif's state of mind.

"As the publisher, I'm sure you have an idea about the *Statesman*'s role," Robin smirked. "So, write something about it, Leif's part in it and what it means to the county."

"That's what I had in mind," he said. "Public opinion might affect the outcome. So, let's put out the facts before someone else frames the story. I've read the management plan. It's a lucid exposition of complex ecological management. It's an example of his mental state at the time of death."

"No problem. The donation is news, and the public should know what's at stake."

"I think it goes along with something you overheard in Rochester," he said. "Wingspan is hot to develop Nielsen's farm. Might be good to know who they are, their investors, officers and so forth. Meanwhile, Jorgenson publicly opposes shifting property to non-revenue uses. A savvy reporter might uncover that Jorgenson finagled tax-increment-financing to benefit his business that others are now paying for."

Ginger gave him a sidelong glance with a wry smile. "Robin, let's put Dub on it. He's dying to cover something besides small store closings and big-box openings."

"It's obvious you think something crooked is afoot," Robin said. She cracked a smile that crinkled about her eyes and told him she was all in.

"Don't know yet," he said. "There may be more stories as this one unfolds."

COUNTY TO RECEIVE OXBOW PRESERVE was the *Statesman*'s lead. The story with Boston's by-line described the two-thousand-acre preserve and profiled the retired forest ranger who surveyed the tract and wrote the plan to manage and protect it. A sidebar reprinted excerpts from the plan, and the editorial underscored the importance of protecting unique natural areas for science and education.

Regina's temper flared as she read the editorial's last lines:

> In simple but elegant phrases, Mr. Nielsen
> described the public benefits and the steps
> needed to protect the area's unique flora,
> fauna and geology. Anyone who reads
> the plan will see it is the product of a
> sophisticated mind that integrates science

and esthetics. The late Mr. Nielsen was a
scientist with the wisdom of a woodsman
and the soul of an artist.

She threw down the paper with a guttural sound of disgust. Then
she picked it up, read it again and spent the day seething and cursing
Meade for the story. When her anger became too much, she drove to
the clinic. Harald was at the hospital in Featherstone, and she used the
clinic phone because it was convenient. Then, she spent two hours
with the young attorney who wanted her political support. She agreed
to back him provided he regularly satisfied her carnal needs. Like
Daddy always said, she thought, give a little to get a little.

The maid was preparing supper when Regina returned home feeling
appreciated as a woman. She showered and changed clothes, but the
satiety from sex soon dissipated as she mixed the cocktails and waited
for Harald in the salon. "Here, read this," she said and threw the
newspaper toward him. "You've got a new problem."

He read the story and then looked up at her. "So, what problem?"

"Is that all you can say? Think, *think*. Don't you see, Meade's
got a copy of the management plan. His summary and the editorial
describe your brother in glowing terms—a scientist with esthetics. *Ha!*
Isaacs will use that to undermine your challenge. Meade is working
with Brewster. You have to do something."

He moved his lips, but no words came out at first. "Well, he only
summarized the plan. It doesn't prove—"

"—Don't be such a dope. Read it again. Judge Knatvold will see
that and make up his mind before he even gets Sam's brief."

"I suppose you're right," he said in a note of concession. "But
Jorgenson told Sandy the county won't let any property leave the rolls.
The economic development department agrees. I think we're covered."

"Don't count on Jorgenson to block the preserve. If he does,
everyone will get upset for taking away something they've just been
told they will receive. And Doug's up for re-election."

The maid answered the phone while they talked and then called Harald. He put down his drink and picked up the call in his den. "What's up, Doug. We were just discussing the Oxbow story. Oh, that's not why you… you say it's on the… Okay. I'll look at it and call you back." He hung up, returned to the salon, and read the *Statesman*'s business page. "Damn," he whispered, shaking his head. "The paper is digging into the way Doug used tax-increment financing. Now he looks bad."

She let out a long cry of disgust. "Everything you've tried has failed, Harald. *Everything!* We'd be moving ahead now if only he had died in that accident."

CHAPTER 43

Though it was only the first full week of January, the Arctic cold gripped the state with a bulldog's teeth and seemed determined to hang on until March—at least. Boston turned the Jeep's heater to high, picked up Isaacs and drove to Wacouta to meet Sandy. On the way, they passed the site of his accident and saw the furrow where the car left the road. The scars on the tree seemed permanent.

"Accident my eye," Boston said. "He had momentum when he went over."

"I agree," Isaacs said. "Best to let the police figure it out." After that, they continued talking about the next steps in proving Leif's state of mind.

"Thanks for coming," Sandy said, lifting his arm in its sling. "I'm still bruised and banged up, but I'm okay otherwise."

"You sound good, despite the shiner," Isaacs said. "Daniels sends his greetings. He'll back us if need be. Now, I think I smell coffee."

"Yeah, and it's real coffee. And freshly ground," he said, laughing. "My classes start at two this afternoon, so let's get at it."

"Before we start, a disclosure," Boston said as they settled into the living room. "Harald is well known, and his challenge is generating a lot of coffeeshop chatter. Ginger hears about it downtown. She wants me to cover the case, but let me assure you, nothing will be reported without checking it with you, Morrie."

"Good enough," he agreed. "Leif's state of mind affects the Oxbow project, so let's go through the evidence. After that, let's talk about what's background and what's news. People don't know much about challenging a will. Maybe outlining that process will be helpful." Then, he listed the requirements. "Harald isn't alleging legal non-compliance or forgery. He's focused on Leif's competence and Sandy's undue influence. So let's lay out the evidence for his competence."

"Leif's tally books," Sandy said. "I've got dozens of them from the seventies until his death. They're not scintillating prose, but the last book is as lucid as the first. Neither words nor thoughts nor penmanship show a decline."

"Good. I know a forensic psychologist if necessary."

Boston held up the coffee pot. Each nodded.

"Look at his last tally book entries," he continued. "He didn't write much in the hospital except to note Karla's visit and her question about a will. He underlined his promise to file one. His guest house notes are cryptic, but he writes about feeling like a prisoner. He didn't want to be there. It suggests he felt being held against his will."

"Harald might back off if he knew we had these notes," Isaac said. "Now, let's turn to the management plan."

"On its face, he was lucid when he wrote it," Boston said. "I would think this alone would undermine a claim of incompetence."

"That will nail our case," Sandy said with a grin.

"But we have a weak spot," Isaac said, removing his glasses. "Leif didn't tell Harald he changed the will. So, he let Harald think he had the power of attorney. In his defense, Harald could claim he acted in good faith based on what Leif didn't tell him."

"But that doesn't let him off the hook."

"No. Not entirely. The pills you found are potent sedatives. A medical friend said the wrong dose could be lethal at his age. A low dose would make him lethargic, dizzy and suppress his breathing. Leif noted your discovery."

"But I want to nail him for the drugs and trying to kill me," Sandy said, frustrated.

"Hold on, hold on," Isaacs said, raising both hands. "You're the administrator of a will, not a prosecuting attorney. That used to be my job. Probate is not the place to raise criminal allegations."

"But he tried to kill me!"

"We don't know that," he said, irritated. "Harald's actions are suspicious, yes. Personally, I don't think he's capable of murder. So far, neither we nor the sheriff have evidence he was connected to the accident. We believe he intended to defraud Leif, but we lack conclusive proof. If we can show that Leif was sound when he made the will, then he has no case. As it is, he's at risk of an investigation into medical malpractice."

"But—"

"—Here's what I advise," he said. "I'll set up a meeting with you, the Nielsens and Sam Willard. Then, I'm going to lay out the evidence we intend to use in defense. That includes the fabricated—shall I say *doctored*—medical records, the tranquilizers, Leif's contract, Leif's letter to you, the management plan and his rework on the draft of the will."

Sandy started to protest, but Isaacs cut him off. "Listen, Sandy," he said sharply. "I doubt Sam Willard knows the medical records are fakes. He's got too much integrity to get mixed up in a fraud. Most likely, he'll back off when he hears about it."

"But without a conviction, Harald gets away with it."

"Son, you're after vengeance—not justice," Isaacs said softly. "The law doesn't provide that. No, he won't get away with it. Defending Leif will hold him accountable. When we do, the Nielsens will see their scheme go up in smoke. That will be hard on them—especially Regina. She'll take it out on him. Their marriage is no secret."

"But that's not fair to Leif or me. They deserve—"

"—Stick to executing the will," he ordered in a harder voice. "Leave the rest to the police if it comes to that. If they fight us in court, the evidence we present will be in the open, where the county attorney can see it. Harald is going down. Accept that."

CHAPTER 44

Harald was dressing when Regina picked up the *Statesman*. COUNTY BOARD APPROVES OXBOW PRESERVE led the news. The board accepted the donated land and enacted the management plan as a county ordinance. In its resolution, the board extolled the plan's clarity in protecting natural resources. A separate column included more excerpts from the plan. Five commissioners voted for the resolution. Commissioners Nielsen and Jorgenson abstained.

She threw the paper at him when he entered the breakfast nook. "Well... you didn't tell me *this* happened," she said in a soft, cold voice. "Why didn't you and Jorgenson get two more votes to kill it?" She tapped her fingers. "Just two more votes."

"It was complicated," he said, swallowing. "The tax-increment story put Jorgenson in a spot. A lot of businessmen are mad at him. He didn't want to look hypocritical, so he abstained. The others... well, they had already promised Daniels and didn't want to cross him."

"*Ugh*," she exhaled and rose to her feet. "Gutless. No balls at all. Jorgenson has to do better if he wants a re-election endorsement—"

"—I supported Doug, so he'll support us if Sandy—"

"—He's not going to prevail. Get that through your fat head. From now on, don't do anything. Don't even think. Just leave it to me. You're hopeless!" She exhaled loudly to expel her disgust. "It's always the women who have to clean up the mess."

"You don't have to be insulting. I was elected many times."

231

"Yes, you were. But you're the kind of politician who wants to please everyone all the time. That's impossible. And that's why you should stick to medicine and business and leave politics to me. I'll have to make some more calls to get us back on track."

Karla heard the phone and suspected it was Harald. He had called her every other day at about this hour ever since Sandy's accident. "Hello," she answered and waited.

"Probate is two days away," Harald said. "I hope you've thought some more about joining the challenge. As soon as the judge rules for us, I'll hand you the check. It's already made out but not signed."

She listened and thought he sounded anxious as he told her how the family must stick together. The money could send Ted to Harvard or Yale. He's desperate if not afraid, she thought and then wondered if Regina was listening on another line.

"I'm sorry. I'm supporting the will Daddy filed. Sandy's plan will do what he wanted. That's what I want. I can't live with seeing the farm developed."

"Give it more thought. Please. For Ted's sake."

Karla ended the call heavy with sadness that her father's estate and Harald had come to this. She phoned Sandy. "I just had another call from…" and then repeated what Harald promised. "Sandy, I'll be at court to support you," she said firmly. Her opinion of him had risen since the accident. He's got guts and integrity, she thought. If he gave me half a chance, I could fall in love with him. But that's not likely.

Sandy and Sophia stayed with his mother the night before probate. In the morning, he left her with Abigail and drove to Isaacs's office in his new car. Though he was healing quickly, he felt twinges of pain, and the cuts and bruises were still visible.

"Willard and the Nielsens are going to propose another settlement," Isaacs said. "I hate playing hardball, but she leaves me no choice. Here's what I suggest," he said and outlined the strategy while they waited. When the challengers arrived, Harald greeted him cordially and asked about his injuries. Regina declined to greet him or make small talk.

Willard nodded pleasantly to each person as if there were no conflict. Isaacs seized the initiative as Willard laid out some folders.

"Before we go over your proposal, Sam, you should know that our defense will raise a few points that could embarrass your client." He paused and picked up several sheets of paper.

"You know our position," Harald said, "We've got records to back it up."

"That depends if your records are genuine," Isaacs said evenly. "In this file," he lifted a folder, "I have Leif's original medical records, the one Harald made when he was admitted in August. They are the same records he ordered destroyed several weeks ago."

"What are you... Harald?"

The doctor stiffened, and Regina's face darkened.

"Sam, the record you have is one he created the day after he learned Doctor Brewster was the heir. The hospital clerk saved the originals because their destruction violated hospital policy. I have a sworn statement to support it." Isaacs looked at Harald and then at Willard. "See what I mean about embarrassing."

"Harald, is this true?" Willard's bland expression turned to puzzlement.

"It's... it's a distortion," the doctor said, squirming in his chair. "He's got no right to those records."

"—The privilege belongs to the patient," Isaacs said. "And it passes to his successor in interest—his estate and its representative." Willard nodded in agreement. "The estate's claim is greater than yours because yours is an adverse interest."

"Well, that's debatable, Morrie," Willard interjected. Then, he studied a copy of the original medical file against the newer one. "I want an explanation."

"It's... it's easy to explain," the doctor stammered. "The urgency of Leif's condition didn't allow time to put down all the information right away. That's... that's right. Afterward, when I realized I... I omitted recording signs of dementia. So... *uh*... I made a new record to update the first."

"Why didn't you add the changes to the original file?"

Sweat broke out along Harald's receding hairline. He licked his lips. Regina shot Isaacs a venomous glare.

"What are you suggesting, Morrie?" Willard's voice and eyes betrayed suspicion that he had been played.

"Withdraw the challenge."

"*Never*," she roared.

"We will offer this in court along with other embarrassing information. After that, it's only a matter of time before the county attorney opens a fraud investigation or the Board of Medical Examiners starts to look at your practice—"

"—You're bluffing," she challenged. "You don't have anything but guesses."

"Oh, but I do," the lawyer said mildly. "Karla's affidavit attests to your promises of ever-increasing amounts of money in return for joining the challenge."

"The little bitch," she hissed under her breath.

"Anything else?" Willard asked.

"Sandy," Isaacs turned to him.

"Doctor Nielsen, you knew he was competent when you fabricated the senility claim. I found the sedatives you dispensed from an aspirin bottle. Then, I found the vial with the prescription from your pharmacy. Why isn't that prescription shown on the medical record?"

Red-faced, Harald yelled, "You don't know anything—"

"—I know they made him lethargic. They made him appear feeble, confused. I also know they depress the bodily systems and retarded his recovery at risk to his life. The autopsy confirms the sedatives in his system. The coroner said an incomplete recovery from pneumonia was an underlying cause."

Harald's eyes opened wide, and the veins in his neck stood out. Regina's face paled, and her eyes seemed even darker.

"Get to the point, Doctor Brewster," Willard sighed.

"Mabel Lund dispensed the sedatives from a Bayer aspirin bottle. She signed a statement affirming that. She was told that an aspirin a day keeps the doctor away."

"We'll sue you for defamation," Regina hissed through lips as tight as a snake's. "We'll get everything you've got or ever will get."

"Morrie, I need a moment with my clients," Willard sighed in a tone of defeat.

Sandy and Isaacs waited in the private office, but even with the door closed, they heard the muffled argument in the conference room. Then they heard the Nielsens stomp down the stairs.

Willard stuck his head in Isaacs's office and shook his head. "They're going to court this afternoon against my advice," he said. "I'm sorry."

"I'm surprised he wants to go through with it."

"Well, it wasn't his decision—as usual."

CHAPTER 45

The county courthouse resembled a half-sized state capitol with a copper dome, bronze doors and floors of polished dolomite. Boston took a seat in the paneled courtroom beneath a WPA mural depicting pioneers breaking Minnesota's prairie. He arrived a half-hour before the hearing to capture the probate preparation and the entrance of the players. Willard and Harald shambled in at 1:45 p.m. They sat at a table in front of the bench. Isaacs and Sandy arrived five minutes later. The lawyers shook hands and spoke but without animation. Karla and Ted sat behind them. Harald crossed the aisle to talk to her and, he gestured, as if pleading. She shook her head. Abigail and Sophia settled into the seats behind Karla. Curious onlookers filled the back rows of seats. Regina strode down the aisle at 2:00 p.m. and sat beside Harald. Boston captured her as: "Erect, imperial, sheathed in a glacial blue suit, coordinated make-up, every hair in place."

He watched Isaacs lean over and whisper to Sandy as he turned to look at Harald. Then, the bailiff entered. "All rise. *Oyez, oyez*, this court is in session. The honorable Judge Ray Knatvold, presiding." Everyone stood. The diminutive judge in large robes took his seat on the bench and rapped the court into session in the matter of *Harald Nielsen v. the estate of Leif Nielsen*. Everyone sat.

"Gentlemen, I have read the will and your briefs. If you wish, you may enter further evidence, call witnesses and cross-examine the same. Mister Willard, if you are ready, you may begin."

Willard rose and adjusted his pale silk tie. "My client will enter evidence that Leif Nielsen, his elder brother, was mentally incompetent when he made his will. He will also assert he made this will subject to the undue influence of Sanford Brewster. For these two reasons, he believes the will is invalid."

"For the record, Mister Willard, you prepared a draft of the will, did you not?" Knatvold interrupted. "Was that at the decedent's personal request to you?"

"No, your honor. My client relayed to me his brother's request that I prepare a will as he was hospitalized at the time—"

"—But you never actually met the deceased," the judge interrupted.

"That is correct. We submit the prepared draft as evidence. Now, I would like to call the plaintiff as a medical expert on the decedent's state of mind."

"Objection," Isaacs said, standing and removing his glasses. "Doctor Nielsen is an internist, not a psychologist. He is not competent to give expert testimony. Further, anything he says violates my client's privilege. Finally, we object to his opinions on his brother's state of mind because he is the plaintiff."

"Objections sustained."

"Your honor, the plaintiff was the physician who cared for the deceased. Therefore, he is qualified to attest to the condition of Mister Nielsen's mental state. That is the heart of our case."

"Your honor, the medical privilege belongs to the patient and his estate," Isaac objected. "Doctor Nielsen is the plaintiff, and we object because his testimony supports a view adverse to my client's interest."

"Point taken, counselor," the judge agreed with a sardonic smile. "Is there any latitude in allowing the plaintiff's testimony?"

The attorney and client huddled for a moment before Sandy nodded assent. "We object to any testimony bearing on the deceased's state of mind. He must limit his remarks to the deceased physical condition that he treated, namely, pneumonia. He may testify only to what he entered on the original medical record."

Willard hesitated and whispered to Harald. "Your honor, we submit these medical records to document the deceased's state of mind at the time of his death."

"Mister Willard, call your witness," the judge said.

Harald walked to the stand, swore his oath and sat down. Willard questioned him, and the doctor gave careful, technical answers in a disinterested voice.

"Doctor, in your non-medical capacity, as his brother, tell us about your brother's mode of life, the way he took care of himself."

"He lived alone on a farm and visited me for medical help. I admitted him to the hospital twice in one month for pneumonia. He was physically weak and had lost his power of concentration. For his safety, I suggested that he recover in a nursing home or at my guest house. He opted for the guest house. I saw him almost daily, and his condition didn't change. When he left the guest house, he wrote a note saying he was going away on business. He told a bartender he was going to fix a hunting shack he didn't own. Then he put out decoys and swamped his duck boat before he went camping."

"And when you learned all these things, what was your non-medical reaction—as his brother?" Willard asked.

"He used to be deliberate in his actions. These acts were so random and non-sensical that I can draw only one conclusion."

"And what is that?"

"That he had lost his mental moorings."

Isaacs studied Harald closely and didn't object. Instead, he wrote notes on a yellow tablet. He seemed unperturbed by the picture Harald was painting. Each time the doctor spoke, he wrote another note.

"Tell us about the undue influence of Professor Brewster."

"I practiced medicine with his father—a fine man who died too soon—but his son was wayward. He hung around my brother's farm even as an adult. His promise to keep the farm unchanged is what my brother wanted to hear. But the fact is, he lacks the resources to keep the farm as it is. Despite that fact, he persuaded my brother to give him the farm."

"Thank you, doctor. No more questions." Willard said and went to the table without a backward glance.

Isaacs approached Harald and studied him in silence until the doctor fidgeted like a man with a case of hemorrhoids. Then he began asking simple questions, whether he was Leif's brother, his physician and had he treated Leif for pneumonia. Harald answered all in the affirmative.

"And you stand behind your non-professional opinion of his mental state."

"Of course. I'm his doctor."

"But you're an internist, not a psychologist. Yet you recognized this the first time you admitted him to the hospital."

"Yes, I did."

"And you didn't make note of it then or during his second admission."

"Yes, that's true, but—"

"—Isn't it true you ordered a hospital clerk to destroy your brother's original medical record and replace it with an altered one?" He moved closer to Harald.

"No, that's not true," Harald said and glanced toward Willard. "We admitted him twice as an emergency. At the time, his survival was more urgent than mere paperwork. I filled in the details later when I had time."

"How is it you didn't change the records until the day after you learned you were not his heir and executor?"

"Coincidence."

"The medical records you gave the court aren't the original ones. Please explain how and why the records you submitted differ from the originals."

"It's merely an updated file, so his case would have a complete record."

"Your honor, we offer the court a copy of the original record, the one he ordered destroyed contrary to hospital policy. With it is a notarized statement from the clerk who preserved that record. Please note the discrepancies between them.

Willard drank deeply from a glass of water. Regina's face stiffened.

Isaacs resumed his questions in his unassuming voice. "Why aren't the sedatives you prescribed shown on this record?"

Harald opened and closed his mouth without speaking. He drew a breath. "An oversight."

"Are sedatives usually prescribed for pneumonia cases?"

"That depends. He needed rest but wouldn't stay quiet. A mild dose was necessary to keep him indoors during recovery."

"You mean, keep him under control," Isaacs said more sharply. "And why dispense it from an aspirin bottle?"

"*Uh…* well, as you know… *uh…* drugs are valuable in the wrong hands. I, *uh*, to make sure they didn't get into the wrong hands… I disguised them as aspirin."

"Are you saying you didn't trust Missus Lund with them?"

"No, but… *uh*, you can't be too careful."

"So, you gave him a sedative daily to make certain he stayed at the guest house. And, when sedated, he appeared *non compos mentis* as intended. Isn't that right?"

Before Harald could answer, Isaac turned to the judge. "Your honor, with respect to Mister Nielsen's state of mind, I offer two sets of contemporaneous documents that show his mind at work just before his death. The first is the Oxbow management plan the deceased wrote, signed and dated on the day he died. The county board of which Doctor Nielsen is a member adopted it by resolution."

"Objection," Willard called, rising to his feet.

"State your objection," the judge ordered.

"It is a technical document. It doesn't address the issue."

"Oh, but it does, your honor," Isaacs responded. "Ecological protection is a complex subject. Even a cursory reading reveals that he had the mental power to explain complex relationships in simple language. I will also mention that the commission lauded the lucidity of the plan."

"Mister Willard, your objection is overruled. Continue, counselor."

"Second, we offer the court photocopies from Mister Nielsen's tally book. You will see that it is listed in the estate's inventory. He briefly recorded thoughts during his time at the plaintiff's guest house. The tally book entries are offered in rebuttal to claims that he asked to stay at the guest house and also the claims of mental incapacity."

The sound of shuffling feet filled the courtroom. Harald sat as still as a rabbit, trying to avoid detection while Isaacs passed copies of the pages to the judge.

"Doctor Nielsen, you testified that your brother chose to stay in the guest house," Isaacs said and handed him several sheets of paper. "Will you please read the highlighted text from this copy of his tally book?"

Harald looked at the pages, sucked a breath and read in an inaudible monotone.

"Louder, so we can all hear," the judge ordered.

Harald loosened his tie, cleared his throat and started over: "September 10: H. gave me will he drafted. Makes him heir & exec. with POA. September 12: Home. September 13: Take will to Morrie. Change heir & exec to Saginaw. Will tell him later. September 21: Home. September 27: Out of hosp. H. moves me to guest house. Don't want to stay. September 30: In bed. Feel weak. Sleepy all day. October 1: Don't want to stay. Feel like prisoner. October 5: Saginaw visits. Finds H. gives dope from aspirin bottle. Stopped taking. October 6: Upset over H. and drugs. Feel better. Exercise in room. October 7: Clear head. Walk at night. October 8: Walk at night. October 9: Stronger. Walk at night. Escape soon. October 10: H. has big party. Leave guest house. October 11: Cover tracks. Go to Oxbow. October 12: Down chasm and back. Finish plan."

The courtroom fell silent. Harald swallowed, his shoulders slumped, his double chin rested on his collar as his body appeared to collapse in on itself. He started to rise, but Isaacs had more questions.

"Your honor, I don't intend to go further into the matter of the sedatives disguised as aspirin. We leave that to other authorities. However, if necessary, we have the decedent's autopsy, a statement from the housekeeper and another from a toxicologist at the Mayo

Clinic with regard to their effect on a man of Mister Nielsen's age and health. On this point, we think it is enough to say the sedatives created the visual impression of mental decline. His notes show he recovered mental acuity after he stopped taking them. We offer the tally book and the management plan as indications of Mister Nielsen's competency despite great adversity. Should it be necessary, we have earlier tally books for comparison if the court wishes."

Harald sat lower in his chair as if trying to hide from Isaacs. He pulled at his tie.

"Now, Doctor Nielsen, let me turn to the issue of undue influence," Isaacs said. "How long has my client known your brother?"

"That's a stupid…" but the judge rapped the gavel and ordered him to answer. "Since he was a kid. Maybe twenty, twenty-five years."

"And how long have you known Leif Nielsen?"

"Well, all my life. Sixty-two years, but—"

"—And who would have the most influence—a brother he has known for sixty-two years or an unrelated young man he has known for a mere twenty years?"

"Well, that depends on—"

"—No, it doesn't. Your honor, this statement from Seabury College affirms that my client was on a sabbatical leave in Massachusetts between January 6 and August 27 of last year. As you see, Mister Nielsen filed his will before that. The only persons who asked about his will were his daughter, who supports our cause, and the plaintiff."

"Is there anything else, counselor?" the judge asked.

"A few more questions, you honor. Now, Doctor Nielsen, after you learned Professor Brewster was the heir, did you tell him certain parties wanted to buy the farm?"

"Well, yes, they approached me. I gave them his number. Just trying to help him maximize the value of the estate." Harald licked his pink lips and swallowed.

"And you decided to challenge the will after that?"

"Well, yes. His decisions aren't in the interest of the estate."

"But you are not named in the will. Describe your interest in this."

"I'm looking out for my brother's daughter and grandson."

"But she signed a statement supporting the will. Explain how you can act in her interest when she supports the will as filed."

"I don't think she knows what is in her best interest," he said, looking at the back of the courtroom. "She's still in shock. The farm has been in the Nielsen family for eighty years. My parents and her father are buried there."

"Who were the prospective buyers you referred to Professor Brewster?"

"Wingspan Associates," he squeaked. "A Rochester group."

"Who are its partners?"

Boston watched with admiration as an unassuming night-school lawyer dressed in shades of brown deftly eviscerated the client of an Ivy League attorney. Isaacs's mild-mannered questions were dissolving the challenge like water droplets on a sugar cube.

Harald named three individuals and then wiped the perspiration from his brow.

"Do you have a material interest in Wingspan?"

"There are four partners. I'm not one of them."

Isaacs walked to the table, picked up a brochure and entered it as evidence. "This is a brochure and an audited statement from Wingspan Associates," he said. Then he handed a second copy to Harald. "Please read the highlighted portion."

Harald droned on with the names of the principal stockholders, including his own.

"Though you are not a partner, you *do* have a material interest in Wingspan, don't you? And you *did* suggest them to Professor Brewster, didn't you?"

Boston watched Harald stare at his hands and then look at Willard, his eyes blank.

"We've covered a lot of ground, doctor," Isaacs said, removing his glasses. "To wrap it up, let me summarize where we are before my final question. You asked your lawyer to draft a will for your brother that gave you control of his estate. Your brother realized this and made changes before he signed and filed it. He didn't tell you about the changes. Why, I don't know, because he refused to tell me. But he had no legal obligation to do so. He also didn't tell his daughter or Professor Brewster of the change. When you discovered this after his death, you falsified his medical records to support a claim he was *non compos mentis*. At the same time, you pressured his daughter to join your challenge. And then you deliberately directed a development company to Professor Brewster in hopes of pressuring him into making a deal—a deal that would have enriched you. Isn't it true you wanted to develop the farm for nine million dollars?"

"No, that's not true… I, it's more like—"

"—I've finished with this witness," he said before Harald could answer.

Boson watched the doctor stumble off the stand and sink between Regina and Willard. The attorney appeared resigned, but she radiated palpable contempt.

"Anything further, Mister Willard?" the judge asked. Willard shook his head.

"Mister Isaacs?"

"No, your honor. We believe the plaintiff's testimony has affirmed our defense."

"We stand in recess for an hour," the judge said and rapped his gavel. The on-lookers milled about the hallway, but the principals and their attorneys remained to await the decision. Forty-five minutes later, the bailiff called "All rise," and Judge Knatvold entered. He put the papers on his bench and rapped the court into session.

"After reviewing the evidence and testimony presented in this case," Knatvold began, "I find the plaintiff failed to present sufficient evidence to void the will either due to mental incapacity or that it was made under duress. Therefore, this court confirms the validity of the will filed by Leif Nielsen. Sanford Brewster may now execute the will according to its provisions. This court is adjourned," he declared and slammed the gavel.

Regina strode past everyone and out of the courtroom with her chin thrust forward. Harald scurried behind her like a whipped cur.

"My compliments," Willard said to Isaacs as he shuffled papers into the calfskin briefcase. He shook his head. "Just between us, you put on a masterful case. I advised them not to do it because they didn't have the goods." He offered his hand.

"Thanks, Sandy," Ted said, shaking his hand. "I'm glad this is over. It's been tough on Mom." Karla smiled with relief and hugged him for a long moment.

"I'm sorry it had to happen at all," he replied and then sat to wipe the tears stinging the corners of his eyes.

Isaacs closed his briefcase. "I'll take care of the paperwork, Sandy. Abby, how about I take you to lunch? I think Sandy needs a moment to himself."

"You did it," Sophia whispered after everyone left. "You deadass did it!"

"No. I didn't do it. It's only round one," he said through tight lips. "I still want them to pay for medical fraud, holding Leif against his will and trying to kill me."

CHAPTER 46

Detective Sergeant Mary Kasson bustled into Jack's office like a wren to its nest. The plump, fifty-ish veteran detective in a bulky turtleneck sweater liked the nitty-gritty of investigations. Every other year or so, she declined promotions to positions that could take her a step away from the scene of a crime. She had mentored Jack when he was a rookie deputy and adored him because he was tall, dark, handsome—and smart. They knew each other's moods, and she was content with a genuine friendship uncomplicated by a romance.

"Good morning, Mary," he said. "Here's a cup of your usual." He handed her a mug of hot water and a tea bag. "Have you followed the Nielsen probate battle?"

She shook her head. "Not really. But I can tell you want me to."

"I'll get to that. For now, I want you to get up to speed on the backstory. My brother has his own sources—as usual," he said with a wry twist of his lips. So, talk to Boston. He knows the players. There are a couple angles to this story that require your attention. But do it with a light touch—"

"—Because of a commissioner and his political wife."

"Exactly. They just lost in probate court. The testimony raised several elements of interest to the county attorney. I hear there are lengthy briefs from both sides, and Glenda is likely to ask us to dig into them." Then he told her the lab was holding the drugs found at Nielsen's guesthouse as evidence. "Down the road, you may be putting together a case that includes a conspiracy to commit murder."

247

Kasson drew an excited breath, fished a notebook from her oversized purse and began making notes.

"The probate documents may have leads with regard to motive. Talk to Morrie Isaacs. I understand he has sworn statements from several people at the hospital and elsewhere, including Nielsen's daughter. Don't talk to Doctor Nielsen or his wife. Not yet. But talk to my brother. Keep it low-key."

"What are the drugs?"

"Prescription sedatives dispensed from an aspirin bottle. It's possible the doctor was holding his brother against his will. Nielsen got away a week after he quit taking them. Brewster can give you the details. Check the tox screen in the autopsy, the prescription and the when, for whom and by whom, etcetera. The murder investigation depends on finding a snowplow driver, the person who hired him and why. That should tell us if the wreck was deliberate or accidental."

Kasson finished her tea and shook her head. "I've got more than enough to get started. I see why you want to tread lightly." She entered her cluttered office, created several sets of files and started working on the accident. If she could find the driver, it might be possible to work her way up to the instigator. Sandy's statement to the highway patrolwoman had few details, except it happened fast inside a snow plume. The crash-site photos showed the car went off the road, but nothing confirmed a deliberate collision.

Kasson drove to the Johansson farm through the keen January wind. A stout woman about her age opened the door and offered coffee and brownies. Then she called her husband in from the barn.

"Oh, by golly," he spouted as he peeled off his barn coat and goulashes. "So, that crash wasn't just some accident, *huh?* Ya know, I thought there was somethin' strange about that one. Yessir, like I said to the missus…"

Kasson instantly realized that Johansson was an incorrigible talker. He had probably told everyone he knew about the accident. She felt equally certain he had embellished his version in the telling. He said they saw the car come out of the snow cloud and fly off the road just as a green pickup raced past them. He was positive it was a

1978 or 1979 three-quarter-ton GMC with dual back wheels, a row of yellow lights above the windshield and a burned-out tail light. The door had a company name in white letters, but he couldn't read it. The rear license plate started with an F, ended with a 6 with a Z in between.

"Well, we stopped, ya know. The missus went home to call the patrol, and I went down to check. Laying across the seat that way, he looked as dead as they come, for sure. I hear he's okay now. I swear, has to be the hand of God."

It didn't take Kasson long to draw all the reliable information out of him. Then she turned to Gudrun, who was more composed but had little to add beyond what he said. When their talk turned to family life, she thanked them for the coffee and left.

The Department of Motor Vehicles gave Kasson more than thirty green GMC trucks with plates that started with an F, ended with a 6 and had a Z in the middle. She spent hours on the phone whittling down the list to a couple dozen possibilities. Twenty were registered to locations more than a hundred miles from Wacouta. That left four pick-ups registered to owners in Wacouta, Rochester, Owatonna and Winona.

Kasson spent the next morning on the phone. The Rochester GMC had been in the shop at year's end, awaiting a new transmission. A farmer owned the Owatonna truck, but it didn't have a snowplow. The Winona truck belonged to a shopping mall, but it lacked dual back wheels. A Wacouta landscape service had one with plates that began with an F, had a Z and ended with a 6.

Kasson gave Jack a written report for the record and then a verbal summary. "I think we have enough evidence for a search warrant," she said. "The accident happened in our county, but the perp lives in Wacouta. We need a search warrant for the records of Riverside Lawn and Tree Service. I want to question the owner, a driver and impound the only green GMC that fits the description."

"What do you know about the owner?"

"He's got a record. Out of prison six years after serving five for assault. He's been clean since."

"Any connections of interest to us, like former cons or others?"

"We'll know when we question him and look at the employee roster. But here's an interesting tidbit. He had a top-notch attorney."

"So, c'mon, Mary, you're leading me," Jack laughed because she often teased him, and he usually enjoyed it.

"Well, his attorney was none other than Regina Nielsen's father."

"And your conclusion is—"

"—Oh, no conclusion," she said, feigning innocence with open hands. "He's entitled to the best lawyer he can afford—if he really can afford it."

"Keep that connection in your purse. I don't want it on the street unless we've actually got something. Which we don't. I'll get the search warrant."

The next morning, deputies Nathan Larson and Bud Schlitz stopped at the Wacouta police station and picked up a city officer to help them serve the warrant. They pulled up to Riverside Lawn and Tree Service next to a green GMC pickup with a snow blade.

"Willis Hanson," the Wacouta cop called when they entered the office.

"Yeah, that's me. What do you want?" called the stocky man with biceps that bulged his Vikings sweatshirt. The cramped office smelled of cigarette smoke. Posters covered its walls, and the calendar featured a topless Miss January seated on a Harley.

"My colleagues are deputies from Alton County. It's about a traffic accident. They have a warrant to search your office and impound a GMC truck, license eff, bee, zee, one, one six along with its service records, mileage log and customer roster. They also want to question you and the driver."

"Hey, my truck wasn't in no accidents."

"We've got a witness who says otherwise," Larson said.

"You can't take my truck. I can't afford to have it out of service, especially with more snow tomorrow."

"We want to question whoever drove it on December thirtieth."

"He's not here. Left for New Years. Then he had to stay because of a family emergency. Don't know when he'll be back."

"Give us his name and where he went. We've got ways to find him. And the sooner you cooperate, the sooner you'll get the truck back," Larson added. Then he picked up the desk phone and called for a tow truck.

"Any more stalling, and I'll arrest you for obstruction," the Wacouta officer said.

Hanson handed over the truck keys. Larson and Schlitz collected all the documents on the warrant while Hanson glowered from behind the counter and lit one Marlboro after another until the deputies were ready to question him.

Kasson briefed Jack after she and an assistant spent a day checking the records seized under warrant. They discovered the truck usually started plowing at four in the morning and finished its route at about one in the afternoon, depending on the snowfall. The driver had a regular sequence of customers he plowed—all of them within the city.

"Hardly the smoking gun, but it is definitely the right caliber," she said. "The truck logged ninety-six miles more than usual on the day of the accident. Roughly the round-trip distance from Wacouta to the accident site. I called some of the customers on the route. They said he didn't plow them until later in the day. Some are still sore about it."

"Who's the driver?"

"Gordy Diamond. He's also known as Gordy the Gimp because of his leg."

"Ex-con?"

"Well, *duh*. With a name like that, yeah. He has priors for assault and attempted murder. And here's another tidbit. He had the same attorney as his boss."

Jack pulled on his lower lip as he digested this. "Two small-time cons had the same big-bucks attorney. There must be more to the connections." He sat back and smiled at Kasson. She was a frumpy, easy-to-overlook woman, but his admiration of her went all the way to genuine affection.

"I think so," she said. "We've got a lead on the Gimp somewhere in Detroit. Their cops are on it." She knit her brows. "Jack, tell me if

I'm in la-la-land for thinking Regina may have hired one of her dad's clients to take out Brewster."

Jack shook his head. "Harald can't inherit a ten-million-dollar farm unless Brewster is out of the way." That's what he loved about Mary. She was discrete but didn't tip-toe away from tough questions. "From what I know of the doctor, I doubt he has criminal connections or intentions. Between us, someone else arranged the hit. Hold that thought until we hear what the driver has to say."

The Detroit police caught up with Diamond, and the deputies booked him into the Alton County jail several days later. The Gimp sat in the basement room with stone walls, metal chairs and fluorescent lights. Kasson made him wait until he began fidgeting. He danced as she probed, telling her one story after another. Someone called Hanson, and Hanson told him to follow the car and report where it went. He followed it until he lost sight of it during the white-out. Later, he told Hanson the car had escaped him.

Kasson ordered him held for suspected assault and asked for Hanson's arrest. Then, she and Jack considered their options. "Unless one of them flips, we're stuck," she said. "So far, we don't have enough to hold either one beyond forty-eight hours. Once free, we may not get them again."

"We both have a hunch who hired him, at least indirectly. Let's put it to a test."

CHAPTER 47

Mornings were sacred to Boston, and he savored the tranquility. He and Ginger rose early so she had time to say her morning prayers, meditate and practice yoga before breakfast. Boston normally walked when it was too cold to run, but this morning was too cold even for walking. His phone rang a few minutes before 8:00 a.m. He picked up the call and barked, "Meade here."

"Good morning, brother," Jack called, sounding more cheerful than anyone had a right to. "Hope I didn't wake you."

"It's still early, asshole," Boston grumbled, pulling the bathrobe closer around him. He coughed to clear the sleep from his throat. "What do you want?"

"Got a hot tip related to Brewster's accident. Stop by when you're in." Kasson wasn't the only one who used "the tease" and Boston fell for it—again.

"I'll see you at nine," he said. "Have coffee for me—fresh this time."

He hung up in a better mood. So much for a cozy day in his PJs, he thought as he dressed in extra layers. The last week of January was usually the coldest of the year, and this morning's temperature felt like an early down payment on that. Colored prismatic bars of ice crystals flanked the sun that seemed in no hurry to rise. Even in the carriage barn, the Jeep needed coaxing to start. "God, it's colder than a witch's tit," he muttered and left it running with the heater on full while he waited in the house for it to warm up.

Jack handed him a mug of office coffee, somewhat fresher than the last time he stopped. "We've got the snowplow driver and his boss. They're both ex-cons who did time for assault."

"So, what's the rest of the story?"

"They both had the same attorney in their priors—Winthrop Belton."

"And who is Belton?" He suspected Jack was playing with him.

"Don't you know? He's Regina Nielsen's father." Jack grinned as if he had just scored a point.

"So, maybe she went through daddy's Rolodex for the expert she needed."

"Possibly. Now, we don't want to get ahead of ourselves. So far, they're saying they were hired to follow Brewster. Neither admits anything definite. Diamond said he lost sight of him in a white-out. It's a 'maybe I did, maybe I didn't' game for a deal."

"You think she hired him?"

"Doubt it. At least not directly. She's too clever. I'm told she strikes with the hidden hand, like Lucrezia Borgia. More likely, she hired an intermediary who contacted Hanson. It might be someone else her father represented." Jack shoved a folder of information toward him.

The revelation intrigued Boston. In his only encounter with the woman, he had gained an impression that she was cold, domineering and manipulative but not necessarily a murderer. Not firsthand, at least.

"Oh, so you want a story in the *Statesman* to flush a bird from cover."

"You read my mind."

"Well, that's never been difficult."

"Oh, fuck you," Jack laughed.

Telling the story straight was always Boston's ideal, and he wanted to tell stories that helped his readers. The monthly column for *American Outlook* put bread on the table, but he wrote for a national readership of people he would never meet. A story in the *Statesman* affected people he knew and who knew him. And though that pleased him, collaborating with Jack might have unintended consequences.

He waited until supper to tell Ginger that two suspects in Brewster's accident were detained in the county jail. "Think it's worth a paragraph?" he asked, careful not to overstep his promise to stay out of running the paper.

"Jack wants this—right?" She scowled. "Yeah, well, I sometimes worry about the ethics of this. Worry, mind you, but I haven't lost sleep over it. Not lying next to you. It is news, but the story is really aimed at an audience of one. And between you and Jack, I sometimes feel like an arm of the sheriff's department."

"Well, if that's how you feel, I'll ask Jack to give you a badge so—"

She hit him with her wadded napkin, stuck out her tongue and laughed. Then, she left for the weekly AA meeting at St. Paul's Lutheran Church.

He worked up a brief story about the criminal career of Gordy the Gimp and his connection to Hanson and his career. Everything he wrote came from a public record or the sheriff's department. The firm of Belton, Hampstead and Shea were their last attorneys of record. He called the firm for a comment, but they refused, citing client privilege. Good enough, he thought. Now I can insert the Belton name.

Harald hadn't slept for more than two hours at a stretch since the court affirmed Leif's will. Ten million dollars was gone, but so what, he thought. We already have more than enough for a comfortable life. It's not the money. It's Detective Kasson's questions about the sedative prescription dispensed from the aspirin bottle. Then the state medical practice board called. If they get involved, goodbye to an invitation from the Mayo doctors, he fretted. Might lose my license. With it, the clinic and the pharmacy. Sedating him wasn't my idea, but I had to fill the prescription and hire Mabel. She followed orders, so I can't blame her. If only I'd ignored Regina. But I could never do that. Never in our married life have I said "no" and made it stick. Too late now, he thought, loathing himself for weakness. I wished we hadn't married. Then he heard the garage door rise and shut. That's her, he thought and felt his stomach tighten.

"Well, tell me, where are we today," she demanded upon entering the salon.

"Where we were yesterday, except I had a call from the medical practice board."

"Bureaucrats," she said with a dismissive hiss.

"I don't think I can avoid sanctions. I'll be lucky to keep my license." But he could tell she wasn't in the mood for a martini or to worry about his career.

"Stop thinking of yourself and think of us," she scolded. "Now that he owns the farm, we have to remove him before he concludes the sale. He's young enough that he probably doesn't have a will."

"Regina, what are you talking about? It's over."

"Oh, shut up! There is risk, and there is reward. Timing is everything. It can be done if we work fast."

"You had a… a… call today at the clinic," he said. "I… I took down the number. He wants you to call him back."

"Well, give me his name."

"He wouldn't give it. Just a number. Why would he call you at the clinic? What's going on behind my back?"

"Mind your own business. I don't ask about your patients—don't ask me about my clients." She turned on her heel and stalked down the hall to her personal office.

There's no way to remove Sandy, he thought. Not unless… and then he sucked in his breath. That wasn't an accident! It was attempted murder. The realization shook him. Regina uses my clinic phone because… the conclusion terrified him. She isn't going to defend me. Not now. She's hanging me out to dry. It's all set up, so I'll take the fall when it comes. Panic overtook him because he couldn't think of any defense. Feeling his bowels move, he rushed to the bathroom just in time. When he came out, she was talking quietly to someone on her private phone, but he couldn't make out her words. He took an antacid and prepared for another troubled night.

Regina remained abed in the morning until after Harald left. Then she picked up the day's editions of the *Statesman, Minneapolis Star-Tribune* and *The Wall Street Journal* that he had left on the bench by the front door. She read them in the breakfast nook with her first cup of coffee.

ASSAULT SUSPECT IN CUSTODY. The two-paragraph piece said Willis Hanson and Gordon Diamond were under investigation in connection with Sanford Brewster's auto accident on December 30. The article said the Belton law firm was the men's attorney of record, but it refused to comment on their arrests. Her hand trembled and rattled the coffee cup in its saucer.

"Oh God," she groaned. "Meade has connected them to Daddy. It won't take long to connect them to me." Regina sipped the coffee slowly and considered her options. Daddy won't say anything, but if I don't act now, I'll be in real trouble. Meade has all but printed my name. He'll do to me what he did to the Ferralls unless I get rid of him, now. And Brewster, too.

She closed her eyes and heard her father's voice saying, the guy you hired to line up Hanson and Diamond isn't the one to do it. No, you need either a real pro or a patsy. Either way, you've got to stay above suspicion. Denial won't be enough. You'll have to lean on political connections for cover. You better look at Harald. He's coming apart a little piece at a time. A little more pressure, and he'll crack. He's your biggest threat. You've made him successful, but he's never done anything for you but make money with your ideas. You don't owe him another thing. Not now.

Regina opened her eyes, set aside the paper and weighed her options. Harald is under investigation, not me. I'm still in the clear. So, Harald owes me a favor. It's risky, but it will keep me in the clear.

CHAPTER 48

The message light on Sandy's office phone was blinking when he entered 301. It was a call from the provost asking him to stop at his office as soon as possible. As he entered, the taciturn official in a gray suit cracked a smile and held out his hand. "Your references backed you up and then some. The tenure vote is on for Wednesday afternoon."

"Thank God," he said and sank into a chair.

"After your lawyer talked to the regents, they felt embarrassed and asked me to convey their apologies. One asked if there was something he could do—"

"—*Yes*, there is something. I'm donating sixty thousand dollars for scholarships to the environmental studies program. It's an anonymous donation. I'd like each of them to at least match it with their money."

"Well, that's generous of you but—"

"—But it's the least they can do. What's the best way to approach them."

"I'll take that up with the president. Good luck on Wednesday."

Sandy dashed across the quad through the ankle-deep snow and bounded up the stairs to 301. Maybe the provost wasn't the jerk he imagined him to be. He had no doubt that Regina had played her last card and lost again. For the first time in months, he felt free of the churning uncertainty over the future—his and the farm's.

Sophia was prepping for class when he burst into the office and spun her around in the chair. "The tenure vote... it's Wednesday," he said, out of breath. "The provost called my contacts… everything is all right. Thanks for standing by me," he said and wrapped her in his arms.

"What a relief," she sighed, holding him.

"I feel so good. Come to dinner tonight," he said. "And stay for breakfast." It was hardly an invitation now.

"You know, the tenure vote isn't the only news on campus. Our affair isn't a secret anymore," she said. "Some of the women think you are happier than they remember. A regular Petruchio—the old Sandy. What caused that, *hmm?*" she teased and put a finger to her puckered lips.

"Yeah, it's probably obvious," he replied. "Especially since women have said you've changed. Your critiques are hilarious, and they noticed you talk about the domestic stuff you used to diss as trivial. And everyone—and I mean everyone—notices you've upgraded your outfits. Now you don't look like an Italian nun. Why's that?"

On Wednesday, while the students wrestled with their first quizzes, the faculty committee voted to recommend a grant of tenure to Associate Professor Sanford Brewster. He took the decision with gratitude, but it felt like an anti-climax. A relief but not a surprise. He went home, called his mother with the news and then Isaacs. After a change of clothing, he walked back to campus for the celebration thrown by the History and American Studies departments. Most of the faculty attended, including the dean, provost and president. He wished Leif could have been there to see it. That would have made it perfect.

He finished his last class on Friday afternoon, gathered his mail and Sophia's from the departmental mailboxes and carried it to their office. The January daylight had already died, the campus was nearly dark and the building was quiet. He sorted the mail and then sat atop his desk to look at brochures for winter conferences in warm locales.

Sophia leafed through her mail and moaned softly.

"Bad news?" he asked.

"Yes… it is," she sighed. "A memo from the dean. We're moving into our renovated offices next week. We'll be on different floors. It's the end of our cozy nest."

He stared at her for a moment and then gave her a rakish smile. Hopping off the desk, he bolted the door and turned off the lights.

"What are you doing?"

"Let's go out with a bang," he said, putting his arms around her and easing her back against the desk. While they kissed, he slid his hands under her skirt and up her thighs. "I want you," he whispered. "If we don't do it right now, we'll regret it."

"Oh, you mean this kind of a bang," she laughed and unzipped his fly.

"Is there a better one?"

CHAPTER 49

Water was already dripping from the eaves when Harald stepped outside after breakfast. The temperature had risen in the night, and the sun shone through a milky haze. It might be the late January thaw the weather geeks predicted. Normally, it would cheer him up, but not today. The mysterious phone call to Regina at the clinic and her muted call from the house last night worried him. *She's up to something.* If she used the clinic phone, it's because… but he didn't like the direction of that thought. The way she set things up, he felt as if he had a noose around his neck, and she might spring the trapdoor. *But would she do that after all these years?* He ignored the question and gave his patients extra attention. *Maybe I'm overreacting. Just a case of heebie-jeebies.*

When he returned home, she met him at the door in winter boots and the heavy wolfskin parka. "Let's go for a walk before cocktails," she said and flashed the first smile he had seen in weeks. "Come on," she said, taking his arm. "It feels like spring."

"*Uh*, okay," he said, uncertain whether her cheer was real. *Oh well, it was a better reaction than he expected.* Right now, he was glad to take what he could get.

The snowdrifts had settled during the day's thaw, and the streets were ankle-deep in slush. Joggers and walkers had packed the river path into a slick, lumpy crust that was beginning to freeze. They crossed the street to the path, and Harald reeled unsteadily in street shoes. Now and then, he windmilled his arms and grabbed Regina to keep his balance. They paused for a moment to talk to a neighbor who was helping his boy build a snowman. Crows cawed in the distance. She pointed to the sky and the thin strands of pastel clouds. "It feels like spring," she said lightly. "If only it were so."

They arrived at the footbridge. She took his arm and hauled him with her to the center of the span, where the ice-free current slipped silently between the icy shelves along the banks as far as the pool at the logjam.

"Harald, you're a failure," she said suddenly in a cold, even voice. "Everything you've done to get the farm has failed. You let Leif get away. You botched the medical records. Brewster didn't die. He won probate and then got tenure. My regent colleagues aren't speaking to me. The medical board is investigating you. Now Meade has linked my dad to the snowplow driver. It's all because you are a failure. You've got one chance to clean up your mess."

"My mess! They were your ideas. What's going on? Who called you at the clinic? I demand to know. It's my neck."

"You have to get rid of Brewster and Meade. If you don't, you'll lose your license and go to prison. It's your only way out—that or suicide."

"*What!* I can't… I won't kill anyone. I took an oath… I'd rather go to prison."

"I can't allow that," she said. "Kill them or jump—"

"—I'm your husband," he said, raising his voice.

"Husband—some husband," she sneered. "A real husband has balls. Like my Dad. That's something you don't have and never did. Not even in bed," she sneered. "I got those needs met with real men— candidates like your friend Jorgenson and even your associate," she smirked.

"*What.* My… why?" Harald gasped in short, shallow breaths.

"You can't get anything unless you fight for it. You've never fought for anything. Everything you've got—your practice, the clinic, the pharmacy, mayor, commissioner, the house—you got it because I planned it. I fought for it," she said through clenched teeth. "You're nothing without me. And now you're nothing to me." She pulled a small automatic pistol from the coat pocket.

"You, you're crazy…" he stammered.

"Back up," she ordered, waving the gun. "You've failed. Ruined us. I've waited too long. I've got to cut my losses. Now, back up."

He stepped back, palms up, afraid but suddenly clear-headed.

"Climb on the railing," she ordered. "Drowning won't hurt."

"Wait," he said, glancing over his shoulder at the six-foot drop into the open water.

She put the muzzle of the gun against his coat. As she pushed him against the rail, his feet slipped. He grabbed her arm. She lost her footing. For a moment, they whirled about on the icy span like dancers in a deadly pirouette.

Harald entered the big house alone. This was the maid's night off, and he reveled in having the place to himself. He mixed a snifter of equal parts rum and Coke because it reminded him of his carefree frat life before he met Regina. Then he lounged in the darkened living room wearing only underwear. He drank it quickly, downed a second and lost track. How many did I have, he wondered. Two or three? He shook his head. Let's see, I said something to the guy with the snowman. It was twilight. Now it's dark. Then someone pounded on the front door. He burped, got up and opened it.

"Doctor Nielsen, please come with us," one of the Waterford officers said.

"Oh, ish you," he said, wavering on his feet. "Wha' took you sho long? I bin waitin'. Lemme finish thish, pleash. I may neber get anudder." It went down in two gulps. He wiped his mouth and held out his wrists to be cuffed.

"Please get dressed," the officer said. "At least, put on some pants." They knew him and were polite because he had treated them and their children. They put him in a cell at the Waterford police station until the city's detective arrived. Two men, both professionals and acquaintances, looked at each other for a moment across a small table without speaking. Harald felt the change in their relationship.

"Have you been drinking?" the detective asked.

"Yesh. Rum 'n Coke. You like it?"

"Were you drinking before your wife disappeared?"

"No. Cold shtone shober. I drank after that. Schelebrating."

"Do you know where your wife is?"

"Yesh, schumplace hot. She and I are in better playshes now."

CHAPTER 50

News of Regina's death reached Sandy in a call from his mother. Abigail had no details about the death except she drowned, and Harald was in jail and under arrest. "Some news moves fast in a small town," he said, turning to Sophia. Then he exhaled a loud breath. "What a sad ending. I'm surprised I don't feel any joy over it. Guess I'm not good at nursing a grudge."

"No, you aren't. And we wouldn't be together if you were."

"Well, I better make some calls," he said and dialed Isaacs, who hadn't heard about it. "Hard to believe how this turned out. It's like God came down and smote the wicked or something like that."

"Remember, I told you justice and vengeance aren't the same thing. There's more to justice than the law," he replied. "There's your proof. Things tend to balance in their own good time. I'm happy to hear you aren't gloating."

Sandy said goodnight to the lawyer and called Karla, uncertain exactly what to say but certainly not condolences over Regina's death. She said the police had already called her with the news. "After all that's happened, I don't quite know what to say," he began. "I feel sorry for Harald. Why, I don't know. He's lost everything. His wife, profession, clinic, pharmacy, the house—everything."

"I know," she said. "He wasn't a strong man, but on his own, he could be a good man at times. His intentions were good, but he didn't have the courage to stand by them. I guess it's a lesson for all of us. And however it happened, she got what she deserved."

After that, news of Regina's death moved across the county by telephone before the *Statesman* could report it. Boston heard about it from Jack, who said he didn't have the full story yet. All he knew was that a neighbor heard her scream, and Harald made a cryptic remark about it. He admitted doing nothing to rescue her.

"Is it tied to the probate challenge or Brewster's accident?" Boston asked.

"We're still looking at that. No connections so far between Harald and Diamond. Someone made calls from the clinic, but Harald was at the hospital when they occurred. It appears Diamond was Regina's gambit, but we may never know for sure. Not unless we find the intermediary."

Waterford's residents let out a collective gasp, followed by a blizzard of rumors. A few in town said, "Good riddance," including several aspiring GOP candidates who had run afoul of her. No one talked of arranging a memorial service. The *Statesman* reported that she drowned, but the sheriff's department was unable to locate and recover her body. Harald was in jail pending charges but cooperating with the police investigation into the accident. Some thought Harald was innocent and had been used or framed or set up. Worried patients called the clinic asking if they would have to find a new doctor. The crassly curious speculated on the chateau's price and who might buy it.

The district court scheduled the trial of Harald Nielsen for second-degree homicide and manslaughter for 9:00 a.m. on the Ides of March. The courtroom seats filled up by 8:15 a.m., and a small crowd waited in the corridor. Boston arrived early, flashed his press pass and took a seat beneath the WPA mural where he could see the faces of County Attorney Glenda Mercer, Harald, Sam Willard and another attorney he didn't know. Karla, Ted, Abigail and Sandy sat near the front. He saw Isaacs slip in and sit at the back with the clutch of onlookers. Reporters who came late stood along the walls.

Boston scribbled quick notes as the deputies brought in the accused: "Nielsen. Relaxed, tranquil, as if about to nap. Appears 20 lbs. lighter." He saw no sign of the intense anxiety visible at the probate hearing. Then the bailiff called, "All rise," as Judge Knatvold entered.

"This honorable court is now in session," the judge said and banged the gavel. "Mister Willard, in the matter of *Minnesota v. Harald Nielsen*, does your client still desire a bench trial?"

Willard and Harald stood. "Yes, your honor, but against my counsel."

The request for a bench trial puzzled Boston. Any jury would probably include former patients and others who supported him as mayor. He would need only one or two holdouts for a mistrial. There was only circumstantial evidence. And what there was had enough ambiguity that the county probably wouldn't try the case after a mistrial. With so little solid evidence against him, a bench trial made no sense.

County Attorney Glenda Mercer stood and looked squarely at the judge. "The defendant's claim of self-defense has no evidence to support it. We will prove the charges are justified because of the defendant's depraved indifference to his wife's peril and his failure to aid her."

Boston noted Mercer's appearance at the moment: "Woman, indeterminant middle-age, short, stout, dark pin-stripe suit. Commanding voice, stronger than the judges." He wondered if Mercer believed the argument she was advancing.

In a smooth, avuncular voice, Willard said the defense would show Regina died of accidental drowning after falling into the river during a scuffle when she attempted to kill the defendant after he refused her order to kill Mister Meade and Doctor Brewster or commit suicide. He said Harald slipped, they struggled for the gun, and then she fell into the river, where the current carried her under the ice before Harald could act.

Mercer then began to dismantle the defense. She said the police didn't recover a gun, so there was no evidence except Harald's claim that she forced him onto the bridge. No one heard her order him to kill anyone. It seemed unlikely she accidentally fell into the river because the railing was too high. However, the state could prove the defendant did not call for help or do anything to rescue the deceased from drowning. That was sufficient to justify a charge of second-degree murder.

Mercer called the arresting officer and the detective who testified to Harald's drunken celebration of her death. Both said he was drunk and elated when arrested. Then she put the neighbor on the stand. "We exchanged pleasantries when they passed," he said. "Fifteen minutes later, I heard a scream. Then silence. A few minutes later, Harald passed us. I asked where Regina was. He said she was under the ice where she belonged." Mercer rested her case.

Willard's defense rested on the neighbor's confirmation that the path was slippery and the Nielsens were chatting happily when they passed him. Though the neighbor heard their voices, he didn't know what they were saying. Several minutes passed between their voices and the scream. He called the police because he thought Harald was in shock and in no condition to do it.

The judge called a recess for lunch.

The attorneys made their closing arguments that afternoon. Mercer made a brief but pointed close, saying there was no evidence that Harald was in danger or acted in self-defense. And while there were no witnesses at the scene, it was undisputed that he made no attempt to call for help or rescue his wife. Further, his statements to the neighbor and the police indicated malice, if not culpability.

"This case is thin," Boston wrote. "Mercer has only inference and circumstance but no motive. Willard has the upper hand."

It was mid-afternoon when Willard smoothed his tie and began the summation. "We who knew Regina recognized her as an energetic and resourceful member of the community. Her death is a great loss to us all. She and her husband, Harald, were leaders who generously gave time and talent to the county. The prosecution would have you believe her husband callously allowed her to drown. But the prosecution has only two witnesses, neither of whom actually saw her death. In fact, he slipped as they stood on the bridge and fell into her arms. As they struggled to get their footing, she fell backward into the river. A scream is the natural reaction to falling. The current is swift and deep at the bridge. Her heavy fur coat and rubber boots dragged her down. The distance to the pool is short, and her fall happened so fast, Harald had no way to reach her before she vanished. He was in shock and said things wholly outside his character. I ask the court to dismiss the charges—"

"—Your honor," Harald called and stood. "I have something to say."

"Mister Willard, before I permit the defendant to speak, I think you should caution him about the consequences."

Willard huddled with Harald for a moment and shook his head. Then he stood. "Your honor, my client wishes to make a statement despite my caution."

"Granted," the judge said. Then Harald took his oath and sat in the witness chair.

"All right, Doctor Nielsen," the judge said. "Tell us what you wish to say."

He squared his shoulders, looked at the judge and then at the crowd in the courtroom. "I want to set the record straight. Regina and I wanted title to my brother's farm to develop it, but he gave it to Sandy Brewster to prevent that. When the court upheld the will, she became obsessed with removing him. I believe she used my clinic phone to hire Mister Diamond to kill him. But I can offer no proof but the phone record." He paused for a moment, took a breath and licked his lips. "On the day she died, we walked to the footbridge and stopped. She said she had to cut her losses. Killing Sandy Brewster and Boston Meade was my only way out. That or suicide. When I refused, she pulled a gun I didn't know she owned. Then she ordered me to get on the railing and jump. When I didn't, she pushed me back. I lost my balance and fell into her. She dropped the gun as we struggled for footing, and she fell back against the railing."

"What happened then?" the judge asked.

"I grabbed her ankles and boosted her up and over."

"Why?" Judge Knatvold asked as observers let out a collective gasp.

"To do right by my brother… to regain my self-respect."

The judge rapped the gavel to quiet the spectators' murmur. "Anything more you want to say?"

"She was afraid of water. The current took her. In less than a minute, her legs slid under the ice covering the pool. She hung on to the edge of the shelf. We looked at each other for a moment. Then the ice broke, and she vanished. I threw the gun in the river and walked home."

Willard stood. "The defense rests, your honor."

"The prosecution rests," Mercer added.

Judge Knatvold recessed the trial for an hour. Boston watched Harald, who seemed composed, almost serene. When the judge returned, he ordered the defendant to rise with all the gravity his thin voice could muster. The defendant and lawyer stood, and Boston thought Willard seemed more nervous than the accused.

"You requested a bench trial," the judge began. "Your attorney has done his best to defend you. The county attorney has done her best to find the truth and see justice served. I take your free will statement as the truth in this case. Therefore, based on the evidence presented in accordance with your own words, I find you guilty of the second-degree murder of your wife, Regina Belton Nielsen. You are remanded into the custody of the county until sentencing. Court is adjourned."

Boston watched as the deputies cuffed Harald and walked him out. The spectators crowded out the door. Those who hoped for the legal fireworks were probably disappointed. Neither attorney seemed eager to savage the other. Instead, they reminded him of dancers performing a legal cotillion for an outcome that neither wanted. He watched Willard shove papers into his briefcase. Then he and Mercer talked for a moment. From a distance, they appeared to be old friends. She gave him what looked like a sympathetic smile, patted his arm and packed up her briefcase. Then he saw Isaacs slip out.

Sandy, Ted and Karla stood about talking like three old friends when Boston left his seat. "Mind if I join you," he asked.

"Please do," Sandy said. "We're going for coffee at the Streamliner. We'd love to hear your take on this." They seemed sad more than triumphant.

Seated beside Karla, Boston noticed something like a cloud drifting across her face. "Are you all right?"

"Yeah, I'm okay, but…" she sighed. "What a sad ending. I never liked Regina because she liked no one but herself. I think she married him because she could dominate him—treat him like dirt without repercussions. She didn't want a husband, she wanted a flunky, like Igor. I can't believe he really meant to kill her, but I believe he regained his self-respect, as horrible as it is."

"He was under a lot of pressure," Sandy said. "Probably felt complicit in Leif's death. Probate exposed him as a fraud. His medical practice was under a microscope. Regina demanded something and he said no. Maybe he saw who he had become and wanted redemption."

"Interesting that you say that," Karla added. "Yesterday, I spent an hour with him at the jail. He apologized for trying to steal the farm. He thinks he'll get twelve years but might serve less with good behavior. He seemed happy. When I asked him why, he said this is the first time in his life he really knows who he is."

CHAPTER 51

The suitcase lay open on Sandy's bed as Sophia packed some spring clothing. She still had an apartment but had moved in with him after the accident. It feels like we've always been together, she thought as she closed the suitcase and lugged it downstairs to the front door. "I wish I didn't have to go," she said as he put the case in his car for the drive to Minneapolis airport.

"Me too, but it's only a week. And this visit is important."

"I know, but I'm mad at myself for letting Mama and Papa put the guilts on me."

"This is your chance to end it. I'm with you. Call if you need support."

As much as he selfishly wished she would stay, he hoped even more that she would confront the cloud of Papa problems that hung over them.

When she didn't call him, spring break seemed even longer. He met the flight at the Minneapolis airport and drove south along the Mississippi River to Wacouta through a light rain. She bubbled over with stories, happy to be with him again. They settled into the house and drank wine before the fire. He was eager to hear about her family.

"Oh, still the same," she said, trying to blow it off. "Haven't changed a whit."

"That's what I'm getting at. We both know you have unfinished business with your father. I hope you made progress."

"Damn you. I just got here. Now you're giving me the frickin' third degree about it. It's none of your goddamn business. I'll sleep in my apartment tonight."

"Sit down," he ordered and pressed on her shoulder. "You've been dodging these questions since the day we moved into 301. If we are to have a future, I need to know how you really feel."

"Is this about trust?"

"You're damned right it is. I need to know if you trust me enough to share your feelings about your father and men in general. I don't want to live with your unresolved anger. It's toxic."

This is it, Sophia thought as she forced all the air out of her lungs. She breathed in and stuck out her chin and felt her face twitch, knowing she couldn't put it off. He's not going to let me off the hook.

"Tell me something you like about your father," he asked.

"When I was a little girl, I felt safe around Papa because he was big and had answers for everything—even when he didn't. He's spontaneous, emotional, romantic, always the master of ceremonies and loves being the center of attention. He plays with children, anyone's children. He makes them laugh." She smiled.

"Sounds like a fine father. Full of fun."

"Yes, as long as it's his… his rules."

"Oh, you mean, like Leif's two ways to do things, his way and the wrong way."

"*Ya huh*. His opinions are the only ones that matter. He does a lot of cooking and sings when he cooks… in Italian, of course. He says men are chefs and women are merely cooks. Men are composers because women lack the talent."

"You're a scholar, an author, a professor. People across the country respect your work. How does he treat you?"

Her expression darkened even more. "It means little to him. I'm his *bella Sophia la zitella*, the old maid." She spat out the words. "When I got my doctorate, he didn't toast my achievement. He said, 'may you marry soon and bless us with many *nipotis*'— that's grandchildren."

She bit her lip, but the tears streamed down her cheeks. A log fell from the fire dogs and sent sparks up the chimney. He put his arm around her, but she pushed him away. "No, I don't want your pity."

They stared at the flames licking the logs. She clenched her fists. Then buried her face in his shoulder.

"And your mother?"

"Mama is reasonable, compassionate. She's proud of me… encourages me when Papa's not around." She wiped her eyes and sniffled. "She rarely disagrees with him. Instead, she tries to keep the peace. It would be different if she asserted herself like your mother. She could do it, but she doesn't know how."

He considered the fact they had both avoided saying an explicit "I love you." But he knew their bond ran much deeper than merely sharing a bed. Sooner or later, it had to be said. But not tonight. They had to get past a question. "Whom do you take after?"

"I'm not like either of them."

"Oh, I think you are," he said in a soft voice. "Everything you've told me points to that."

"Well, if you're so frickin' smart, tell me, whom do *you* think I take after?"

"You're the reverse image of your father. He thinks men are superior. You flip that and demean men to prove that women are equal if not superior."

He saw a sudden fury blaze in her dark eyes and put up his hand to stop her protest. "You love and hate your father at the same time. You love your mother and fear you'll end up like her. Not all men are like your father—"

"—Most of them are," she pouted. "Except you."

"And not all women are like your mother," he said, unable to tell if her rage was aimed at him, her father or all men. No matter, the boil had to be lanced.

"You *bastard*," she screamed. "Look what you've done." She jumped off the couch and picked up her coat. "Things were so good. Now—"

"—What's changed? We're talking about your family. That's all."

She stood with the coat in her hand and sobbing so hard her shoulders shook. "It's not you," she blubbered. "It's them."

He took the coat and led her back to the couch. "It's all right," he whispered. "You're all right. Nothing's going to hurt you."

"I don't want to be my mother, and I don't want to be the reverse of Papa."

"You aren't—you are you. But you can't hold onto the anger forever. It leaks out, and I feel it."

"Like what?"

"Sarcasm, barbs, snide remarks… pent-up anger hurts you and me, too."

She stared into the fire for a long time as the flames licked at the wood, and she chewed her lips. "Oh God," she moaned. "I've been angry with him for years. I've never confronted him. Just kept my mouth shut."

"He doesn't know how you feel."

"No, I've never told him." She sighed, and her shoulders dropped. "I'm disgusted with myself."

"You're an adult. I think it's time to say something—one adult to another."

"I don't know if I—"

"—Standing your own ground, that's what you say it means to be equal."

"You *are* a sonofabitch," she cried. "You're deadass sticking it to me—put up or shut up. That's it, isn't it?" she snapped. "I want to hate you, but I can't."

"I don't want a future for us filled with free-floating anger. It'll poison us. I let go of Becky because I want to go forward with you. Either you hang on to your old hurts, or you grasp our future. One or the other—but choose one. And soon."

She knew he meant it and let out a long, loud breath. "You're right. I've been avoiding it. I thought I'd be all right if I got away from him. It doesn't work." She put her head on his shoulder and groaned softly. "I feel like a frickin' hypocrite."

278

"Hey, easy on yourself. You aren't a hypocrite. Just a late bloomer."

"I feel so… so naked."

"You're beautiful…"

CHAPTER 52

Plans for the Leif Nielsen Environmental Studies Center advanced. Sandy persuaded the program to offer Karla a seat on its board of advisors as an integral part of the program. Not only as Leif's daughter but because she took a risk to make the center possible. Meanwhile, Sophia and the scholarship committee completed their decisions on financial aid requests. Before the college sent Ted its official acceptance, Sandy and Sophia felt it needed some ceremony. Karla welcomed them into her townhouse with coffee, and they talked about the upcoming dedication of the environmental center.

"Come sit by me, Ted," Sophia said and patted the sofa. "I haven't talked to you since the burial." He glanced at his mother and took a seat beside her. "I'm vice chair of the Seabury scholarship committee. We were all impressed with your application. Especially your essay. So it is my honor to tell you the committee chose you to receive the first four-year environmental studies scholarship."

Ted's mouth dropped open, then closed and then opened again. He looked at his mother with the large, innocent eyes of a calf. Karla reached out, put her hand under his chin and kissed him.

"*Wow*," he hooted. "That's awesome! Like I can never thank you enough."

"Ted, you did the important part of it yourself," Sophia said. "Besides your grades and accomplishments, your essay on the cultural importance of environmental protection put you way over the top."

"When we filled out the applications, we wondered, you know, would it happen," Karla began.

"I know," Sandy said. "It had to be that way. Now, there's something else, and I don't want it to overshadow Ted's news. But besides the money Leif left you, you will receive twenty thousand dollars from the sale of the farm for your own use."

"Thank you," she whispered as her mouth gaped open. "Now I can finish law school. But... but what about you. You deserve something."

"I already got it during the years I spent with your dad."

Dedication of the Leif Nielsen Center was scheduled for the farmhouse on the first Saturday in June. Sandy and Sophia went to clean and air the building over the Memorial Day weekend. Dressed in shorts and T-shirts, they opened the windows to flush out the warm, musty air. Then he began sweeping out mouse droppings, cobwebs, dead flies and dust. Sophia bound her hair in a large scarf and attacked the filmy kitchen windows. Then she washed the sink, cupboards, stove and refrigerator until they gained a presentable patina. She hated housework because it consisted of menial tasks, and it seemed only women did it—mostly by women lacking talent. It was only out of love for Sandy that she got on her knees and scrubbed the kitchen's linoleum floor.

Then she gasped as if in sudden pain at the realization she discounted women based on what they did. I've judged them by their titles. That's hierarchy. Just like the patriarchy. She paused in wonder at the thought. What entitles me to more respect than a charwoman, she asked? Right now, I'm both. Cleaning is necessary, so it isn't demeaning. And I'm not less for doing it. You frickin' fool! I bought into the hierarchy without knowing it. Well, now I know, girl. She stood and looked around the kitchen, proud of what she had done. Overcome with joy at this revelation, she tuned the radio to an oldies station and returned to scrubbing. The grime didn't give up without a fight, and neither did she. On her knees, she scoured the linoleum, happily rocking her bottom in time with the music.

Sandy spent hours on the mower cutting the grass around the house, then along the driveway, the gravesite and some walking trails along the shore and the prairie. He entered the kitchen unseen and stood behind Sophia and watched her derriere groove to the beat of *My Girl*. "Wow," he said. "That's one gorgeous sight."

Startled, she turned and looked at him over her shoulder. "Meaning what?"

"I've never seen such a… such a clean kitchen floor."

"Oh yeah, right," she said and got to her feet. "You're a liar."

"I meant that."

"Well *damn*, I was hoping you were admiring my ass."

"I do," he said, running his hands over it.

"Not until we're done," she giggled and pushed him away. "Work before play. If I were running this, you'd be scrubbing the floor, and I'd be on the mower."

"Yeah, but seeing you barefoot in the kitchen brings out your sexy femi—" but a wet rag stifled the rest.

They sat on the porch and drank beers with their lunch before returning to work. When the heat broke later that afternoon, a fresh breeze shivered on the lake's surface. Gazing across the water, Sophia tried to measure the emotional distance she had traveled in Sandy's company. We've been through so much together so fast. Is the idea of a commitment still closed, she wondered. Is it time to reconsider independence? We're comfortable living together. I'm forty-one, he's thirty-nine, and it's too late to think about children. Maybe a commitment is compatible with independence. He has all but said it, and I know how he feels. I made the first move before, and I won't wait now. It's time to say—

"—Hey, help me get the canoe out of the shed," he called from the barn door.

His request upended her thoughts. She wanted to talk about their future, but not when his mind was elsewhere. He lifted the canoe onto his shoulders, she put the paddles under her arm and they walked to the lake. Then he returned to his car and lugged a huge canvas pack to the canoe.

"What's all that?"

"Tent, sleeping bags and air mattresses."

"Are you going to sleep outside?"

"No... *we* are going to sleep out. Haven't you ever camped?"

"You mean, like sleeping on the ground. *No*," she shuddered. "There're animals and snakes and creepy-crawlies."

"Nothing here can hurt you. We can lie in the tent, look at the stars and listen to the night birds. Maybe a coyote. It's magic."

He was so eager that she shrugged and went along to please him. They paddled slowly down the shore, and she admired the clumps of wild irises, the sandpipers, turtles and the courting display of grebes. He beached at the lake's far end and hauled the pack to an oak knoll that gave them a view down the lake.

"I used to camp here. It's special, and I want to share it with you because there's no camping after the dedication." He raised the tent under the solitary oak, laid out the bedding and zipped the tent shut. Then, they paddled to the house where he grilled steaks. Afterward, they sat on the porch with wine and listened as the orioles and doves closed the day with their evensong.

"I love it here," he said with his gaze fixed on the far shore. "The lake, the farm and all it stands for. That and the man I owe so much to. This is everything that's good in the world or could ever be good. You're part of it, too."

"I am? I've only been here a couple times."

"You are part of it because you took this journey with me. Supported me when it was tough. Besides that, you open up out here. Here—especially here—you aren't laced into your ideological corset. You aren't struggling to fit into your professional girdle. You are simply your natural self, and you're beautiful."

"This is paradise," she whispered, especially when it's just us. "I'm kind of sad it's going to end."

"It doesn't have to."

"Well, of course, it does," she replied. "You're giving it away."

"I mean, I want to spend my life with you. I love you. I want to marry you."

"Say… that… again," she said, eyes wide and lips parted.

"Sophia, will you marry me?"

"*Yes, yes, ya huh!*" she yelled, and her answer echoed from the far shore.

"I hope your father will accept me. I can't sing, I'm not Italian or Catholic."

"He won't care, I promise. He'll love you like his other sons-in-law. You're a scholar, a writer. He'll admire that. More importantly, you've rescued his *bella* Sophia's womanhood from neglect." She laughed from her belly. "Here's a promise. When we get home, I'll call and confront him about… well, you know."

"Thank you," he said. Then he gave her a small velvet-lined box."

Her jaw dropped at the sight of a large lapis gem.

"I don't know your ring size," he said. "But it's also beautiful in a pendant. I chose it because it signifies wisdom. It's a match to the meaning of Sophia."

She held it to the light and wept. He closed the house, and they paddled to the tent.

CHAPTER 53

Sandy and Sophia spent the second day at the farm sorting and organizing the clutter of Leif's equipment. He had already taken the personal items he wanted and set aside the rest for Ted to make choices. Seabury could use the tractor and some of the tools. What they didn't want, he would sell in an auction and donate the money to the program.

They slept in the house that night and rose early enough to watch the dawn break over the lake. "I didn't tell you before, but Karla and I have a lifetime lease to use this house," he said. "It won't be part of the center program until we pass. That means we can stay here whenever we like."

"So, we'll have a lakeside cottage? Can we honeymoon here?"

"Yes. A perfect spot. There won't be anyone here."

They were dressed and ready when Putnam and the environmental studies director arrived with the schematic diagram of the Leif Nielsen Center. The funds Sandy donated would pay for moving the barn to the twenty-acre hayfield near the road, where it would be incorporated into a larger dormitory and classroom building. The house and knoll with its pink boulder and the graves would remain off-limits to students and staff.

Everyone arrived by mid-morning, including the Seabury faculty and the two regents who had questioned his tenure. Karla and Ted, Isaacs, Daniels, Boston and Ginger, the wildlife refuge manager, newspaper reporters and others took the rows of chairs under a tent set in front of the porch. It was 11:00 a.m. when Sandy welcomed them and introduced Karla. She spoke of her father, his love for the lake and his vision for the farm. Then Putnam and Seabury's president spoke of their collaboration as a way to train a new generation in ecosystem protection. The president said an anonymous donor created an environmental studies scholarship that several generous trustees had double matched it.

Sandy watched the ceremony proceed as he had hoped. The focus was on the lake, the preserve and Leif as he intended. He made certain Karla was the queen of the ball, but receiving congratulations for giving the land gave him a lump in his throat. After the catered lunch, Ted, Karla and Sandy led groups of guests to special sites around the preserve. When the crowd thinned out, Sophia and Sandy remained with Isaacs and Abigail, Karla and Ted, Ginger and Boston in the shade of an oak.

"C'mon ladies," Sophia called. "There's something I want to show you." She led the women into the kitchen and took a bottle of champagne from the refrigerator. "I have wonderful news and can't think of a better group to share it with. You are the first to know— Sandy and I are getting married." Cheers and squeals followed. She showed them the gem and they *oohed* in unison.

"You go, girl," Karla yelled and held out some plastic cups. Abigail wanted a double and wiped away a tear. Ginger passed up champagne for a Sprite, and then they toasted her.

"Are you next?" Sophia whispered to Ginger.

She shrugged. "Time will tell."

"My advice—don't wait. Act," she whispered.

"Don't you think it's time to let the men in on the news?" Karla asked.

"Well, if we must," Sophia laughed and emptied the last champagne into their glasses. "All right, now call them in."

The men came in and were more than happy to finish off Sandy's whiskey in toasting the couple.

***

Sandy downed his congratulatory drink and left the house, longing for a moment of solitude. He walked down the knoll toward the lake and glanced at the boots nailed to the oak. Then he sat on the pink boulder, rested his elbows on his knees and gazed across the water to let his emotions settle.

God, if only Leif could have been here, he thought and sighed. He would have loved it. Of course, he would've been the center of attention. He could've told his stories. This is his heaven, his Valhalla, his eternity. The center's program will teach others just as he taught me. Looking into the distance, he felt joy and sadness mingled like some strange cocktail of peaceful emotion. It was a moment without a past or present but an instant that might go on forever because the past was never past.

A gentle touch on his shoulder brought him out of the trance. He looked up and into Karla's eyes.

"It startled me to see you sitting here leaning forward. For a moment, I thought it was Dad sitting here."

"I keep thinking he'll appear," he said.

"I know. I'm sure you'll see him again because you know where to look. The boulder is here, his ashes are here, you are here… the son he always wanted, the brother I never had… until now. They are all here. He will be here because you embody him, him and his stories and this ethos." She squeezed his shoulder. "And wherever he is now, I know he's pleased with you."

"Thank you," he said and put his hand over hers. "I'm honored to call you kin."

She pressed down on his shoulders so he couldn't rise. "Stay. It's a comfort to see you here. Dad was a lot of things," she said quietly. "Kind and understanding but also harsh and even cruel—but always authentic. And so are you. I'm grateful for what you've done. For this memorial, for Ted's college, for defending Dad's values. You remember what he said—you won't know your true self until you give someone else the thing you value most. He taught you well. Taught you to love the farm. He gave it to you to give to others. He set an example that you followed. That is his legacy."

Acknowledgments

The inspiration for this story owes much to the late Ed Iversen, a friend with whom I fished, hunted and camped during my formative years. Like Leif, he was a retired forest ranger and consulting forester who told stories and introduced me to woodcraft and the natural web of life that makes up the heart of this story. I am also indebted to my critical readers. To Geoff Barnard and his stellar career with The Nature Conservancy and other conservation organizations, my deepest thanks for his perspectives on the realities of saving species and ecosystems. To Peter Haijinian, my sincere thanks to a fellow writer whose cheery and constructive comments in brewpub outings helped me refine the stories while raising my spirits. To my brother Alan, for a critical and affirmative reading from one who knew Ed. To Susan Thurston-Hamerksi, my editor whose comments continue to improve my craft. And last but not least, to my wife, Sue Stavig, my children Hannah and Maren and the friends who have supported me. Thank you.

ABOUT THE AUTHOR

Newell Searle grew up on a southern Minnesota farm, and his writing includes a variety of pieces on Minnesota's history, culture and natural environment. *Copy Desk Murders* was his first novel in a mystery series set in southern Minnesota during the 1980s farm crisis, a period when he worked in agricultural organizations. After a vocational school education, he received a B.A. from Macalester College. His first book, Saving Quetico-Superior, was an award-winning narrative of wilderness protection. He continued writing while working as a public affairs professional in corporate, government and nonprofit organizations. Now he writes wherever he is, at his home in Minnetonka, volunteering in Mexico or at a forest cabin north of Lake Superior.